Copyright@2015 Ron

All rights reserved. This includes the right to reproduce any portion of this book in any form.

CreateSpace

1st Edition

ISBNN: 13:9781515127864
Title ID: 5625422

Also by this author:
Hamburger for One

Legacy

Acknowledgements

We all have countless influences on our individual lives, and I am no exception. There are no age constraints on learning. It's an endless process that only stops when we choose to stop it, and I'm grateful that I was encouraged at a young age to be curious about everything. I had a great hometown and good people of all ages around me. This book is a reflection of and a tribute to them. Of all the influences I have had, two stand out above all the rest and I would especially like to dedicate this effort to them.

The first is my mom, Karen, who has never failed to be there for me. Her intelligence, wisdom, kindness, and amazing unselfishness has always impressed me, and someday, if people tell me I am a lot like her, that will be the best compliment I could ever receive.

The second is my Grandpa, Everett, a man I was very lucky to get to spend a great deal of time with in my youth. His casual and low-key outlook on things showed me that life is meant to be enjoyed and lived and appreciated, not spent worrying about things that are out of our control. He taught his lessons so subtly that it wasn't until I became an adult that I fully realized how much he had impacted me.

This book is for them and for everyone who made Gowrie, Iowa, a great place to grow up.

I tried to create a work that combined some of my memories, some fiction, some fun, and some lessons in leadership and personal growth that come from Jim Rohn, Andy Andrews, Zig Ziglar, and Dr. John C. Maxwell. They get the credit for the wisdom and the lessons you will read. Reading and listening to their ideas has also greatly impacted me. Personal growth is intentional, not automatic, and it's a journey for which the destination can never completely be reached. Knowing that, it is still a journey well worth taking because doing so changes each of us in positive ways and can make our lives better in countless ways.

LEGACY

How much can you learn after you know it all?

By Ron Underwood

CHAPTER 1

  The tension at the kitchen table rose to an unbearable level for me and more than anything else I wanted to bolt through the door and escape. I didn't know what kept me sitting there listening to Mom go on and on about her apparently sudden and total disappointment in me. Maybe it was the fact that she never raised her voice. Maybe it was the strange mix of hurt and hope I read in her eyes as she spoke to me. Some unseen force kept me in my chair despite hating and resenting nearly everything I heard.
  "Eli, you could be so much more," continued Mom. "I wish you could see in yourself what I see in you, but right now you can't. All you seem to think about are things that don't matter, things that will lead you to the wrong places. I know you think I'm crazy and have no idea what I'm talking about, but I do. Your world right now is your small group of buddies who are nothing but trouble and who are going nowhere."
  "That's not true," I interrupted. "They're good guys. You don't know them well enough."
  She calmly placed her hand on top of mine and smiled. "Oh, but I do know them. I've seen them and their power every day for the past year as I've watched you change. Their effect on you is far greater than you realize or understand, but that's normal. We rarely notice the negative qualities that we possess, even when we see and dislike the same qualities in others."
  "What are you talking about?" I asked angrily, even though I was pretty sure I understood what she meant. Something inside me compelled me to at least try and defend my boys from her verbal assault.
  "What am I talking about?" she continued. "That's easy. I'm talking about how we tend to judge and evaluate ourselves based on our intentions, which we generally believe are always good, yet we judge others by their actions and rarely take into consideration that from their points of view they believe their intentions are as noble as ours. I'm talking about you changing from a boy who was kind and caring and thoughtful and generous into a crude, tactless, thoughtless, selfish bully who I have trouble recognizing as my

son. The Eli whom I knew for seventeen years made me proud and you had me incredibly optimistic about the man you were about to become and then it all changed."

"Everything changes," I explained. "I know who I am and I know what I'm doing. My boys and I rule the street. We've got things figured out, so you can stop worrying about me. I'll be fine."

"Oh, honey, this talk is so overdue. I should have never let things go this long." She then squeezed my hand tightly, as if to make sure I stayed where I was and heard the rest of what she had to say. She sat erectly in her chair and wore a confident, yet nervous look as her eyes locked onto mine. Following a brief, silent pause she spoke again. "Here are some hard truths that you need to face, and you need to face them right now. You don't know who you are and you can't see where you're headed, but I can and that scares me a lot. I want my old Eli back. I miss him greatly. I know he's still inside you somewhere and I believe with all my heart that he's worth finding again. Do you believe that I want the best for you?"

I shrugged my shoulders. "I don't know. Yeah, I guess you do."

"You guess?" she asked. "Have I ever done anything to even suggest otherwise?"

"No," I stated. "I know you want the best for me. What are you getting at?"

"I know a way to revive the old Eli and that's what we're going to do. Do you remember how much fun you and I used to have? How easy it was for us to talk? Do you remember when your world didn't revolve around ruling the street?"

I looked past Mom and my eyes were fixed on a shelf full of trophies and ribbons and a wall covered in pictures of Mom and me together. "I remember."

"In two days I'm going to put you on an airplane," she explained. "I'm going to show you there is so much more to life than you think there is."

"Okay," I responded. "Where are we going?"

"Not we," she answered. "Just you. You're going to spend the summer in Iowa with your Grandpa."

"No way!" I shouted. "I don't want to go to Iowa. Summer is the best time here in the city. Why would I want to go waste summertime on some farm? I finally graduated and am done with school and learning and now it's time for the fun to really begin. My boys and I have big plans."

"Oh, Eli," she spoke through a sigh. "Learning never ends. Do you really think that your new diploma means that you now know all there is to know? It doesn't mean that at all."

"What does it mean then?" I asked with a hint of frustration.

"It means you've finished the first part of your life-long learning process. It means you have a foundation to build on, a foundation that not long ago was solid. Lately it has gotten somewhat shaky and that worries me. I want you to go to Iowa for the summer so that we can make that foundation solid once again. If you stay here I'm afraid of who you'll become."

"And you think a summer with Grandpa will make everything better? I'll hate every minute of it. How can that make anything better?"

"You'll have to trust me on that one for now. Spend the summer there and if you still believe that you want to do the things you're doing now, then you can come back and I will not get in your way at all. There will be no nagging, no complaining, no anything. You will be your own man, free to choose whatever life you want for yourself without any interference from me. Deal?"

"A whole summer is a long time," I stated.

"It's not that long," she replied.

"I'll hate it. I know I will. What can I possibly learn on a farm?"

"You might be surprised," she said with a soft smile. "You might be very surprised."

I sighed loudly. "I spend the summer there and then you'll let me do whatever I want to do right?"

"That's the deal."

"I can't believe you want me to be on a farm. Just because you grew up there doesn't mean it will be something I'll like."

"Shall we start packing?"

I paused for a moment before I answered. "I guess so. Let's get this started so I can get it over with and get back here."

Legacy

Chapter 2

I looked out the window of the plane but had no way of knowing what state we were flying over at the moment. I was so mad I almost didn't get on the plane, but mom's eyes were such a mix of sadness and optimism that for her sake I had to at least give her idea a chance. I never wanted to hurt her with anything I did or said, but when I was honest with myself I knew that I had gotten very good at doing just that. When you're eighteen and live in the city, and when you run with the boys every night, you have to act and talk a certain way, and I had always fit in very well. I knew how to walk tough, talk tough, and act tough, though I had never really had to prove my toughness to anyone.

She hated my friends, my boys, and she never allowed them into our house, which irritated and embarrassed me. I resented it every time she told me how much trouble they were and when she tried to explain and predict all the horrible places they would take me if I continued to hang out with them. What she didn't understand was that nobody led me anywhere. I made my own choices, and I knew what was what. I had told her that many times, and when I did she just sighed, shook her head, and told me that one big secret to success was how much a person learned after he thought he knew it all. I never quite understood what she meant by that, but she said it was one of the best lessons she had ever been taught.

Mom kept trying, no matter what I did, and though I didn't like it all the time, I guess I'm glad she never gave up on me. I was not a guy who liked rules much and she had plenty of them. She could have just turned me loose on the world to find my own way. That would have been a lot easier for her and she could have worried a lot less about me, but she thought spending a few months with Grandpa Carl would make a difference for me. Part of me thought the time here would at least give me a little insight into why mom thought the way she did on things.

It all looked the same from the plane. I tried to make my bags of peanuts and my Coke last as long as possible, and I looked out the window and wondered what I was about to get into. A summer on a farm. I couldn't even imagine how horrible that would be. I knew

Legacy

nothing about farming or gravel roads. I knew the city and the streets. What could I possibly do or learn there for a whole summer? "What a waste of time," I mumbled to myself as I continued to stare blankly at the endless squares of land so far below me. If I had had a parachute I would have jumped right then. Whatever place we were flying over at that moment had to be better than spending several months in a small town in the middle of nowhere. The thought of all the fun I would miss out on in the city and not being able to run with my boys made me furious.

I had never been on a jet before and didn't want to be on this one. The guy next to me was sweating, so I tried hard to avoid any contact with him. He coughed a lot too, which was also annoying. I had no idea where he was from and didn't really care. The poor guy was headed to Iowa, just like I was, so I had to sort of feel sorry for him.

The pilot announced that we would be landing soon, and before long the vague squares I had watched for several hours began to turn into trees and homes and vehicles. It looked to me like we could drop onto the interstate at any moment, but the plane glided smoothly onto the runway, and a few minutes later we were at the gate. I was now actually in Iowa.

I grabbed my jacket from the overhead compartment and made my way up the ramp into the terminal. I had seen pictures of Grandpa Carl but had not seen him in person for eleven years, not since I was seven years old. That was when Mom and Dad had gone through their divorce and I could barely remember him coming to stay with us for a couple weeks. I knew Mom had mailed him some of my school pictures, so I figured he would recognize me. I still wasn't sure why mom had put me on this plane to come here, but I knew I was about to get my first taste of whatever the summer was going to be like.

I spotted him the moment I walked through the terminal door. He wasn't as big as I thought he would be, but he was formidable just the same. From the stories I had heard from Mom, I had pictured a giant waiting for me, but he was just another guy standing in the terminal waiting to greet someone from the plane. He stood quietly and didn't look fully comfortable in the middle of the airport crowd. He wore jeans and a blue button shirt that hung loosely around his frame. His arms were dark, no doubt from spring days in the sunshine working his fields. He wore a hat that covered most of his gray hair, but it still showed through on the sides of his head. His belt seemed to not fit his pants or his waist. It was buckled but it was as if it was two holes too long. There was extra belt just hanging loosely by itself. Somehow he looked older than I had expected, but I hadn't paid much attention to too many sixty-two year olds, so I couldn't be sure.

When our eyes met and we were both sure, he smiled at me. I didn't return the smile. Instead I just walked with my jacket draped over my shoulder to where he was standing, and I stood quietly, not really sure what to say to him. He reached out and shook my hand, which surprised me a bit. "How was your flight?" he began.

"It was okay," I answered. "Any flight that lands without crashing is a good one."

He laughed at that comment and added, "I guess that's true. Never quite thought about it that way before. We need to get your luggage don't we?"

"Yeah, I stated. "I've got three full suitcases. I think Mom packed everything I own."

"She is usually pretty good at thinking things through," he continued as we began walking toward the baggage claim. "I'll bet she has most of what you'll need here, but we will still need to get a few more things for you."

"Like what?" I asked curiously. "What do I need that I don't already have?"

With that question he stopped walking and looked me straight in the eyes. "From what I hear I'd say you need patience, humility, and gratitude, but we can work on those things. If you were talking about clothes, we will need to get you some work boots, a couple pairs of gloves, and some work shirts." Without waiting for a reply from me he again started walking toward the baggage claim.

I stood speechless for a minute, trying to digest his answer to my simple question. "Patience? Humility? Gratitude? Where did that come from? And what did he mean we could work on those things?" I shook my head and then hurried to catch up with him. I think he could tell that his answer had puzzled me, but he did not elaborate further. I guessed the answers would come with time.

We threw my suitcases into the back of Grandpa Carl's lime green Chevy pickup. It had a white topper on it, so that nothing would blow out the back, and the bed of the truck was dirty and cluttered, filled with tools and hoses and other things I could not identify or recognize.

"How far is it to your house?"

He turned the pickup out of the airport and answered softly, "About an hour and a half. You can look at the scenery on the way. Here is your first chance to see what life looks like outside a city."

"What makes you think I'm interested at all in life outside a city?" I asked a bit arrogantly. "I like the city."

He replied confidently. "Oh, I'm sure that at this point you're not interested at all, but that will change. I'll be curious to see how long it takes you to get over that angry and hurt feeling you're carrying around with you. For future reference, self-pity doesn't look good on a guy no matter who is wearing it."

"I doubt my interest level in anything here will change," I exclaimed defiantly. "I like my life just the way it is now. This is just an intermission to humor Mom."

Grandpa just grinned at me knowingly and drove on.

"Can I at least turn the radio on? You do have music here in Iowa right?"

"Help yourself," he said as he gestured to the dashboard of the truck.

I turned the radio on and found a rock and roll station. Fleetwood Mac was playing *You Can Go Your Own Way,* and I looked out the window as the song filled the truck cab.

Grandpa asked, "You like that song?"

"Yeah, I guess. Why?" I inquired.

"Going your own way. You think that's the answer for you in lots of things don't you?"

"What do you mean? Go my own way with what?"

Without taking his eyes off the road he began to explain what he meant. "Go your own way - do your own thing – be your own man

– do what's best for you first. Do you think that's the secret to success?"

"I don't know," I continued. "I guess so. Doesn't everybody look out for himself first?"

Without hesitation he turned to me and softly said, "No, not everyone does that."

"Where I come from," I added, "if you don't look out for yourself, you get stepped on. I don't like being stepped on. That's just how it is."

"And you think that's how it should be? You think that's the right way?"

"What else is there besides taking care of number one?" I asked with a selfish pride.

"In three months you won't ever need to ask that question again because you'll know the answer. I won't have to tell it to you."

Most of the rest of the drive was spent without conversation. The scenery we passed was so different from what I had known every day for eighteen years. There were endless fields of dirt in every direction separated by a different small town every ten miles or so. The tallest things I saw were silos, though I wasn't totally sure of their purpose.

We finally made a turn off the highway and were on a gravel road. Grandpa pointed to the field on the right side. "That's one of mine."

I wondered again to myself, "What have I gotten myself into? Why would Mom send me here?"

A third of a mile down the gravel road he pulled the pickup into the driveway of a small farm. "Here we are!" he exclaimed proudly.

I looked around, trying to take in as much as I could in a matter of seconds. "Oh, good," I sarcastically replied.

CHAPTER 3

Grandpa Carl was ready for bed at 9:00 my first night there, which totally stunned me. I had never heard of anyone going to bed that early. Most of the time my boys and I were just getting our nights started at that time.

"You're really going to bed already?" I asked him in disbelief.

"I really am," he replied with a yawn. "5:30 comes early."

"5:30? What's going on at 5:30?"

He grinned at me. "That's when you and I are getting up. It's planting season and every hour of daylight in the field matters. We've got a full day ahead of us tomorrow. If you want to stay up be my guest, but you're not going to be standing on a street corner all day tomorrow. We've got work to do. The TV channels turn off at midnight, all three of them, so suit yourself. Goodnight." With that he turned and walked into his bedroom.

I didn't know quite what to do next. Where was I? Some backwards land that didn't understand what nights were for? I had never gone to bed that early, and I certainly could never remember waking up at 5:30. If I had ever thought this trip was meant to be a vacation for me, I had just been shown that I was wrong. I stayed up for another hour and then headed upstairs to bed. Nobody really got up at 5:30 in the morning did they? I still couldn't imagine that, but once I got comfortable in my new bed I fell into a deep sleep far more quickly than I thought I would.

> *Oh, it's nice to get up in the morning,*
> *It's nice to get up in the morning,*
> *It's nice to get up in the morniiiiiiinnnggg...*

I woke suddenly to that horrible song coming from the bottom of the stairs. When my eyes worked their way into focus I grabbed my watch from the nearby nightstand. The hands on it displayed 5:20. I stretched and groaned and tried to come to life, but it wasn't easy. Eventually I put on my jeans and a clean t-shirt and sauntered down the stairs. When I got to the bottom of the stairway I could smell breakfast cooking.

Legacy

Grandpa stood at the stove flipping the eggs in one skillet and adding more slices of bacon to the other one. As I entered the kitchen, two slices of bread popped up in the toaster. "Butter those would ya?" he began.

"Sure," I replied without really thinking. "You were right. It's definitely early."

"The sun is already almost up and we've got lots of acres to plant today. Gotta get your belly full before we start. Don't worry, you'll get used to being up at this time of day."

"I doubt that," I stated. "Has the rooster even crowed yet?"

"I don't have a rooster," he smiled. "Had one but he turned mean, so I shot him."

"Nice," was all I could think of saying.

After breakfast we filled two Coleman coolers with ice water and headed out the door to begin the first day of farm work I had ever done. The May sky shone brightly over the entire farm. The chill of an Iowa winter had long since gone away, and the fields, covered for months in layers of snow, now ached for activity. It was time to put to use all the stored moisture the land had been hoarding in order to bring the newly planted seeds to life.

Grandpa Carl had already filled the fuel tank on his John Deere tractor and everything had been greased and oiled in preparation for many hours of hard use. The wagon filled with soybeans sat idly, waiting to be pulled to the field and emptied as the day wore on, as the planter bins were filled, emptied, and filled again.

I hopped onto the tractor and stood beside Grandpa as he drove us to the field. He had not told me anything about the process of planting beans, and I had no idea what my job or jobs would be all day, but I knew I would find out quickly. The tractor ride seemed bumpy to me, but Grandpa appeared totally comfortable and at ease in the driver's seat. I still wasn't happy about being up so early in the morning, and the rough ride to the field only added to my personal frustration. I found myself still wiping the sleep out of my eyes, and when I looked to the east, the bright morning sun made me squint.

Once we got into the field he parked and unhooked the wagon near the fence. I helped him hook the tractor up to the planter which was already there. He then drove near the wagon and tossed me two five-gallon buckets. "Time to start. Let me show you how to do this so you'll know and you won't spill any. There is nothing worse than wasting something of value, and it's the same whether it's soybeans, talent, or time."

"What does wasting time or talent have to do with standing in an empty field?" I asked, a bit confused by his comment.

"Well, I'll tell ya," he said as he grabbed one of the buckets. He lifted the bucket and held it up to a small door on the back of the wagon and he raised the door just a little bit. "Spring is the most important time of the year in farming and in life. It's the time of opportunity and possibilities, and you can't waste that."

"I understand opportunity. You plant and then you get a crop. That's the opportunity of farming. Simple, right?" I asked.

"Simple, huh?" he continued. "Just put the seed in the ground, relax for a few months, then bring in the crop when it's ready. You really do know everything don't you?"

"Well, I'm sure there's more to it than that," I stated, realizing how illogical and simplistic my comment had been.

"Just a bit more, as you'll find out," he added as I raised the wagon door and the soybeans quickly filled the first bucket. "Close the door!"

I didn't get it shut in time, and a pile of soybeans suddenly appeared on the ground near the wagon. He looked at the pile and then looked at me scornfully. "There, that's waste. That's what I was talking about. You have to think farther ahead than a couple minutes or a couple days at a time. If we're sloppy and careless today, do you think that helps or hurts the results we'll get in the fall?"

"It would hurt them," I said solemnly.

"That's right. You have to do it right in the spring or all you get in the fall is regret. Even if we do everything right this week, how many things do you think can go wrong between now and harvest time? Start thinking of a bigger picture. You don't build a house from the roof down."

I looked down at the pile of beans on the ground, not fully understanding what house building had to do with beans, but I didn't ask any more.

"Let's get all the bins filled and see if you can do that without adding to the pile on the ground."

I lifted the full bucket and emptied it into the first bin on the planter then I repeated the process until the planter was full and ready to go. Each time I raised the wagon door I spilled less than the time before, which made us both happy, but as Grandpa climbed onto the tractor to begin, there was a considerable pile. He turned to me before driving away and directed, "Clean up as much of that pile as you can without getting any dirt mixed in with the seed. I'll be back when the planter is empty, and we'll do it all over again."

"Okay, I replied. "What do I do while you're driving up and down the rows?"

"Whatever you want," he explained with a hint of a grin. "See you in a bit." And with that he drove away and left me standing beside the wagon.

"Anything I want," I said to myself with disgust. "Like what?" My boredom set in almost immediately. I had the spill pile picked up quickly, and after that I just sat down on a wagon tire and watched the tractor moving steadily toward the far end of the field. What was I doing here in Iowa in the middle of a field? Just two nights ago I was hanging out with my boys in front of Giletti's Pool Hall without a care. I still couldn't understand what Mom had been thinking when she put me on that damn plane to come here.

Throughout the day, it took nearly an hour to empty the planter each time, so I had far more time than I wanted to just sit and watch nothing and to think. When I had filled the planter for the fourth time, Grandpa told me to walk back to the farm and bring the pickup down. After the next load we would go to town for some lunch. I was shocked. He had no idea whether I could drive or not, and he just blindly trusted me with his truck. Nobody had ever done that with me before, and I wasn't quite sure how to feel. It was a half mile walk back to the farm, but I welcomed the

14

diversion and any change from sitting by the wagon throwing dirt clods.

I had the truck back twenty minutes before the planter was empty, and for some reason the time passed more quickly than it had just sitting on the wagon. When he was ready, he parked the tractor, turned it off, and climbed down. He checked a few things on the tractor then walked to the truck. "Hungry?" he asked as he wiped sweat and dirt from his forehead and face.

"Big time," I smiled.

"Let's go eat."

CHAPTER 4

Three miles later I got my first look at Grandpa's town. At first glance it looked pretty much like all the other little towns we had driven through on the way from the airport, and I again wondered to myself why anyone would ever want to live in such a place, though at the moment I wasn't worried about that. I was tired and hungry and thoughts of food were in the front of my mind. We drove into town from the southwest side and to the left of us I could see a large cemetery just outside the city limits. The only cemeteries I had seen before had been small and dark and were usually surrounded by some kind of really high fence. The one I looked at now appeared almost sunny and inviting and was obviously well taken care of, and I thought it odd to have a cemetery that looked like a cheerful place. There had been many times when my boys and I had gone into cemeteries in the city late at night to drink a few beers or hide out from somebody who might be chasing us, and being there had always given me the creeps.

One block into town we arrived at a stop sign. The road sign on the corner read Main Street, and I laughed out loud. "We're already on Main Street? What, is this town three blocks wide or something?"

Grandpa was unmoved by my question. "It's a few more than that. Why?"

Legacy

"It's just so small," I continued. "The whole town is the size of my neighborhood."

"You don't think much of small towns and small town people do you?" he asked. "Are you always that sure of yourself when you talk about things you know nothing about?"

"What do you mean by that?" I fired back at him quickly.

"Well, I'll tell ya," he continued quickly. "You've never seen any of the world outside your precious neighborhood and your city, and you have convinced yourself, or you've let others convince you, that nothing could compare with that. You think acting tough and running the streets is going to turn you into somebody important. That might make you a big man with your little group, but what a sad, short-sighted plan that is. You think you know where you're going in life, but if you would ever tell yourself the truth, you'd see that you have no real plan right? You know what happens when you just float along not really knowing where you're going?"

I was intrigued. "What happens?"

"You end up somewhere else," he finished confidently.

I didn't know what to say, but I felt like I had just been scolded for no reason, and I didn't like it. We had now entered what seemed to be the middle of town and Grandpa pulled the truck into a parking space in front of what appeared to be a café.

We walked into the café and I immediately saw that it was full of people. I couldn't decide whether it was full because the food was good or if this was the only place in town to grab some lunch during the day. The smell of grease filled the air, but I seemed to be the only one who noticed or cared. Everyone appeared to be talking at the same time, and as I looked around the room, I wondered if anyone was actually listening to anything he heard. Each conversation that I could hear bits and pieces of seemed to deal only with crops and machinery and fields, how far along planting was, the latest breakdowns of some piece of machinery, and other similar topics.

There were eight stools at the counter on the right and three booths on the left, all of which were filled with customers devouring their food whenever it was someone else's turn to lead

Legacy

the conversation. Grandpa greeted two or three of the men as we made our way to the back room where there were several more tables. Two men immediately raised their hands as we entered the room, and we headed toward them. "Sit down Carl. We saved your chair for you," exclaimed one of the men. "Didn't know if you'd be in today or not."

Grandpa pointed at me and explained. "Breaking in a rookie today, so I'm running a little bit behind." Everyone at the table laughed at his comment, but I didn't see the humor. These guys didn't even know me, yet they had no trouble laughing at my expense. "He'll get it figured out before long," Grandpa continued.

I sat down at the table without an ounce of enthusiasm, and I began to silently examine each man at the table as their conversation cheerfully went on around me. Kenny, the one who had welcomed us to the table, couldn't sit still. He squirmed and fidgeted continuously and spoke much faster than the rest of the men. He was a large man, and he sat very upright in his chair. His overalls were new and underneath them he wore a long sleeve white shirt.

Herman sat next to Kenny, and in my opinion the two couldn't have been more opposite. Herman was much smaller and slender. He wore a blue and white striped hat that looked like one I had once seen somewhere in a picture of a railroad conductor. In the top pocket of his overalls there was a red can of Prince Albert tobacco. He seemed to laugh, or at least chuckle, at nearly everything anyone said, and once he even tried to tell a joke he had heard, but he struggled with it because he made himself laugh so often while he told it that he had trouble getting to the punch line.

The third man at the table was a smaller man who wore jeans and a clean shirt. The others' footwear showed evidence of prolonged work time, yet this man wore Hush Puppies that shined in stark contrast to the boots near them under the table. Everyone called him Captain, though nobody bothered to explain to me what he was the captain of. He seemed to know more than the others no matter what topic was brought up, and he even interrupted the other men several times while they spoke in order to share his knowledge with the group. It took about two minutes for me to conclude that he was nothing more than an arrogant blowhard who had evidently done something of significance somewhere in the past and had spent every day since living on his reputation.

The burger and fries tasted just fine to me, and it wasn't until the food had been placed in front of us that Grandpa actually got around to introducing me to the other men. He put his arm around my shoulder and announced to the group, "This is my grandson Eli. He's going to be here for a while. This is his first full day in Gowrie, and he has just gotten his first taste of planting beans."

The others smiled and Captain spoke up. "Make sure you keep him busy!"

"Oh, I will," replied Grandpa. "No worry there."

On the way out Grandpa let me have a malt. It seemed that Hazel's Café had a different special malt flavor each week, and this week the flavor was lime. That was something new for me, and as we walked back to the pickup I wondered how long my list of new things would grow while I was here.

The afternoon was as monotonous for me as the morning had been, though I was happy to no longer to be hungry. I filled the planter several more times before we stopped just before sundown. When we finished, Grandpa drove the tractor back to the farm and I drove the pickup. I could feel the new sunburn on my face and arms, and Grandpa's tan arms had a new reddish tint to them. He also wore a layer of dirt on his face and clothes, remnants of driving through clouds of dust he had stirred up all day long.

After supper Grandpa dropped himself into his recliner and was asleep in just a few short minutes. Looking at him suddenly made me realize how tired I was too. I could never remember putting in that long a day doing anything that resembled work, and since I knew we would do it all over again tomorrow and the next day, I now had a better understanding of why he was ready for bed so early in the evening.

We planted for two more days, two long full days, and then we were finally finished. The seed wagon was nearly empty and I was definitely tired of filling the planter bins over and over. We had stopped and gone to Hazel's for lunch each day and we had always sat with Kenny, Herman, and Captain. It was easy to see how close

18

those four men were, and each day as I listened to them talking and laughing, I wondered about my boys back home in the city. What were they doing without me?

CHAPTER 5

The day after we finished planting we were again up early. The eggs were cooked and eaten, and I had already learned to walk straight for the toast and make sure each slice was buttered. We had quickly developed a morning routine though I had not yet gotten used to waking up so early. In fact, I hated it.

It took all morning to hose down and completely clean the planter, and I was more than happy to see it returned to its storage place. Grandpa then spent another hour working on the tractor, checking everything from the air pressure in the tires to the spark plugs and the hydraulic hoses. As I watched, somewhere inside me a level of curiosity rose. "Why do you do all that stuff?" I asked. "It seemed to me the tractor ran just fine all the time we were planting."

He put down his grease gun then took a rag out of his back pocket and cleaned his hands with it. "You've never had to deal with anything that was even close to something long term have you?"

"I don't know. What do you mean?"

"When you're at home and you start a week, do you ever look past that day or the next day or the weekend? Looks to me like you spend all your time just thinking about the moment you're in and what you can do to make it easy on yourself."

"I never really thought about it," I answered. "I guess I like living one day at a time."

He just shook his head at me and gave a look of great frustration. "One day at a time is the only way any of us can live, but the people who get things done in the world are smart enough to not think one day at a time. You have to think ahead and plan ahead. There is absolutely no substitute for preparation with anything, but not everybody prepares. Can you guess why that is?"

"No," I said a lot more quietly than I had asked my initial question.

"Because it's tedious and it's not glamorous and most of the time it's not fun. Yes, I could ignore the oil and the grease on the tractor, and I could put the planter away without cleaning it, but those little bits of inconvenience will help that machinery last a lot longer, and to me that's just being smart."

"I kicked some gravel and tucked my thumbs inside the pockets of my jeans. "I guess that makes sense."

"You guess," he answered. "You talk about the important things you and your friends do. Do you ever sit with them and talk about goals or is it just what's good at the moment?"

"I can't remember ever talking to them about any goals."

"I didn't think so. Think for a minute. What if I would have decided to plant three days ago without any preparation? We would have been ready to go, but we would have had no seed, the field wouldn't have been ready, and the tractor and the planter may or may not have worked as well as they did. Ignoring all those things and expecting good results would have been foolish. It's even tougher for short term thinkers to do all the work and spend all that time, and then not get to see or enjoy any of the rewards for five months."

"Yeah, that sucks," I added, thinking I understood what he was telling me.

"No, it doesn't suck," he quickly corrected. "It's just the process. There is no harvest without the planting, and I want a good harvest in the fall. I want it enough that I'm willing to work at it now and wait for it. I'm willing to put in the time now even though I won't be paid until much later. That's how you need to start thinking. Stop thinking all rewards happen instantly in life. It doesn't work that way, especially on the things that matter most."

I looked toward the field we had just planted. "I don't know about that," I said. "Sounds like what adults have to do, but I'm only eighteen. I've got plenty of time."

"How naïve that is," he continued. "How much time do you have? You're eighteen. Guess what? A year from now you'll be nineteen and you'll be somewhere. Will it be time to start thinking about your future then or will you still be just a kid? There is no magic age to start thinking smarter. If an eight year old wants a bicycle he may get creative and set up a lemonade stand and over time he will get that bike a dime and a quarter at a time. Can you imagine how satisfying that day would be for that kid? It starts with a goal and some discipline, and the discipline is crucial because many of life's big goals will cost a lot and they will almost always make you wait for the payoff. Whether you like it or not, you're an adult now and it's time to stop thinking like a little kid."

"Sounds tough," I spoke with a shrug of my shoulders.

"It's brutal," Grandpa said with a smile, "but when you set a goal, work for it and reach it, the feeling is amazing. I'm about to give you a real chance to know that feeling of doing the work now, protecting it, and waiting for the payoff."

"What are you talking about?" I inquired with suspicion in my voice.

He set the rag on the tractor and walked into the garage. In just a few seconds he emerged again carrying two shovels and a hoe. He held one of the implements out for me to take, which I did, and he spoke deliberately. "Today you and I are going to plant a garden."

"It never ends here does it?"

"Nope," he said with a sly grin. "Are you ready?"

The garden took two days. I learned how to run a tiller and hated it. I wanted to go fast but Grandpa kept telling me that fast was no good. The best ground for gardens was tilled thoroughly and was not just a lot of big clumps of dirt that had been separated a little bit. I swear he could already see the vegetables in his mind as we planted the seeds, but all I saw was more dirt. Everything here seemed to revolve around dirt and dust and work. I wished every day that I was back in the city, and though I knew I had to stay here for some unknown length of time, nobody could make me like it.

When we finished planting everything in the garden we stood together and admired our work. We had rows of lettuce, radishes, potatoes, beans, tomatoes, carrots, kohlrabi, and a huge section of sweet corn. As we stood looking over our infant garden, I remembered something he had said before we started the work.

Legacy

"What did you mean by protecting this before the payoff of eating what we just planted?"

"That's easy," he replied. "Remember what I told you in the bean field? A lot of things can go wrong between now and harvest time. Same thing here. These plants are living things, and living things needs lots of care, especially when they are just getting started. If it gets too dry, we'll have to water it. Weeds will pop up and try to choke the new plants to death, so we will have to keep them out. Animals like deer and rabbits will come here for a meal, and we'll have to keep them away too. There's a lot of good eatin' we'll get from this, but we'll have to protect it."

"That just sounds like more work to me," I added as I looked down at the rich black ground.

"It is, but a full garden is something to be proud of. A garden is good, and you need to figure out that anything good in our world will be attacked in some way. I can't tell you why that happens. That's just the way it is."

I looked up, still not quite sure what he meant. "You're not just talking about gardens now are you?"

Grandpa grinned. "Your Mom told me you were quite intelligent and picked up on things quickly when you wanted to, and I can already tell that she was right. No, I'm not just talking about gardens. Remember when I asked you if you had ever set any goals for yourself? What do you think your buddies back home would say and do if you told them you wanted to be a doctor or lawyer or even a farmer. It doesn't matter what profession, just pick one. You think they would jump for joy and cheer you on and encourage you?"

"Doubtful," I concluded. "They'd either laugh at me or tell me how stupid I was being thinking like that."

He continued. "You know them and I don't, but you're probably right. Think about that for a minute. These are supposed to be your best friends, people who claim to want the best for you, so if you told them you wanted to achieve something, why would they want to tear that goal down?"

"I really don't know," I added as I kicked a couple dirt clods. "I'm not sure."

"Yes, you are," he stated firmly, "but you don't want to admit the truth."

"I guess that's right," I conceded.

"If you raise the standards for yourself, then your friends have a decision to make. They either get ambitious like you have and raise themselves up, which is often way out of their comfort zone, or they do all they can to keep you down where they are, which is a lot easier and a lot more comfortable for them."

"So what do you do when your friends try to keep you down?" I asked, now very interested in what we were discussing.

"Then you make your choice. You either let them drag you down to stay with them or you stay true to your heart and realize that sometimes, quite often actually, for something good to happen, we have to leave things and people behind."

"Even if it's your best friends?"

He paused there for a moment. "If people don't want you to succeed, are they really your best friends? You've got to learn to surround yourself with people who share your goals and want you to succeed. Trust me, you have more of those people in your life than you realize right now. You'll figure that out. Your Mom and I believe there's a lot of good in you, and she sent you here so she and I could work to protect you. She could see where you were headed with your city buddies and that scared her. All good is attacked in some form, so you and I are going to protect our garden and see how good it can become. Time for you to realize and appreciate that you are your Mom's garden and sending you here is her way of protecting you so that you can grow too."

I smiled at him. "Okay."

CHAPTER 6

The next two weeks were completely filled with work and they were exhausting. It seemed that Grandpa had a list a mile long of chores to do around the farm, and he intended to get to all of them. I repaired several boards in the hayloft, scooped out the corn crib, mended several sections of fence, mowed and trimmed the yard, and completed a host of other tasks.

"Have you been saving all this stuff for me?" I finally asked him one night.

"You are smart aren't you?" he grinned. "You're learning and you don't even realize it."

I asked sarcastically, "What exactly is it that I'm learning?"

"Discipline and pride," he said confidently. "Look at the yard, and what you did with it. It looks great. You could have done a half-assed job but you didn't. That's showing pride in your work."

I squirmed a bit as he talked. I couldn't remember ever doing anything that someone had described as great. All I could think to say was, "Thanks."

The last Friday in May changed everything. All day long the sky was a deep, pure blue and the temperature was oppressive. Sweat covered me all day long with every task I did around the farm. We went to Hazel's for lunch and most of the talk there was about the storms that had been forecast for that night. Each farmer seemed to have heard the same reports because they were all antsy and genuinely concerned. As I listened to everyone, I had a hard time believing any of them knew what he was talking about because at that moment there was hardly a cloud in the sky.

After lunch we returned to work and the heat continued to overwhelm everything. Around 5:30 that afternoon a breeze began to blow. It was quite welcome to me because it cooled me down a little bit. Thirty minutes later we quit for the day, and Grandpa lit the charcoals on the grill so he could barbeque some chicken which we would eat outside on the picnic table, something we did regularly.

We finished eating and were ready to go inside and settle in front of the TV for the rest of the night. The breeze stopped without

Legacy

warning and it suddenly became extremely calm. I didn't think much about it other than I again felt uncomfortable in my sweaty clothes. Grandpa knew better though, and he moved faster than I had ever seen him move before. "Come on, let's get this stuff inside," he ordered in a very serious tone that I had never heard from him. He began gathering up the plates, glasses, and utensils incredibly quickly.

"What's going on?" I asked quite puzzled by his sudden change in behavior.

He pointed to the western sky as we hurriedly gathered everything up in our arms. "Look over there."

I looked at the sky but all I saw was a solid gray bank of clouds, and I was unimpressed. I had seen rain clouds before. "Are you that afraid of getting wet? It's just rain isn't it?" I continued, still not comprehending the full gravity of the situation.

"Not this time," he continued. As he spoke the breeze returned, except this time it was much cooler than before, almost cold. "Hurry up!"

We got everything put into the house, and he quickly gathered several flashlights and candles which he placed in my arms. He shoved a box of matches into his pocket then grabbed a cooler and started filling it with food from the refrigerator.

"What the hell are we doing?" I asked nervously.

He didn't answer. He looked around the house one more time for anything else he might want to bring, and then spoke out loud, more to himself than to me. "Water." He quickly filled a gallon jug and then we were apparently ready, but I still had no clue what we were ready for.

"Let's go," he stated. "Quickly." He rushed out the door and I followed as fast as I could with my arms full.

When we got outside, I was shocked at the change. The peaceful sunset had surrendered to total blackness, and the once gentle breeze was now a violent wind that was already tossing loose things around the farm yard. I could hear the boards on the barn and the garage creaking, and for the first time I got scared.

It was only thirty feet to the cellar door, but it definitely seemed farther. Grandpa opened the door and instructed me to go down first. I needed no convincing and was down in the underground room quickly. He was right behind me, and he lit several candles to erase the cellar's darkness. The cellar was quite small, just twelve feet long and four feet wide, and it was lined on both sides with shelves. The shelves were full of glass jars that contained some things I couldn't identify. I decided I would ask about them later, but right now they were not the most pressing thing to worry about.

"Okay," he said more calmly than before. "We're as ready as we can be. Let's go have a look. It's not quite here yet." He walked back up the steps and I unwillingly followed.

"What's not here yet?" I nervously inquired.

"That's a tornado sky. Something you don't see in the city, but we don't monkey around with them here. We take them seriously. Remember this. When you fight a tornado, the tornado will always win. Always."

We stood together just outside the cellar door, and the cold wind now blew even harder than before. I was still amazed at how quickly everything about the weather had changed. I stood shivering and watched Grandpa examine the gray sky which now looked like it had been painted an almost sick mix of green and orange, and as I was about to comment on the color the rain began. There was no warning. It just started pouring, and we were instantly soaked.

"Down!" he cried. "Now!"

Again we retreated into the cellar, but this time he latched the door from the inside. Outside the door, the sounds again changed. It sounded like continuous knocking at the door, which was extremely eerie to me. "What is that sound?"

He replied knowingly. "Hail."

"We should have come down a couple minutes sooner. Then we'd still be dry," I complained as I shook the wetness from my hair.

"Let's hope being wet is as bad as it gets for us tonight," he replied unsympathetically.

I felt helpless but somehow safe in this cramped little room. The noise outside the door intensified and both of us sat very still and quiet, as if waiting for something we didn't want to hear. I was very happy to have the candles and the flashlights with us. Sitting there in the dark would have been unbearable.

Ten minutes…. Twenty minutes…. Fifty minutes…. As quickly as it had arrived, the outside noise left, and it was suddenly silent. Grandpa edged his way toward the door so he could listen more closely. Much to my dismay, he unlatched the door and began to inch it open.

"Are you sure?" I asked from the back wall of the cellar.

"Nope," he replied, "but I think it's past us."

The door opened farther, and I still couldn't hear any of the weather sounds that had been so steady just moments earlier. He poked his head out of the cellar and looked around, and then he stepped up and all the way outside. I lagged behind and waited.

"Come on out," he stated. "Blow out the candles first though."

I blew out the candles, gingerly walked up the steps, and was quite surprised by what I saw. The huge dark bank of clouds now filled the sky to the east of us and the sun once again shone on us. I had never seen weather like this before. We stood together and looked around the farm. The garage was leaning to the right, almost like someone had tried to tip it over and had changed his mind in the middle of the process. A few other things had been blown around, but the garage appeared to be the extent of any major damage to the farm. He continued looking around and wore a far off gaze of concern. We could both see tall flames in the distance, and he wasted no time.

"Let's go, he commanded. "That's Kenny's place."

We both immediately got into the pickup, and the man who did everything slowly and methodically sped down the gravel road. "I hope it's nothing big," he added, and that was the extent of our conversation. There was nothing of substance that I could add.

Kenny's farm was less than three miles away, so it didn't take us long to get there, but when we reached the driveway I wished we had not come. Nearly everything on the place had been flattened and totally destroyed. There was no longer a house or a barn or any sheds or cribs or anything. Apparently something had exploded in what used to be the work shed, and that had caused the fire we saw from our farm. It still burned brightly in the twilight, but appeared to be in no danger of spreading.

There was no sign of life, and I was not excited about the very real possibilities of what we might be about to find. "You think they're okay?" I asked timidly.

Grandpa grabbed his gloves without hesitation and started walking toward the rubble of Kenny's house. "I sure hope so," he replied. "Let's go find out."

I also put on my gloves and we both began hollering at random for anyone, hoping against hope that we would hear a reply of some sort. We stepped carefully over and through all the debris, but we heard no answers to our calls. Every step into the mess gave my stomach another knot. "Do they have a cellar like yours?" I asked. "Surely they do."

"It's around back," Grandpa responded. "Come on."

As we walked through what we thought was their back yard, four more vehicles pulled into the driveway. A dozen men I had never met piled out and wore the same look we had worn when we first arrived. "Are they here? Are they hurt?" one of the men asked excitedly. "What can we do?"

Grandpa waved them to where he thought the cellar was, and the entire area was covered by pieces of debris. He hollered again for Kenny, and this time we thought we heard a muffled reply. "Come on guys," Grandpa ordered. "Get this stuff off the door so we can get it open."

There was a sudden flurry of activity. Boards, pieces of insulation and everything else in that pile was tossed aside. The cellar door finally came into view and was at last unobstructed and clear. "Unlatch it Kenny and open 'er up. It's okay now."

The anticipation outside the cellar was intense. We heard the inside latch slide over, and the door began to open. Kenny emerged first, followed closely by his wife Dorothy and their daughter Denise, who was thirteen years old and obviously terrified. Everyone lent a hand and helped them all come out to get their first views of what used to be their entire life.

There were no words that could help, so the group of men waited in a respectful silence as the family began to absorb what had just happened to them. Dorothy, a short round woman with a tender heart of gold, nearly buckled under the weight of what she was seeing. Kenny and two others quickly moved in to support her, but her tears began to flow without reservation or apology. Kenny held her tightly and did his best to console his distraught wife, though he himself was equally devastated. "We're all alive, honey," he said softly. "We're all okay."

"It's all gone," she whimpered as she rested her head on his chest. "Everything is just gone. Why?"

"I don't know why," replied Kenny as he squeezed her even more tightly. "I just don't know, but we're okay. We can fix this."

"All our things," she continued through her sobs. "Our pictures, our clothes, our furniture and beds. What are we going to do?"

Grandpa looked at the group that had come to help. "We've still got some daylight left. Go get your tractors and put the scoops on the front of them. Jerry, go get your big truck. Al, you too. Let's start cleaning this mess up."

In less than a minute all four vehicles had disappeared down the road. Grandpa then turned to me. "Think you can drive a tractor all the way over here?"

"Yeah, I can do that."

"Go get it and come right back. Bring the Minny and be careful." The Minny was a yellow Minneapolis-Moline tractor that had its bucket already on the front end.

When I got into the pickup I noticed Denise for the first time. She just stood there almost in a trance. She hadn't moved or cried or spoken. I drove away trying to imagine her thoughts at that moment, but I couldn't do it. There was no way I could get into her heart and mind and emotions. I had never seen anything like what I just saw.

It took me twenty minutes to return with the tractor, and when I drove it into the yard two other tractors and one of the big trucks were already there and busy with the cleanup. The sun was setting fast and I wasn't sure how much we could get done before the night's darkness completely set in, but Grandpa waved me to a spot on the east side of the yard, and I drove to where he had instructed me to go. I dropped the bucket on the front of the tractor to almost ground level and tipped it back a bit so it could hold more. Then I turned off the tractor, got down, and began my part of the cleanup one item at a time.

When I had filled the loader I raised the bucket and drove the tractor as near to Al's truck as I could get, then I dumped the load into the back of the truck and returned for more. Several others were doing the same thing, and there was no good way to do the work more efficiently. Three spotlights had been turned on and they partially lit the area, but the darkness had really set in and that made the sorting and sifting difficult. Still we worked on. A neighbor needed help and there were no questions asked by anyone. At 11:00 that night three women drove up with a carload of food and some blankets for Kenny's family. We stopped our work briefly but I knew, without having to be told, we would soon return to our task and the darkness would not slow us down.

Grandpa was with Kenny and his family. They each carried a large flashlight and they stepped everywhere they could and looked for anything of theirs that could be salvaged. Twice I stopped and watched them for a moment, and I saw them find pieces of things that meant a lot to them. Nothing was fully intact, and Dorothy cried each time a broken item was retrieved and examined before she tossed whatever it was onto the pile again as trash. I couldn't stand to see and listen to her sorrow, so I returned to my job and tried to pretend that I couldn't hear her. The work continued on all through the night.

CHAPTER 7

We cleaned up the mess for the next two days, and we never left Kenny's place during that time. People brought us food several times a day, we slept anywhere we could when we needed a rest, and we disappeared to any private spot we could find when nature called. Fuel to keep the tractors running was brought from other neighboring farms. The amount of debris was incredible, because the house and four other buildings had been destroyed. The fire had taken care of some of the wood that would have been hauled away, but there was still an amazing amount to remove, all one piece at a time. Our original group of workers had grown to over fifty people, each doing what he could to help Kenny, Dorothy, and Denise.

By mid afternoon, three days after the storm, all the debris had been picked up, dumped onto a massive pile and burned. Word had reached us that two other farms had been hit as hard as Kenny's, and several other farms had sustained minor damage. There were equally large groups of people cleaning up the other farms, and we were told that the cleanup on those places was at or near completion too. I had never seen anything like what I had been a part of the past three days and would have had a really difficult time explaining this to any of my boys back home.

We were all filthy and utterly exhausted, though we felt an odd satisfaction and pride when we finished the cleanup. When the last truckload of debris was dumped onto the fire we all sat quietly on the ground and watched it burn. Nobody had wanted a situation like the one we were in, but once the terrible reality had appeared it had been immediately dealt with. There had been no waiting around to decide on a plan. Everyone had acted swiftly and with a purpose. As I sat and watched the fire burn, I thought how nothing like this would ever happen in the city. It would have taken weeks or months to do what we had just done in three days. Small town ways were still very different to me, but I couldn't help but be impressed by what I had just witnessed in this crisis.

Kenny and Dorothy had already talked with a local construction firm and had chosen plans for their new house. Insurance would also replace the garage, the barn, and the work shed, and each would be rebuilt even better than it had been before the storm. The family was still sad about losing so many of their personal things, but the outpouring of help and support had allowed them to also find some smiles and count their blessings.

We were finally ready to leave for home, and since all we had was the tractor, we would both have to ride it back. Grandpa found Kenny before we left and reassured him one more time that things would be okay.

"I know they will Carl," smiled Kenny as he shook Grandpa's hand vigorously. "I don't doubt it at all. Is there anything in the world better than great friends?"

"No, sir, there isn't," responded Grandpa. "I'll talk to you very soon."

We walked to the tractor and Grandpa surprised me. "You drive. I'll stand beside you."

"Are you sure?" I asked. "The other night was the first time I had ever driven a tractor."

"Did you have any trouble getting it over here?"

"No, not really."

"Then drive us home," he continued. "I need a bath in a big way. You could use one too!"

I smiled in agreement. "That's a fact. Are they gonna be all right? I can't even imagine how scared they must have been."

"They'll be fine now. That's why it was so important for us to clean up everything so fast. Now they can turn all their attention and energy to what's ahead of them and not think so much about what they just lost. You can't look ahead if you're still holding onto yesterday's stuff. Let's go home."

I started the tractor and drove us back to the farm. We had a few things to tend to and clean up there too, specifically emptying the garage and knocking it down, but that would keep. Right now it was time for a bath, some food, and a long sleep.

The insurance adjuster priced a new garage for Grandpa and after we removed all the contents, which was not a minor task, we were ready to push it over and have our own fire. I had been given the

Legacy

assignment of destroying the garage with the bucket of the tractor, but I was unsure of myself.

"You really want me to do this instead of doing it yourself?" I asked with an uncertainty that was foreign to me. I never lacked confidence with things I understood, but everything here seemed to involve machinery and tools I knew little or nothing about. "Maybe you should do it."

"You can do it," was Grandpa's only response. "Let me show you." He walked to the side of the garage and pointed to a couple spots where he wanted me to push on the building. "Just go slow, and if you do it carefully you'll get it right. You'll find that when you understand something you'll almost always lose your fear of that thing."

"I guess that's right," I responded. "How long has this garage been here?"

"Oh, let me think a minute," he said rubbing his chin. "We built it in '44, so I guess it has been here over thirty years."

"It sucks that one storm can tear up everything and change so many lives," I stated.

He stood very erect beside the garage. "Well, I'll tell ya," he began, "life is full of moments like this. Things happen, both good and bad, and they happen to everyone. Doesn't matter if you're good or bad or rich or poor. If you're living, life will happen. You can count on that without fail. When it's bad like this storm was, the thing that happened is not the real issue. It's how we choose to respond that matters. I've seen people lie down and never get back up when life deals them a bad blow like it just did to Kenny and Dorothy, and that kind of response is weak and pitiful. Each person's response is a personal choice. He can feel sorry for himself or he can understand the situation, handle it, and move forward. You can learn a lot from how Kenny chose to respond. They will be fine and probably even stronger because of how they chose to deal with that horrible night. Now get busy and knock that sucker down."

It didn't take long to reduce the garage to rubble, and the pile of wood burned for several hours. Grandpa smiled as he looked at the bare spot in the middle of the farm, and I thought he was probably imagining the layout of his new garage. These Iowa people continued to surprise me. They just kept going no matter what, and nothing seemed too big for them to tackle or overcome.

Mom called two nights later. It was the first time we had talked since I had gotten on the plane to come here, and she was more than a little surprised at how talkative I was on the phone.

"Did you hear about the tornado?" I began. "It destroyed several farms, and we helped clean one of them up. The beans we planted are looking good, or so Grandpa tells me, and the garden we planted is doing well too."

"Wow," mom continued. "Sounds like you've had quite a start there. I had no doubt Dad would keep you plenty busy. I remember doing all that stuff too when I was growing up."

"You mean you worked in the fields too when you lived here?" I asked.

"Of course I did," she laughed. "Every single year. I actually miss that at times. When a person grows up with that life it becomes a part of him that never really leaves, and my office here is a poor substitute for the fresh air of the country and the atmosphere of a small town."

"Yeah, being here is nothing like what I am used to. I still haven't figured it all out, but I'm getting some of it. I'm not used to everybody being so nice to me, even if they don't know me. I'm a lot more used to people yelling and taunting each other and just worried about their own stuff."

Mom laughed again. "It warms my heart to hear you talking like this. Can you understand why I put you on that plane? The things you were doing and saying here scared me, and I didn't want you to get so far down that road that I wouldn't be able to bring you back."

"At first I thought you sent me here to be a work slave of some kind, but I think I understand more now. At least I have more of an idea than I did the day I left. I was so mad at you for making me leave everything I knew and come here."

"I know you were, but I'm not sorry I did it. I can already tell that your time on the farm has been good for you. You had never seen any kind of life other than what you knew on the streets here, and there is so much more. So much more than just hanging out and accomplishing nothing. You're starting to see that, and I can't wait to see who you become in another month or two. You can become an amazing young man if you choose to. In the end it's up to you."

"Grandpa talks a lot about choices too," I interjected.

"He's right. Choices are everything," continued mom. "Everything we do is a choice. Even choosing to do nothing is a choice, and each choice carries with it its own consequences that can be either good or bad. Whoever and wherever we end up, it's primarily because of our choices."

"You really did grow up here didn't you?" I laughed. "You sound exactly like Grandpa."

"He taught me the same lessons he's teaching you now. I tried to share some of those things with you here, but you weren't too eager to hear me or listen to what I was telling you."

"I know," I replied softly and then I swallowed hard. "I'm sorry." It took more courage that I had imagined to apologize to her. I couldn't even remember the last time I had said those two words, though looking back I remembered dozens of times when I should have.

"It's okay Eli," she answered tenderly. "All part of growing up. I need to get busy here. It has been really great hearing you, and there's something else. Grandpa has a big surprise for you. It's something he and I discussed, and he thinks you're ready. We'll talk again soon."

I felt different after I hung up the phone, but I wasn't quite sure how to describe, even to myself, how I felt. I still felt out of place here, a city boy tossed onto a farm, but it felt good to hear the pride in Mom's voice. I wasn't sure I had ever before admitted to myself that I wanted her to be proud of me. Would I really keep changing just by being here and being around Grandpa and the other people in this town? I had no way of knowing, but somewhere inside myself I felt the same anticipation that Mom had talked about.

Grandpa was outside during my phone call with Mom, so I rushed outside to find out what this big surprise was. I found him bent over in the garden pulling every weed he came across. "Mom said to tell you hello," I began. He smiled but continued to pull the weeds.

"Jump right in here. Remember what I told you about having to take care of the things you start? The weeds are already here wanting to hurt what we planted, so we have to stay ahead of them," he replied.

I began in a row a few feet from him and attacked the weeds with a fervor. After a couple minutes of silence my curiosity got the best of me. "She also said something about a surprise for me."

"Oh, she did, did she?" he laughed. "I'm afraid you'll have to wait until tomorrow for that, but I promise it will be worth the wait."

"You won't even give me a hint?" I begged.

"No."

"Damn," I muttered under my breath. I could see his chest moving as he tried not to let me see him quietly chuckling to himself. After that, no weed in the garden stood a chance against me, and when we finished he lit the grill so we could eat.

When we sat down at the table I tried again. "Not even a clue?"

"Tomorrow."

"Damn."

CHAPTER 8

Grandpa was evidently extra tired because he didn't yell up the stairs for me until 6:30 the next morning. My sleep had been restless anyway, as I tried to imagine what my mysterious surprise could be. I had visions that ranged from some new clothes to a plane ticket home, but the truth was I had no idea what it could be. When I got downstairs he was sitting at the table casually drinking his morning coffee, and his demeanor showed no signs of any unusual excitement, though with him it was hard to tell. I had no doubt my disappointment showed, because I was keyed up with anticipation.

"After breakfast we need to run into the elevator," he began. "I need to get some things, and I'm going to contract some beans."

"What does that mean?" I asked curiously. "Contract?"

"It means that I lock in a price for a certain amount of the crop. If it goes up after that I miss out, but if it goes down then I did good."

"Gotcha," I replied. "And you think right now is a good price?"

"It's as good as it has been. Beans are up to $6.71 this morning, and I thought about holding out for $7.00, but today's price is good, and I'm going to take it."

"I hope it works out then," was all I could think to say. I understood the basic idea of what he had explained, but I didn't know anything about crop prices.

We cleaned up the breakfast mess, put our hats on, and went outside. It was a warm June morning and a slight breeze blew across the yard. For first thing in the morning it was quite comfortable. I saw our trip to town as a further delay of the news I was most interested in, and as we made our way to the pickup I asked. "So what's the big surprise you made me wait 'til today to see?"

Without looking at me or breaking stride he replied calmly, "It's in town. You'll see what it is soon."

"In town?"

"In town. Just relax a while longer and you'll see."

"If you say so," I replied as I opened the truck door and climbed inside.

The elevator was already in full swing even though it was just 7:30 in the morning. Workers were loading trucks for farmers, larger trucks were being filled by chutes that ran out of enormous bins, and a handful of farmers stood around the coffee pot in the lobby discussing the usual topics, crops and the weather. Until I came to Iowa I had probably drunk five cups of coffee in my entire life, but that had changed dramatically here. It seemed that everyone hear drank coffee, so in order to fit in I had begun drinking it regularly, and I actually had grown to like the taste a lot.

Grandpa went to the counter to deal with his contracting business, so I joined the farmers near the coffee pot. "Morning men," I began as I poured myself a cup.

Captain was among the group, and since he was already familiar with me, he replied first. "Morning Eli," he said. "What are you and Carl up to this morning?"

"Actually I'm not sure," I laughed. "Most of the time I don't know until we're ready to start doing whatever it is."

The others laughed at my comment too. Wally, a short slender man in his fifties, spoke next. "Knowing Carl, I'm sure he has something lined up. He's always thinking and planning and usually has several projects going at once." Wally's overalls were too big and loose for his frame, and he looked like a nervous boy in man's clothing. He shuffled his feet back and forth as he talked.

Captain spoke again. "Are you getting the hang of this small town farming life yet? Boys, old Eli here is a city clicker. All these tractors and crops and hogs and cattle are new to him."

"Sort of," I replied. "It's different for sure in lots of ways, but not so different in others. There are times when I wish I was back home, but I'll figure it out here before long."

At that moment Kenny walked through the door. He looked more cheerful than I would have imagined he could be so soon after everything he owned had been destroyed. When he approached the group, the men slapped him on the shoulders and welcomed him. Everyone was curious regarding any updates of Kenny's situation,

Legacy

and he didn't disappoint the group. He told us the insurance company had responded quickly due to the severity of his loss, and construction had already begun on the rebuilding of his house. His smile was only partially convincing, but I had seen first hand evidence of his and his family's resilience, so I felt somewhat certain that the excitement he showed was real.

It took a little over ten minutes for Grandpa to finish his business, and as he walked toward us I finished my second cup of coffee. "Men," he said casually, greeting the entire group at once.

"Carl," they replied almost in unison.

Captain, who had been watching him at the counter far more closely than the others, didn't hesitate. "Doing a little contracting today?"

"Oh, I don't know," replied Grandpa in a non-committal tone. "Thinking about it. Do you think I should? You're the wise one of the group."

Captain seemed to relish the question and the pedestal to which he had just been elevated, and even I felt bad for him for a moment since he seemed incapable of detecting the sarcasm in Grandpa's comment. "Might be a good idea, but I think beans will go over $7.00, maybe $7.50, so I'd wait."

"Interesting," was all Grandpa said to him. He then turned his attention to me. "Are you ready?"

"Yeah," I said eagerly. I really wanted to know what my big surprise was, and I was tired of waiting for it. If patience was one of the things I needed to learn, today would not have been a good test for me.

Before we drove away from the elevator I laughed to myself. I looked at all the pickups parked in front of the business, and there was no order to them at all. It was totally haphazard. Some were parked facing the building, some were diagonal, and some were parked end to end still in the road. "Only in a small town," I thought to myself. We drove away but did not go in the direction of the farm. Instead we headed toward uptown.

"Is there anything that Captain isn't an expert on?" I asked without too much seriousness.

39

"You picked up on that did you?" Grandpa smiled. "I guess if you asked him that, he'd probably tell you that he knows a little bit about lots of things. We all understand how he is, and we just take him with a grain of salt. If it makes him happy to feel like he's the smartest guy in the room, that's fine with me. He's harmless and his heart is in the right place. Remember how hard he worked at Kenny's the night of the storm?"

"Yeah, I guess," I responded. "Some of my buddies back home are like him. No matter what anybody says, they seem to have a better answer or something more important to tell everyone. Drives me nuts when people think they always have to play top the story."

"Good," he stated. "Topping someone's story is very rude, and you shouldn't do it. First of all it shows that you heard but you didn't listen, and when people do that to me it tells me they put no value in me or the things I tell them no matter how important I think it is. When someone immediately dismisses something I tell him and turns the conversation to his story instead, I usually decide right then to always be on my guard around him, and to speak very little, because I know I won't be listened to anyway. If Captain can teach us anything it's that listening is more important than talking. Did you ever consider that we have two ears and one mouth for a reason?"

We both laughed, but I understood what he had explained to me. I didn't enjoy being around Captain, and when I looked back honestly, I didn't enjoy the people back home who acted like he did. I guessed that people like Captain were everywhere.

Grandpa pulled into a parking spot in front of the post office and we both got out. Are you ready for the surprise?" he asked, though he was already certain of the answer.

"It's at the post office?"

"No," he said. "It's across the street. Come on. It's time for you to pick out your car."

I stopped in my tracks. "No way!" I exclaimed. "A car? Really?"

He was halfway across the street and turned back to me. "Are you coming?"

"You bet I am. Outstanding! I get a car?" I couldn't believe it.

CHAPTER 9

I ran to catch up with him and we entered the car lot together. My mind raced a thousand miles an hour, still not quite believing what appeared to be about to happen. It took less than thirty seconds for a salesman to approach us and shake hands with Grandpa.

"Good morning Carl," boomed Curt, a local thirty-something man who had once dreamed of traveling the world. He had made it halfway across town to spend his life fulfilling the dreams of others on the car lot instead. "The cars you asked about are over here." We followed him to a corner of the lot where Curt waved his arm and pointed to a specific group of four cars.

There was an El Camino, a Dodge Dart, a Satellite, and an Impala in the group. I looked them over and turned to Grandpa for a sign that I really got to choose one of them for my own. He nodded and said with a smile, "Whichever one you want. Your mom and I talked about it, and we agreed that it was time you had a chance to have a bit more freedom. From what I know of your behavior back home, you were nowhere near ready for this, but you've earned the chance by how you've acted here. Use your chance well, because if you blow it, I'll take the car away from you."

"I understand," though at that moment I was sure I would have agreed to any terms he would have presented to me.

"Which one do you want?" asked Curt, who could not contain the smile of his impending commission.

I sat in each one and pictured myself driving it everywhere. The El Camino didn't really interest me, but it was a difficult choice between the other three. In the end I chose the Satellite. It was olive green with a black top, and I could tell it had more power than the others. I made my decision out loud, and just like that I owned a car. Grandpa then gave me another surprise. He told me there was nothing really pressing to get done on the farm and he thought I should get to know Gowrie and the area better. Now that I had a car I could do that, and I liked the idea of spending a whole day driving around doing nothing in particular. The papers were signed, my gas tank was full, and I headed off to nowhere.

Legacy

Most of my time in Iowa so far had been spent only with Grandpa and his friends, and he was smart enough to realize that if I was going to be here for an extended period of time, I needed some friends of my own. I had no idea where to begin, and it was still early in the day, so I just started driving.

There were three main roads in Gowrie that ran east to west. Two of them ran the entire length of the town, exactly one mile. The intersecting north-south roads all varied in length, from one block to seven blocks in length, and I was determined to drive down each one of them. My feelings of independence overwhelmed me as I drove, and I wore a smile that could not be wiped off my face. I had my window down and my left arm rested proudly in the morning sun.

I saw so many new things in the town that it was a challenge to absorb them all at once. Many homes had gardens that were showing the same signs of future food that our garden was. Most of the yards were mowed and neatly trimmed, and I laughed as one man cussed loudly at his weed eater because it wouldn't start. A few yards in town were totally neglected, though there were obvious signs that people lived in the houses. The grass in those yards was very tall and the weeds had overtaken nearly everything else. When I saw those homes I immediately thought of Grandpa's lesson of keeping the weeds out of our garden. Apparently the people who lived in those places had no interest in any kind of long term things, and I was a little surprised that I could so quickly recognize that. Back in the city I would have given the overgrown yards no thought at all.

There was a city park that filled an entire block. I had seen it as we drove by on all our lunch trips to Hazel's Café, but I had never really paid much attention to it. I pulled my car along the curb on the east side of the park and shut off the engine. I wanted a closer look at the park, so I got out and began to walk around. A man across the street, whom I didn't know, raised his hand and gave me a friendly greeting. He then got into his white van and drove away. In the center of the park there was a concrete basketball court which looked like a lot of our city courts. The backboards were beaten up and the nets were made of wire. On one side of the court, connected to it, there was a covered stage of some kind. The floor was wooden, but the outside was rough, dark stone. Just west of the basketball court was an area filled with children's playground toys that included swings and a sand box. Just south of that was a covered shelter house filled with green picnic tables. In the middle of the park there was a drinking fountain that was set inside a brick base. Water gurgled from the fountain though nobody had turned it on. It looked to me like it had a small leak that needed some attention. The only other person in the park was a city employee on a large mower who was cutting the grass as quickly and efficiently as he could. He kept an eye on me every time he passed me on the mower, perhaps because I was a stranger to him, but when our eyes actually met he found a smile to share with me. There was a lot of grass to cut in the park, and I didn't envy him his job.

I had examined the park for about twenty minutes, and after I got a drink from the dripping fountain I started to walk back to my car. There was a lot more to see in town, and I was ready to see it. When I reached the curb a white car went by, and I suddenly heard, "Hey, Eli!" I was caught by surprise, and even more so when the car made a U-turn in the middle of the road and pulled in behind me. The driver grinned at me, turned his car off, and got out.

It took me a second but I remembered him from the two days at Kenny's house. He had shown up to help with the cleanup. He was in his mid twenties and had long straight hair. His build was similar to mine, tall and slender, and I remember that he had worked very hard at Kenny's house after the storm. His name was Darren, but everyone whom I had heard talk to him called him Rock. He started talking immediately. "What's up? Whose car?"

"Nuthin'." I replied, "and it's my car. Just got it this morning. Thought I'd try to learn my way around this place since I'm living here for a while." I turned around and looked at the park again. "That's a big park for the middle of town."

"Yeah, it's all right," he stated. "Wait til you see on the 4th of July. It'll be totally packed."

"Why? What happens here on the 4th?" I asked innocently.

Legacy

"Oh, man, the whole town comes to life. The whole area actually. It's like a non-stop three day party, and this year will be huge because of all the stuff going on."

"What kind of stuff? Not sure what you mean," I continued.

"Let's see if I can remember everything. There's a carnival here in the park, a parade of course, fireworks, a golf tournament, a softball tournament, a talent show, a tractor pull, a demolition derby, and who knows. I'm sure there's more."

"Nice," I smiled. "I saw some guys putting up decorations over main street a while ago. I guess they are getting a head start on 4th stuff."

"Yep," Rock continued. "Come on, I'll show you around. I wanna see how this new car of yours rides."

I smiled proudly. "Sure. I'll drive and you can tell me where we are."

"Okay," said Rock. "Let's go to Casey's first and get a soda. I'm thirsty."

I was happy to show off my new car and start building a friendship here. We got in and I drove to Casey's, a new convenience store in the center of town. Just like at the elevator that morning, there was no real order to the parking and the lot was full. I found a space somehow and we got out to get our drinks. One of the employees was outside changing the gas sign to fifty-one cents a gallon. "Man, gas is getting high!" exclaimed Rock. "It cost me seven dollars to fill my car up yesterday. It sucks."

We headed east out of the Casey's parking lot. "So, Mr. Tourguide, what are all the sites I should see here?"

"Let's see. There's the Gambles store and the phone company. You can see the Mobil station and here on your right is our awesome Dairy Sweet."

"Thank you so much for pointing out the obvious," I snipped. "How about some things that aren't quite so easy to figure out?"

"Okay." As I drove he started pointing toward homes and giving me a quick rundown of some of the people who lived in them. "That's the funeral home…That house on the corner is supposed to be haunted. Nobody has lived in it for years…That guy does construction…The couple there just got divorced, and I hear she already moved back to her hometown…That guy was in Viet Nam when it finished. Good guy but he won't talk about being over there or what he saw and did…"

When we reached the east end of town I turned left, and the guided tour continued. "The school superintendent lives there…That guy runs the meat market…" One block later I turned back west and drove on. The only thing on our right was one lonely farm house up on a small hill, and it looked very isolated and out of place. Near the middle of town there was more… "The Sinclair station. The guy who runs it is the mayor. Turn right here." I did and Rock continued. "Our skating rink. Lots of good times there."

Just past the skating rink was a sports complex that included a baseball field, a football field, and a track. The baseball team was having a practice when we drove by. At the end of this dead end street was the town's swimming pool, and beside the pool were two new tennis courts and some horseshoe pits. I was extremely intrigued by the high diving board and looked forward to conquering it before summer ended.

"You guys have a lot of things to do here," I stated with great sincerity.

"Yeah, I guess so," answered Rock. "Never really thought about it. Probably cause I've lived here forever and see it all every day."

"I like it," I continued. "We've got a couple pool halls near my house, but none of this stuff."

Rock beamed with a sudden community pride. "There's more," he continued. "We've got a bowling alley and a golf course too."

I shook my head in amazement. This was no ordinary little town. I turned back south away from the pool, and we drove up on two heavyset women who walked together on the side of the road. As I drove past them Rock whistled sarcastically in their direction. They both looked at us, and I didn't know what to do. I sped up and Rock laughed out loud at his joke. I, however, was not amused. "That was pretty rude," I said sternly. "Why did you do that?"

"Oh, come on man. That was funny," he sneered in return. "Did you see them? I probably made their day."

I looked at him coldly. "Would you have done that if we were in your car? It's easy to be brave and stupid if nobody knows for sure who you are. They'll remember my car though. Thanks a lot."

"You wanted the tour of the town, and they are part of the town, a big part of it," he continued to laugh. "What's the big deal?" he asked. You sound like my dad. It was just a joke."

I surprised myself at my reaction, but my feelings were genuine. I had taken an instant liking to Rock working at Kenny's house, and ten minutes earlier I had thought I had found my first friend here, but a guy older than I, who got a kick out of making others feel shame and embarrassment for his own fun and amusement instantly changed my mind. What had appeared to be a friendly and easy time between us now oozed with an unspoken tension.

He remained unapologetic as I steered my car toward the park. "People who look like that invite rude comments. Lighten up man. It's really not a big deal."

I pulled in behind his car. "I need to get back out to the farm," I stated coldly but as politely as I could.

Rock got the message and got out, more than a bit surprised by how I had reacted to his whistle and his comments. "Later," he said as I drove away.

"Yeah, later," I replied.

I wanted to keep driving my new car around, but I knew there would be plenty of time for that, so I turned toward the farm. It was already 85 degrees, and I decided that I would go swimming that afternoon if Grandpa really didn't have any work for us to do . It felt great driving my new car down the highway. I cranked my window all the way down and turned the radio up loud. I could never remember such a feeling of independence before, and I liked it.

I stirred up plenty of gravel as I neared the farm, and I hadn't thought about it, but when I slowed down to turn into the driveway, the dust caught up with me and poured through the passenger window, covering everything in my car including me. I began to cough and my vision was temporarily gone. The dust all

Legacy

settled in just a few seconds, but it seemed like a much longer period of time to me. When the dust was gone I wiped my eyes and slowly drove my car the rest of the way into the yard. Grandpa, who was working on the cultivator, had witnessed my entire episode, and he had a hard time containing his laughter.

"I'm guessing that's a lesson you'll have to learn just once," he began. "Funny isn't it how that dust will chase you down and get you?"

"Yeah," I answered, still wiping myself off and removing bits of gravel from my hair. "Only once."

"I thought you'd be gone all day," he continued. "Nothing to do in town?"

"Sort of," I stated as I walked up to where he was working. "It was fun driving around and then I got irritated."

"Oh?" he asked. "What happened?" He put down his wrench and gave me his complete attention as I told him about Rock and the women on the street. "And why do you think what he did made you mad?"

"Because the women were just minding their own business, out for a morning walk. They had nothing to do with us, and he just casually made them feel bad. Their feelings meant nothing to him, and I felt really bad because I was an unintentional part of it. Even when I called him on it he didn't care. He still thought it was just a funny joke."

"What Rock did was wrong," explained Grandpa, "but stuff like that happens all the time. I'm sure you've seen plenty of things like that back home – when passing construction sites, kids your age teasing old folks, little gangs in the halls at school, and so on."

"True," I said. "How come all this stuff is so much more obvious to me here than it ever was at home? I haven't figured that one out yet."

"You'll have to come up with that answer for yourself, but I'm glad you're noticing. Maybe it's the slower pace here that gives you more chances to notice the details as well as the people. All people deserve to be treated with respect no matter where we are. What Rock did today was cowardly, and it was easy for him because he was in your car and he knew the women wouldn't retaliate. He would have never had the guts to do that if you two had been walking beside them instead of driving away. Insecure people grab any moment they can find to make themselves feel superior or important, even if it's for a few seconds. I'll bet he didn't like your reaction at all."

"No, not much," I answered. "Especially when I drove straight back to his car and basically told him we were done for the day."

"Here, grab a wrench. Let's make sure all the bolts on this thing are tight. About time to get back into the field and make sure those crops are cared for as much as our garden is." I did as he asked and while I worked, out of the corner of my eye, I caught him looking at me and smiling. I pretended I hadn't seen it, but inside it made me feel very good.

CHAPTER 10

Grandpa had told me the truth about not having any real work to do on the farm that day, and I still had the rest of the afternoon and evening to do whatever I wanted. I decided I would go back into town and get acquainted with the swimming pool. I didn't have a swimsuit though, so I would have to buy one, but that would be easy. We finished working on the cultivator, had some lunch, and I was on my way into town, this time at a much slower pace on the gravel.

My first stop was at the local variety store uptown, and I quickly chose a suitable swimsuit to buy. It cost me four dollars for the suit and another dollar to get into the pool for the day, but I didn't mind. The afternoon was hot and I was ready for the water and the diving boards. There were a lot of people already there, mostly kids, but also several adult women who worked on their tans while their children swam and played. Most people just splashed around without a purpose, but there were also some groups who played a variety of water games. Some of my initial eagerness and brashness left me as I looked for a place to lay down my towel. When I looked at all the people in the pool it struck me that I

Legacy

didn't know any of them, and I was alone. I got a few looks because none of the people knew me either.

  I tossed my towel down along the chain-link fence and headed for the deep end and the diving boards. I dove in and swam in one breath to the other side of the pool. When my hands reached the wall one of the lifeguards was waiting for me. "Have you been here before?" she began.

  I looked up a bit puzzled. "No, why?" I asked.

  "You can't be in the deep end until you pass a test."

  "Really?" I asked.

  "Yes, really. Do you want to take it?"

  "I don't know. I guess so. What is the test?"

  "You swim twenty lengths of this part of the pool then you tread water for five minutes with me watching you."

  I thought for a second and then exclaimed, "I can do that. Let's get started."

  Ten minutes later I had successfully passed Gowrie's deep end swimming test and I had access to the entire pool. I started with the low board, and the first time I was on it I bounced high on the end of the board and did a slow, lazy flip. Now that I had my bearings I was ready to give these Iowa swimmers a lesson on how fun a diving board could really be. My buddies and I swam a lot back home during the summers, and we all got really good using diving boards. In the city we didn't have a high board though, and I couldn't wait to show off once I got on the one here. I was amazed at how different everything looked from up there, and it made me think of cliff divers I had seen on TV. Standing on the edge of the high board, I could not imagine how those people calmly dove from heights much greater than where I stood. At the edge of the board I turned around, bounced once, and did a perfect back flip into the water.

  Several of the kids in line for the board cheered me when I surfaced, and I smiled at them. I immediately got back in line and in a short time I had shown them the entire array of my diving board skills. I did a 1 ½ flip, a cutaway, a running gainer, and a long range can opener from which the splash was so big it reached the lifeguard's chair and got her wet. Everyone at that end of the pool, except the lifeguard, cheered that one.

I was now part of the group and was accepted, which made me feel good. Several others tried my board stunts, and a few of them did quite well. Some of the other attempts led to awkward belly flops and other types of painful landings. Overall it was a very fun afternoon for me, and I had met about ten people whom I liked a lot. Eventually I got tired and hungry, so I got ready to leave. I knew there would be more fun days here at the pool, and I looked forward to them.

I walked back to my car and was quite surprised to see Rock standing beside it waiting for me. "Hey," I spoke casually.

"Hey, yourself," he replied. "How's the water?"

"It was great," I continued. "I can see me being here quite a bit. What's up with you?"

"Just hangin'." His feet began to shuffle back and forth a bit, and his eyes were looking at the pavement. "And I wanted to apologize for earlier. I don't know why I did that. Seemed like the thing to do at the time, but it was bad, especially in your car. What's worse is I know those ladies, and they're pretty nice."

"It just really caught me wrong and burned me pretty fast," I replied.

"I know man. Sorry."

"Thanks Rock. I've done lots of things like that back home too, but the city is so different. Don't think I'll do it any more though. Until today I had never thought of the other people's feelings."

"Me either," he added. "What are you gonna do now?"

"No plans," I smile. "Why?"

"Wanna finish that tour?"

"Sure," I said. "Hop in."

Rock and I drove away, just as we had done that morning, except we shared a better understanding of each other. I concluded that sometimes a shaky beginning that gets quickly resolved can turn out to be a good thing in the long run. Perhaps at times, with some humility, a person really can get a second chance to make a first impression.

Legacy

    This time I got the detailed tour of the north and west sides of town. I saw a chicken hatchery that I might have never found on my own, an old railroad caboose in a yard, a log home, the local nursing home, an oddly shaped triangle-looking house, and the local school building. It was interesting noticing the details of this lively little town and hearing Rock's description of the people and places we saw. He was far more careful now than before to not be quick to point out the negatives, and I appreciated that. I just wanted to get a better feel for the town and the people and he had helped me do that.

    Since my car was still new to me I checked the odometer a lot, and I laughed when I realized we had ridden around for about an hour and had driven only a little more than ten miles. "It feels like we're just putting around here like turtles," I stated.

    Rock laughed and answered, "We do this all the time, especially at night. We shag the drag a lot. I'll show you our loop." The loop, as he called it, was one end of the business district on Main Street to the other end, turning around at the funeral home corner when driving east and turning around at the park when driving west. I didn't see much fun in doing that for an entire night, but if that was what people here did, then I would join them.

    On the bench in front of Hazel's Café I saw a man who made me very curious. The afternoon was very hot, yet he sat on the bench there wearing blue jeans and a long sleeve shirt, and whenever the person next to him spoke, the first man roared with laughter and slapped his own knees repeatedly. "Oh, that's Russell," explained Rock. "He sits there a lot. He's a little different but basically a nice guy. Loves to talk with people and laugh. His favorite thing is to have you pull his finger when he needs to fart. That really cracks him up."

    "I'll remember that," I said.

    We drove around for another half hour and then I got bored and was ready for something different. "So what is there to do around here this weekend besides shagging the drag?"

    "Well, there's a big hog roast and kegger tomorrow night. There's gonna be a lot of people there having a good time. Wanna go there with me?"

"Sounds fun," I replied. "Will it be a problem if I just show up with you?"

"No, not at all. When somebody has something like that here everybody is welcome. A girl I've been dating a little bit is coming and bringing a friend with her. You can hang out with her."

"We'll see about that," I stated skeptically. "Not sure if I'm into a blind date or not."

"She's cute and really nice. Trust me," Rock grinned.

"Right," I replied cynically.

When I got home Grandpa was standing beside the foundation of the destroyed garage, and he was talking with someone I didn't recognize. I approached them and he promptly introduced me to the man. "Glen, this is my grandson Eli. Eli, this is Glen. He's going to rebuild the garage." We shook hands and the two wrapped up their conversation. Glen then got into his pickup and drove away.

"When is he going to start?" I inquired.

"Monday morning," replied Grandpa.

We walked together toward the house and were both struck by the incredible noise that came from a row of five trees just south of the house. It was so loud and so constant that we both stopped and looked up into the trees. "Man, they are extra loud tonight," I started.

"I can fix that," he answered. "I'm tired of hearing that constant squalling."

"What do you mean?"

"Wait here. I'll be right back."

He walked into the house and I stood outside, completely puzzled. The birds continued to get louder as more of them gathered in the tree tops. In less than three minutes he returned carrying a shotgun and some shells. He wasted no time and quickly loaded both barrels. Then he positioned himself a few feet away from the middle of the five trees, raised the gun and fired twice, once toward the right side and once toward the left side. What happened next seemed surreal to me.

Some birds flew away because of the sudden deafening gun shot, but many others never got that chance. Birds began dropping from

52

the trees and fell with a gentle thud onto the ground near us. They just kept falling, and I silently watched in awe. Five birds, then ten, then twenty, and more fell to the ground dead. The noise in the trees had stopped.

Grandpa turned to me and simply said, "If you have something that you perceive as a problem, you don't just sit around and gripe about it and hope that it magically fixes itself. You face it, get a plan, and then meet it head on."

The ground under the trees looked like it had been carpeted with birds, and I still didn't quite know what to say. I looked back and forth between him and the birds and unconvincingly blurted out, "Got it." He walked purposefully back to the house and all I could do was quietly follow. He grilled some chicken that night and we again ate outside on the picnic table. Neither of us was surprised by the silence in the trees.

CHAPTER 11

The next morning Grandpa was in the field with the cultivator, and since there was really nothing I could do to help with that, it was my job to mow and trim the yard. Before I could mow, however, I had to get an empty bucket and pick up all forty-three dead birds. I had the lawn looking great by 1:00 that afternoon, and the rest of the day was mine. I got more excited every time I thought about the hog roast that night, but I also got more nervous about the apparent blind date Rock intended for me.

I made a couple sandwiches and took them out to the field so Grandpa could have some lunch. He had covered a lot of ground in five hours and was happy to take a break.

"Get the yard done?" he asked me in between bites.

"Yeah, it's finished. Took a little longer this time because I had a lot of dead birds to clean up first."

He grinned slyly. "Head on, my boy. Always meet things head on."

Legacy

I told him about the hog roast that night and he said it sounded like fun. It would also be a good way for me to meet more people, but he warned me not to drink and drive. "You've had that car for a day and a half, and here's your first chance to be stupid with it. Don't do it."

"I'll be careful," I told him, though in my heart I couldn't be quite so sure that I really would be.

7:00 that night took forever to arrive, but it finally did. The party was only two miles from our farm, but Rock and I had agreed to meet in town and go to the party together. His car was parked in front of Casey's, and I pulled in next to him and saw that there were two girls in the car with him, one in the front seat and one in the back. Both of them studied me carefully while Rock and I talked through the car windows.

"Ready to go?" he asked with a big grin.

"Yeah, I guess so," I replied. "I'll just follow you.

Rock then paused for a second. "Hang on, I've got an idea." He then turned and said something to the girls, but I couldn't hear him. A few seconds later the passenger door opened and one of the girls got out and walked around toward my car. "Pretty silly for three of us to go in my car and you go by yourself. Kathy can ride with you."

Kathy got into my car and smiled shyly. I smiled back at her and silently wondered if she felt as awkward at that moment as I did. If she felt that way she hid it well. She appeared full of excitement for what lay ahead at the party. I felt certain Rock had planned that little car switching move ahead of time, but I wasn't mad at him for doing it. Kathy was pretty, and I liked the idea of arriving at the party with a girl.

It didn't take long to get to the party and we were nowhere near the first ones to arrive. The gravel road in front of the farm was lined on both sides with cars and trucks, and the yard held as many vehicles as it could. I found a parking spot on the road and we walked a quarter mile back to the party. Kathy and I walked closely together and that was the first time I realized how short she was. She was nearly a full foot shorter than I, and she had to take much faster steps to keep up with me. Loud music greeted us when we arrived, and I saw at least a dozen people standing around a huge cooker drinking and laughing loudly.

There were nearly a hundred people inside the enormous Morton building. I had never seen a storage or work building like it before. The doors were wide enough and the ceiling was tall enough to hold a combine, and there were lawn chairs and square hay bales scattered all over so the partiers had places to sit. I could see five or six different groups sitting together throughout the building and we were easily among the youngest people there. Most were in their twenties and thirties, but quite a few people there were much older than that.

Rock seemed to know everyone, which didn't surprise me, but Cheri, Rock's girlfriend, Kathy, and I were mostly strangers to all the others at the party. We milled around without any real purpose and watched Rock shake hands with and greet a dozen people before we finally met the party's host, Josh. Josh, in his early thirties, was definitely in his element as he made sure everyone had a good time. He was a big man, over six feet tall, and solid but not overweight. He toasted his guests with every drink of beer he took, and he went from group to group making sure everyone had eaten some of his pork.

Rock had known Josh for as long as Rock could remember and after a handshake between the two, Rock introduced all of us to him. Josh, who had obviously been drinking for quite a while that day, could not have been kinder. He greeted us warmly, offered to fill our beer cups, and complimented Rock and me on the girls we had with us, which was a bit embarrassing for me since I had known Kathy for less than an hour.

"Josh, Eli is Carl's grandson," stated Rock. "He's a city boy and is staying here a while."

"Excellent!" replied Josh as he shook my hand again. "Carl is a good man. I've known him since I was a little kid, and he has helped me out many times."

"Yeah," I said. "I didn't know him too well 'til I got here, but I'm figuring out that he pretty much knows what's going on. He just gets in my face and tells me what he's thinking, good or bad."

55

Josh began to laugh. "He will for sure do that," he continued, "but he's good to everybody. Hard to go wrong listening to what he tells you."

He shook my hand for the third time, told us all to drink up, then left us in order to talk to some others at the party. We four stood by ourselves for a few minutes, then Rock grabbed Cheri and took her to talk to some other friends. Kathy and I were left alone, and I motioned to an empty hay bale. She smiled and we sat together on it and watched the others for a minute. I was definitely nervous there with her, but at the same time it felt quite comfortable. I wasn't sure I had ever felt that mix of emotions before.

"Pretty good party," I offered in a weak attempt to break the ice.

"It is," replied Kathy. "Everybody seems to be having a good time."

"No doubt," I agreed. "I've never actually been to a hog roast at a farm before. You probably do this a lot don't you?"

"Nope," Kathy smiled. "My first one too, but I like it so far. Rock told Cheri it would be fun and she didn't want to drive down by herself, so she asked me to come with her."

"You two aren't from Gowrie?"

"We live twenty or so miles away in Dodge. Have you been there yet?"

"No, I haven't," I stated. "Never even heard of it, but that's not saying anything. I don't know much at all about Iowa. Lots of firsts for me here."

She leaned in closer to me and spoke softly. "Don't tell Rock, but we got lost coming here. Neither of us had a clue where we were going and we ended up in some other town fifteen miles away and had to ask someone for directions."

I laughed with her. "That's a good one," I said. "I don't know any of the towns here either, but you've lived here all your life."

"I know," she continued, "but neither of us ever drives out of town so we just took off and hoped!"

After Kathy leaned in to tell me her secret she stayed close, and though I was a still a little nervous, I tried hard not to show it. I liked her. Both our beer glasses were empty, so I went to the keg and filled them. I returned to our bale of hay and Josh walked by with a beer in one hand and a huge pork sandwich in the other. When he saw us sitting there he gave us a big smile and a thumbs up.

Four beers later Kathy and I had made our way off our bale and onto the makeshift dance floor. It was the floor of a hayrack that had been taken off its axles. One of Josh's friends was in charge of the music and he kept it going continuously. We danced three fast songs and I had broken a sweat. The next song was slow and without hesitation Kathy wrapped her arms around my neck and pressed herself extremely close to me. We moved together in a very slow circle, and I liked how my arms felt around her back. Several other couples danced near us, but I didn't really pay much attention to them. I had no idea where things might go with her, but I liked our beginning.

The song finished before our embrace did and we stared into each other's eyes with a purpose and a longing unnamed. I suggested we stop dancing for a while and go for a walk, and she quickly agreed. We walked from the building holding hands and we left the other partiers behind and headed toward an unlit area of Josh's farm. We came across several buildings and pens and the night was much quieter several hundred yards away from the music.

I was even more nervous now than before, and I didn't know for sure what the right thing to do was at that moment. My boys back home and I always talked like we were big ladies' men, but the truth was I was quite awkward and unsure of myself. I squeezed Kathy's hand and said, "You're a good dancer."

"Thanks. So are you," she smiled back at me.

I turned so we faced each other. "I know this was all a set up deal, but I'm glad. I like you being here with me."

Kathy continued smiling. "I'm glad too. Cheri told me to take a chance because there would be all kinds of guys here. She said if you and I didn't hit it off, I could find someone else I'd probably like."

"Interesting. So, you wanna go back and check out the others?" I asked, almost half afraid of her answer.

Without hesitation she said simply, "No."

I leaned down and kissed Kathy for the first time and the kiss lasted until I was nearly out of breath. I could not imagine any girl anywhere having softer lips than she did. The sensation of kissing her helped remove my remaining nervousness, and I was really glad of that.

Suddenly there was a noise in the pen behind us. We walked to the fence and saw several pigs asleep on the ground. One had evidently stirred for some reason, but overall the pen was still. A large sow rested just inches from where we stood and Kathy jumped back a little, not quite sure of what she was seeing.

"They're just pigs," I stated as reassuringly as I could. "They won't hurt you."

She gingerly returned to where I stood. "Are you sure? They look so big. I've never seen one up close before. They won't come through the fence will they?"

"No. Wanna touch her?" I asked.

"Really? Yeah, I do. Really? She continued excitedly.

"Sure. Why not?" I said. We leaned down and reached between the boards in the fence. Kathy was hesitant but she finally talked herself into putting her hand on the sow's back. She giggled uncontrollably as she continued to run her hand across the coarse hide of the sleeping pig. Before long the sow stirred and unexpectedly started to get up. Kathy jumped back so quickly she fell on her back, still laughing.

"That was so cool," she declared. "Cheri will be so mad she missed that." I reached my hand out to help her up and when she was again on her feet we shared our second kiss, which was every bit as good as the first had been. Something had definitely begun between us.

We slowly walked back toward the party and I felt great. I looked at her and innocently commented, "You're a lot of fun. Hard for me to believe you don't already have a boyfriend."

Kathy's entire demeanor changed in an instant and she let go of my hand. "Well," she started, "I kind of do have one. I'm actually engaged."

Legacy

I could only imagine how surprised my faced must have looked after that news, and I certainly didn't know how to respond. I just kept walking beside her and quietly uttered a weak reply of, "Oh."

We emerged from the darkness and rejoined the others, and it seemed to me that the party had gotten even louder while we had been gone. There was still a group near the cooker who continued to eat hunks of pork, but most of the people milled around and told stories. We quickly found Rock and Cheri and stood with them again.

"Take a little walk did ya?" grinned Rock knowingly.

"Yeah," I replied. "Kathy had never pet a pig before, but now she has."

"You did what"? asked Cheri with great curiosity. "Pet a pig? You mean you pet it like a dog?"

Kathy giggled uncontrollably again. "I did. I really did. It was so cool."

"I wanna do it too," moaned Cheri. "Where are they?"

"Good grief," replied Rock. "Another time okay?"

"Oh, all right," Cheri said, "but I wanna do it for sure."

Rock answered her with a wry smile. "Got it. I've already made my mental note."

"I'm going for another beer," I stated. "Back in a few." I then walked by myself to the keg and while I waited to fill my cup I met a few others whom I did not know.

Maxie was tall, dark haired, and very loud. He also seemed to find everything he heard funny and he talked nearly non-stop. Maybe it was too much beer. Maybe his talking all the time was just the way he normally was. I couldn't tell. He was in his late twenties and had spent the entire night close to the keg talking to everyone who came to fill a cup.

Wally was a little older than Maxie, and he was definitely a farmer. Despite the heat of the June night, he wore his blue overalls and boots almost as if for him there were no alternatives. His blue Fontanelle seeds hat was dirty and worn and his hands showed that he didn't worry much about his appearance. He spoke little and instead had roving, penetrating, thoughtful eyes that seemed to take in everything possible that he saw around him. He smiled while Maxie talked, but he appeared to me to be a man who always kept his emotions in check.

Zeb was the tallest of the three and seemed to be the most athletic. I suspected that somewhere in his past were some high school glory days that he enjoyed reliving. It seemed those days had been replaced with the sad eyes of his adult reality and a strong love of alcohol. He slurred his words and had very little balance as he stumbled to the keg for another refill.

This was the cast of characters at my first Iowa hog roast and kegger. I was also struck by the intense familiarity everyone seemed to have here, something totally foreign to the city parties I had attended. Everyone here seemed to have at least one nickname, and I tried my best to learn them. There was Crusher, Moses, Deacon, Lennie, Red, JB, Fish, Woody, Legs, Slim, Arch, Gasser, and at least ten others I had already forgotten.

I stayed with these three a few more minutes, introduced myself, and mostly just listened. I figured I would hear the usual talk of rain and crops but I was wrong. The group talked about Carnies and fireworks and bicycles and motorcycles and yard things, which I found really odd. They all agreed that the 4th of July was the best time of year because it was really profitable. I didn't have a clue what they meant, but when they fully comprehended that I was eavesdropping on their conversation, they changed the topic back to beer and pork. I got the message and returned to Rock, Kathy and Cheri, still unsure exactly how to feel about Kathy telling me she was engaged, a fact that certainly changed the mood between us. I again stood close to her but there would be no further romance between us, at least not at the party.

It was after 1:00 AM and the crowd was thinning out. I was also tired and ready to leave. The girls had over twenty miles to drive, assuming they could find their way on the first try, so they needed to go too. The good-byes were fairly quick and I left the other three near Rock's car. It wasn't until I sat behind the wheel in my car that I began to realize just how many beers I had drunk. Grandpa's words returned to my thoughts, and I knew he was right. I shouldn't be driving and it was stupid to try, but I had confidence in myself. After all it was only a couple miles.

CHAPTER 12

The first mile was easy. I kept my speed around forty miles per hour on the gravel and I drove a fairly straight line. During the second mile I twice found my car on the left side of the road before I corrected it. When I turned the final corner toward home I felt vindicated and confident, so I sped up. In just a few seconds I realized I was again on the left side of the road, so I swung my steering wheel to the right really hard. Too hard. I was now unsure how to correct my situation so I turned the wheel to the left again, and I now found my car fishtailing on the gravel and I had no control of the car at all. Eventually the car slid into the ditch on the right side of the road and I put my foot on the brake pedal. I came to an abrupt stop less than a hundred feet from the farm and it felt like my heart would jump out of my throat. My entire body shook uncontrollably and sweat covered me everywhere. A moment later, when my breathing returned to normal, I looked for the best way to get out of the ditch. It was extremely steep where I was and it seemed to me the best solution was to drive in the ditch the rest of the way home and enter the driveway there, driving up a much smaller bank than the one I faced at that moment.

The grass in the ditch was tall and I drove slowly. When I reached the parking lot I put both hands on the wheel and shook my head, frustrated with myself. "Stupid, stupid, stupid," I repeated to myself over and over. I walked into the house as quietly as possible, climbed the stairs, and fell into bed. I had luckily made it home safely and would worry about tomorrow when I woke up. Sleep came quickly, despite my near catastrophe. Such is the power of alcohol.....

> *Oh, it's nice to get up in the morning....*
> *It's nice to get up in the morning....*

My eyes fought back when I tried to open them, and my head throbbed painfully. That awful little song was the last thing I wanted to hear but it continued until I grunted a response. It took several more minutes for me to gather my thoughts, put some clothes on, and walk slowly downstairs. Beside my breakfast plate I found a glass of water, two aspirins, and a glass of tomato juice, apparently an old Iowa remedy. Grandpa had evidently anticipated my condition and I had no real desire to attempt any kind of verbal denial. I took the aspirin with the water, then drank the tomato juice, but I was unsure of my ability to put food into my unsettled stomach.

"Eat," was all Grandpa said to me.

"I'll try," I responded weakly as my fork played around in my eggs.

Grandpa looked at me with a sarcastic grin. "Looks like you had a little too much pork last night."

"Yeah, that was it. Bad pork."

"Look," he continued. "Going to a party is not an excuse to take a day off or mope around like you're the only one who has ever felt bad. Nobody forced those beers down you last night, and nothing is for free. This is a good example for you to remind you that everything in life is a trade off and comes at a price. Everything. When the sun comes up you have to answer the bell. We've got work to do today, so eat and let's get going."

"So you've never been hung over before?" I inquired.

"Oh, once or twice I've gotten into a bad batch of peanuts, but it has been a while."

"I feel like crap."

"I know," he answered. "Let's get going. Time to answer the bell."

The morning sunshine instantly hurt my squinting eyes but I trudged on, not knowing exactly what the job or jobs of the day would be. Grandpa and I walked past the pickup and past the garden and continued toward the driveway. I wasn't aware of his purposeful steps until he stopped near the ditch and we both looked at the matted down grass and the tire tracks that extended a long way down the ditch. My mind suddenly engaged fully, recalling the last part of my drive home just a few hours earlier.

We both stood quietly while Grandpa assessed all that he saw. His face then turned serious and I felt sure he was about to yell at

Legacy

me, but he didn't. He looked at my car, then at the ditch, then at me and simply said, "Got away with it, didn't you?"

I wasn't sure how to respond, but through my guilt and embarrassment I mumbled a feeble, "I guess so."

"I told you last night was your first chance to really be stupid with your new car and you were. Tell me how it feels to believe you're bullet-proof and invincible."

"What do you mean?" I asked.

"You need to figure out what's really important to you. Is it your car? Your life? Others' lives? Your mom? What?"

"All of those are important. Why?" I responded.

"Bull. You still don't think at all. Your car isn't a toy and the road is not a playground. When you drink and drive you're dangerous and that car becomes a weapon. It was easy to convince yourself you were in control wasn't it?"

"I guess so. I don't really remember it all."

"That's even worse. Look, I can see your fishtail marks from here. Think about this. What if another car had been coming toward you at that moment? Your foolishness could have ruined or ended a lot of lives." With that he turned and began walking back. "Let's see if you hurt the car. What do you have to say for yourself?"

I didn't immediately answer. I hadn't even considered those possibilities, but after he said those words I wondered if perhaps I had torn something up as I drove through the ditch. To my relief we found no damage, just a lot of grass stuck to the front bumper and the under side of the car. Grandpa looked directly at me. "You were very lucky all the way around, but if you ever do that again I'll take you to the police myself. Just when I think you're starting to grow up, you show me you're still just a cocky kid who can't think two hours ahead. Give me your keys. You have no business driving a car. You can spend the next week thinking about last night."

"But it wasn't all my fault," I pleaded.

"Oh, really," he sneered back at me. "Whose fault was it then?"

I hadn't planned on having my bluff called so quickly, and I didn't have a good answer ready to use. "Josh kept filling up my beer cup, and I didn't realize I had drunk so much. Everybody there just kept drinking and having a good time."

"That's your answer?" he asked me with a real look of disappointment. "That's pitiful. Grow up. You sound like a little kid. It wasn't my fault. It wasn't me. You've still got a long way to go don't you? You have no clue how to take responsibility for your own actions. Wanna try again? Whose fault was all this?"

I slowly reached into my pocket and relinquished my keys. I stood silently beside my car as he walked toward the barn. I felt ashamed because I knew everything he had said to me was true. I didn't want to be a kid who just lived in the moment anymore, and I pledged to myself right then that I no longer would be that boy. It was time to grow up. Another of Grandpa's lessons had been learned, this one the really hard way.

CHAPTER 13

The day was long and miserable and my headache remained with me until mid-afternoon. Every so often I glanced at my car, and knowing that I no longer had the keys made me feel even worse. By late afternoon our work was done, and I took that opportunity to lie under a shade tree and take a nap. The grass was soft and the gentle breeze was soothing, and I had no trouble at all falling asleep.

When I woke up the sun was nearly down and I had no energy for anything that night. Perhaps something to eat and then some TV, but nothing more than that. The party continued to take its toll, and as fun as it was the night before, I had to stop for a moment and let the cost of the evening fully sink in. I felt bad, I no longer had my car keys, and I had spent some romantic time with an engaged girl whom I really liked. All in all it was quite a first Iowa party for me.

Since I had no transportation for a week, which was the length of Grandpa's punishment, my next few days were spent working around the farm and the yard. I mowed and trimmed the yard again and gave the garden some extra attention. The vegetables were growing nicely but so were the weeds. It seemed to me that the process of protecting one's garden was never-ending, and I was amazed at how quickly the grass and the thistles grew around the plants we wanted to protect. I still had no idea what kohlrabi was but Grandpa assured me I would like it. The radishes and carrots were showing their leaves above the ground and the green onions were several inches high. The tomatoes were always more work than the rest, as I had to keep the vines up in the air and frequently rearrange the chicken wire we had placed around them for their protection. Besides the weeds that had sprouted up, there were other signs of garden predators. Tracks in the soft dirt showed that rabbits and deer had visited, though I had never personally seen either. Apparently they were clever enough to come to our garden only when they felt sure that no humans were around. Grandpa once told me that sometimes the things that attacked "good" did it for their own survival and sometimes they did it because of their fear of the unknown or fear of change. With the animals it was for survival, but with people that was rarely the reason. After two hours of my attacking all the weeds I could see, Grandpa brought me a glass of iced tea and we sat together under a shade tree. "The garden looks good," he said as he looked around. "So does the yard."

"Thanks," I answered, feeling an unusual bit of pride in both things. "I've put in a lot of time on them."

"I know," he replied. "That's what ownership does to a guy. It makes him care more and do extra things. A guy will almost always do whatever he has to do to make something good if one of three things is in his mind. Can you guess what those things are?"

I thought for a few seconds. "Three things that make a guy do extra…Let's see…Money?"

"That's close," he said. "How did I know that would be the one you would get first? It's not just money though. That's too narrow an answer. I think it's when someone believes there is something extra in it for him, something he wants or needs, and that doesn't always mean money. What else?"

I thought again. "I don't know. The only thought that popped into my mind was the money."

Grandpa laughed at my answer. "Think bigger. Haven't you learned that one yet? Money is good and necessary, but it's temporary and it should never be the primary goal for anything you do. Think bigger. What would make a guy do extra?"

Before I realized it I blurted out another answer. "Pride. If someone is proud of something he wants it to be excellent. Is that one of the three?"

"Now you're thinking, and here's the real test. What if nobody else ever sees or knows about the thing you're proud of? Do you still do the extra things for yourself?"

"I don't know," I said, trying to decide on my answer. "I probably would sometimes, but I don't know if I would all the time."

"Interesting," replied Grandpa as he took off his hat and wiped some sweat from his forehead. "What's the difference between when you would do the extra and when you wouldn't?"

I aimlessly began to pull some grass around me and tried to formulate my response. "I guess it would come down to how much I cared about whatever I was doing and how good it would make me feel when I finished it."

"That makes sense," he continued. "Do you think you'd feel good because you finished in general or because you knew you did your best?"

I laughed at him. "One thing always leads to another with you doesn't it? You can't stand any answer that's simple. There's always more to consider."

Grandpa smiled back at me, looking like he had achieved some small silent victory in his teaching. "A guy has gotta think or he gets left behind. So which is it? When you finish the yard, do you feel good because you're done or because you know you did it well?

"I feel good because I did it well."

"And that's the third reason. Self-satisfaction raises your self-esteem, which in turn gets you excited about doing other things in your life equally well. So you see, I hope, that your first answer of money is the least important reason to do something well. If you take pride in everything you do because you feel good doing your best, then I promise the money will find you."

"I like that," I replied as I rose from the ground. "There's still a few more weeds to get out of the garden."

"Let's get to them then," he smiled.

CHAPTER 14

My week without my car finally ended, though it seemed much longer to me than just seven days. Everything on the farm had been cleaned and picked up and arranged, and I think Grandpa was as ready to turn me loose again as I was to regain my freedom. The only times that week that I left the farm were the three trips to town with Grandpa for lunch at Hazel's.

Kenny's house was going up quickly and he was justifiably excited, which made him talk even faster than usual. Captain, of course, never ran out of ideas and suggestions for how Kenny could be doing things better, and I was to the point where I hoped Captain would not be at the table when we arrived, but he was always there. Each day when I sat down I was sure I'd get lectured on my behavior after the party, but nothing was ever said. I found out later that Grandpa never told anyone else about my driving in the ditch, and I greatly respected him for that. It was a secret that stayed just between us.

The 4th of July was fast approaching and Gowrie was buzzing with preparations. Everything seemed cleaner than I had seen it before. The store windows all sported patriotic themes, and nearly everyone in town appeared to have a lot of extra energy. I had never experienced a Gowrie 4th of July celebration before, but the overall enthusiasm I saw around me was contagious. No longer was the talk at Hazel's only about crops and weather. It was now about all the plans and the upcoming activities during the holiday. It was, after all, America's birthday, and it should be a special occasion. The 1978 Gowrie 4th of July would be a very special one.

Legacy

I could not contain my smile when Grandpa gave me back my car keys, and before he let go of them he reminded me of a very real truth. "If I have to take these away from you again, I'll sell the car. You understand that, right?"

I looked him directly in the eyes. "Yes, I do. That won't happen."

"I think you know how lucky you were that night. Just remember that most people don't get that lucky twice," he added. "A car is not a toy."

"I know," I answered quietly.

"Okay," he grinned. "Get out of here."

"Yes, sir!" I replied with great enthusiasm. Twenty seconds after I again had my keys I was on the road and on my way to town. I had not talked to Rock since the party and I was anxious to be anywhere besides the farm. It was a hot morning, but as I drove down the highway I rolled my windows down anyway. The breeze of freedom felt good against my face.

It was Saturday morning, but when I got into town I could see it was not an ordinary day. It was the final weekend before the 4th of July and people were all busy with various preparations. I drove around town without any real purpose, quite content to use the gas that had sat idly for so long in my tank. Every third yard I saw was being mowed and spruced up to look as nice as possible. Litter and other long-neglected trash was being picked up. The entire town had apparently decided to put forth their best efforts and to do their parts to make Gowrie look as good as possible.

I had listened to enough conversations at Hazel's to understand at least part of everyone's excitement. Apparently for the three celebration days, July 2-4, this sleepy little town of 1,200 people turned into a town of 12,000 people. I found that hard to believe but it was easy to see the townspeople preparing for something they viewed as a big deal.

On the south side of the Main Street businesses there was a grass park that was larger than the one I had walked through the day I got my car. When I drove past I could see a great deal of activity but I wasn't sure exactly what the group was doing. There were nearly two dozen men, several tractors and pickup trucks, and a flatbed loaded with railroad ties. Three of the tractors had buckets on the front of them and they were tearing up the top layer of grass in two different areas of the park. One area toward the middle looked to be circular while the other one, on the north side of the park was long and straight. I slowed my car to watch the work and I noticed Rock's car parked among several others, so I assumed he was somewhere in the group of workers. I pulled in and parked my car because my curiosity had been aroused and I hadn't seen Rock for a week and wanted to talk with him.

I had seen several of the other workers before, mostly at the shed party, but I couldn't remember many of their names. I did recognize one guy, however, named Lennie, and I walked to where he was standing.

"Hi," he said when I got close to him.

"What's up?" I asked.

"Getting everything ready for next week."

"What is all this? Why are you tearing all this ground up?"

"Well, the big area is for the demolition derby and the other one is for the tractor pull."

I laughed at his answer. "I have no idea what either of those things is."

"Show up next week and you'll find out. The demo derby is always a good time," he added. "The crowd will be huge. This is the easy part here. We've still got to haul in all the bleachers.

At that moment Rock saw me and waved. I smiled, excused myself from Lennie, and walked toward where Rock was standing. "Hey man, where ya been?" he began.

"Pretty much at home," I replied. "We had a lot to do this week."

"Gotcha. Now you can see the annual routine here with getting all this stuff ready. Kind of a pain year after year, but we make good money and everybody has fun, so we keep doing it."

"So is this just volunteers or a certain group?" I asked. "Who gets all the money?"

"It's a couple groups really, but there's a few people here just because. Most of the money goes to the Legion, but the Jaycees get a good chunk of it too. I'm in the Jaycees, so I have to be here helping."

Legacy

We stood for a few more minutes and watched the tractors, then everybody loaded up in the back of a couple pickups and went to get the bleachers. I quickly realized that I had volunteered to help. I was about to become an active part of a Gowrie 4th of July.

A few blocks from the park a black pickup began to follow us. I recognized the three passengers in the truck from the party. They were the trio at the keg who had suddenly stopped talking when they thought I was listening. I asked Rock about them. "Who are those guys?"

He looked back at the truck. "They're trouble, that's who. No way they were invited to Josh's party, but they showed up anyway for the free beer and food. They're always starting crap, and none of them work but they always seem to have plenty of money. There are lots of guesses as to how that happens."

What do you mean by that?" I asked curiously.

"They steal," Rock answered directly, "but they're good at it. Good enough not to get caught, so far anyway. It's kind of like everybody knows but nobody can ever pin anything on them. Why are you worried about them?"

"Oh, no reason. I just talked to them for a second at the party and they seemed pretty mysterious about everything."

"My best advice is to just stay away from them."

"That's the plan," I stated.

It took ten people, a tractor, several chains, and twenty minutes to get a large section of bleachers loaded onto a huge flatbed trailer, but we got it done and started back to the park so we could unload them. There were five sections of bleachers we had to move, so I knew I wouldn't be going anywhere for quite a while. On our way back to unload the fourth section, Rock began to grin for no apparent reason.

"What"? I finally asked. "What's that stupid look for?"

"What exactly did you do with Kathy besides pet some pigs?" he asked.

"Not much. Why?"

"Whatever it was, it must have been good."

"What the hell are you talking about?" I asked, starting to get a bit impatient. "Just spit it out already."

Legacy

"Okay. For starters, she's no longer engaged. She gave the ring back to the guy Monday."

I had no immediate response after hearing that. "You're kidding right?" I finally asked.

"No, I'm dead serious Romeo," he laughed. "Her wedding is off."

"Holy shit!" I exclaimed. "That's hard to believe. We had fun but not that much fun."

"They will be down next week for the carnival and the demo derby," continued Rock. "Looks like my buddy Eli won't have to look for a date."

I stared down at the road. "Great," I said without any real conviction.

We finally finished the work in the park around 5:00, and I was extremely hungry. I had made several new friends and was beginning to get excited about the upcoming celebration. I laughed to myself about the immediacy of Grandpa's lessons. My whole perspective had changed once I started to help, and even my small feelings of ownership in the process had made me feel good. Some of the workers went home, but a dozen or so of us walked the short distance from the park to Sherm's tavern to get some food. I had driven by the tavern before many times but had never been inside, so I had no idea what to expect.

I walked up the five steps and through the heavy wooden door and was bombarded by red. Red booths lined the east side of the narrow aisle that ran through the center, and red stools took up all the space along the bar on the west side. Right inside the door a fat, hyper man was playing a pinball machine and was working the machine hard as he talked to it and to himself. Several of the stools were occupied, mostly by men in coveralls who had ended their work day early, if they had begun one at all. There was a large back room that contained both a pool table and a foosball table. Along one wall in the back room six men were playing cards, and even with a quick glance I could see that they were playing for large amounts of money. I didn't recognize any of the card players, but a small man sitting at one end of the table left an immediate impression on me. He caressed his Budweiser bottle like an old friend and his head and neck were oddly shaped, somewhat like a

Legacy

light bulb. When he talked he slurred his words, and I immediately felt sorry for him. Drinking and playing cards were probably the highlights of his life.

Our group claimed three of the booths and we all ordered a beer and some food. It felt refreshing to sit in the air conditioned room and the beer tasted good. Ten minutes later I was devouring my cheeseburger and fries and enjoying the laughter with my new friends. Every now and then though, a bit of worry would sneak into my thoughts, remembering that Kathy was no longer engaged and wondering what exactly that meant for me. I liked her but we had only been together for a few hours. I remember I had felt uncomfortable when I found out she was engaged. Now I felt equally uncomfortable when I found out she wasn't.

The tavern door was thrown open and the trio in the black pickup entered noisily, slapping each other on the back and making sure everyone noticed them. Most of my group ignored them but I watched them as they sat down on stools not far from us. They loudly ordered beers and seemed oblivious to anything or anyone outside their private world. The bartender demanded their beer money up front and that made them angry.

"What's this all about?" demanded Zeb. "You know we all got money, always do. Probably got more than you, and before long we'll have even more."

Maxie slapped Zeb's arm. "Shut up, you idiot!"

Zeb turned quickly toward Maxie. "Oh, who cares? This dumbass doesn't have a clue. I'll say whatever I want."

I pretended to pay no attention to the trio, but Maxie's and my eyes met once and he gave me a threatening glare, trying somehow to intimidate me with his dark look. Bad guys didn't scare me. I had spent nearly every day in the city dealing with guys like him. As I sat there an odd thought occurred to me. The trio reminded me of my friends back home and for the first time I could see how silly we must have looked standing on street corners trying to look and sound tough. I was tempted to leave the booth and ask Maxie if he and his buddies ever talked about long term goals. I was pretty sure I'd get a stupid look similar to the one my friends back home would have worn if asked the same question.

Legacy

My visual exchange with Maxie lasted only a couple seconds and then I rejoined my group's conversation. Zeb's statement about soon having more money kept replaying in my mind, and even though it could have been a totally innocent comment, something told me it was far more than that. Time would tell.

CHAPTER 15

A Gowrie 4th of July. Would it live up to all the hype I had seen and heard? Back home we didn't have carnivals and tractor pulls and demolition derbies. Sometimes we had a parade in some section of town as well as some fireworks, but I had never gotten excited about any of it. I had no idea exactly what the tractors here pulled, even when Rock told me they pulled something called a muleskinner. The demolition derby definitely had me curious to see cars intentionally crashing into each other.

There was little to do around the farm in the final days leading up to the celebration, because I had done most of the work during my week with no car keys. There always seemed to be more work to do in the garden though. It was like that never ended. Grandpa told me that the weeds were always there and they never totally went away. The best a guy could do was to know they were there and pull them out or knock them down every time they showed signs of taking over the garden. I had now been around him enough to know he spoke with a double meaning whenever possible, and he never missed a chance to equate our garden with my life.

The fact that Kathy was no longer engaged nagged at my thoughts quite a bit too. Had she given her ring back because of our night at the party? Had she fallen that quickly for me, or had she just been looking for an out and I had given her that final, needed push in that direction? Did she expect an immediate serious future with me now? I wasn't ready for that. Rock seemed to think the whole thing was hilarious, but I saw no humor in any of it, and I had no idea how to act when I saw her again in just a few days.

Legacy

On July 1 the carnival began rolling into town and I was impressed with how fast the rides were put together. I sat and watched the speed and the skill of the Carnies and their tools, and it took just two hours for the Ferris Wheel to go from nothing to thirty feet high. I also watched the Scrambler and the Tilt-a Whirl assembled and tested, and when I finally drove away from the park I had a new appreciation for those who made summer carnivals their lives. For a short time I thought it sounded like a great life, full of traveling and adventure, but when I thought a while longer I didn't like the idea of living in a camper for months at a time, being dirty most of every day, and dealing with an ungrateful public in dozens of different small towns like this one. Grandpa had deep roots on his farm, and my temporary envy for the nomadic Carnies turned more toward a form of pity for the good things they might never have or know because they had no such roots put down in their lives.

All around town there were reminders that the 4th of July was special, our country's birthday. Red, white, and blue streamers and banners were everywhere, and the local newspaper, which came out on Wednesdays, was filled with ads and stories and news of the exciting weekend ahead. At night when Grandpa and I had the TV on, we saw President Carter celebrating as only a President could do. Night after night, for thirty seconds at a time, he encouraged all Americans to enjoy themselves and to show their pride in our nation at this very special time.

I hadn't thought much about my boys in the last few weeks, and it surprised me how little I missed them. I was pretty sure they had gone on just fine without me too, and I doubted their routines or behaviors had changed much since I left. My boys and I had never really been a part of anything except ourselves, and it wasn't until I got to this vibrant little town that I could see how pointless that had been and how many things of substance we had all missed out on. I was already determined to not become that person again.

Nobody here seemed to ever be alone or seemed to do things by himself. Here it was always a group of people working toward something, which was totally unlike life in the city. Everyone back home seemed to spend so much time avoiding people, getting away from others, and not getting involved, that it was still amazing to me when I watched people here go out of their way to get involved and help each other with everything.

As I drove down Main Street I tried to imagine 12,000 people fitting into this town, and it seemed impossible to me that that could actually happen, but I took people at their word and looked forward to being in a crowded place once again. It wouldn't be quite the same as a city crowd but it would be as close as I had been since I had left. People milled around all over town, getting in their final preparations. It seemed like the entire town was on the same page, and I had never seen anything like that before.

I turned north onto Pleasant Street and found an area the locals called Bum's Jungle. The name itself fascinated me and every time I drove by there I secretly hoped to see a hobo peeking at me through the thick trees, but I never saw one. At the far end of the street I saw Maxie's black pickup driving unusually slowly and that got my attention. Nobody ever drove too fast through town, but his truck was going at an unusually slow pace. I slowed my car down too and kept pace with Maxie, keeping a safe distance. I wasn't sure why I wanted to follow him, but some inner sense told me that I should.

Every so often I could see Zeb, who was on the passenger side of the pickup, point and nod his head, which made no sense to me, but seemed odd. I knew if I followed them for very long they would eventually see me, and I really didn't want that, so I turned a different direction and decided to just stay in the area for a while in case there was something more to see with them. When I had circled the same block multiple times I got tired of that and decided to head back to the farm. I got out of my car and Grandpa looked at me from under the hood of his pickup. "Whatcha doin'?" I asked.

"Changing oil. Just finishing up," he replied. He was fanatical about the oil and the other fluids in everything he owned that could be driven. "Have you checked the oil in your car?"

I laughed slightly. "No. This is the first time I've driven it for a week, and I only had it for a couple days before that. I'm sure it's fine."

He just shook his head at me but pursued the issue no further. "What's going on in town?"

"The carnival is starting to get set up. I watched them put a couple rides together which was pretty cool to see. Everybody is making their yards all pretty."

"I suppose so," he responded in a disinterested way. "I'm sure there will be plenty for you to do the next few days," he continued. "Next week, though, we start walking beans."

"Walking beans?" I asked. "We have to walk through the beans? Is something wrong with them?"

He gave me another grin. "City boy. You'll see soon. Just be careful this weekend and don't spend all your money on junk."

"I'll try not to," I smiled. "Everybody actually has me excited about all this stuff. Are there really 12,000 people that show up here?"

"I don't know. Could be. There'll be a lot, especially for the parade and the fireworks."

"Are you going to any of it?" I asked. I had thought of all I wanted to see and do, but this was the first time I had wondered what Grandpa would do over the weekend.

"I might go to the parade and the tractor pull. Maybe the fireworks too," he said. "Are you hungry?"

"Yeah, I am," I replied.

"Come on, lets go eat something." He slammed his truck hood down and we walked into the house together, ready to settle in for a quiet night before the three day storm of celebration.

CHAPTER 16

The only activity on the night of the 2nd was the carnival, so I parked my car and joined the enthusiastic crowd in the park. The rides I had seen assembled the night before were now alive providing thrills to and producing screams from children who had waited an entire year since the last 4th of July. Cotton candy and caramel apple smells surrounded me as I strolled through the midway and listened to the calls of the barkers attempting to draw customers into their games of skill and luck. "Just fifty cents…shoot out the little red star…win a prize" – "Only twenty-five cents…use your skill to operate the little crane…pick up your prize right here."

Guys with their girlfriends on their arms were easy prey because they already wanted to show off and win some exotic stuffed animal for their girl. Some did and were heroes, but most just spent more and more money, and they usually left the carnival games poorer and embarrassed. Often the male ego kicked into gear and overrode whatever shame the guy might have felt, and many returned for more tries, much to the delight of the Carnies running the games. I watched person after person get frustrated with small cranes that would stop on their own instead of where the person wanted them to stop, yet many persisted, quarter after quarter, in their attempts to claim victory over the tiny machines inside the glass case.

I could hear the noise from the bingo tent which was toward the west side of the park. It was by far the biggest of all the games in the park, and as I got near I could see the players were marking their cards with kernels of corn. I stopped a few feet from the players and was surprised to see Wally, one of Maxie's secretive buddies, working there as if he were one of the Carnies. Wally wore a money pouch apron and hustled quickly in between games to make sure his side of the tent was ready when each new game began. It took only a minute before Zeb and Maxie took seats on Wally's side of the tent and got ready to play bingo. I decided to hang back and watch, just to see what might unfold, and I wasn't disappointed.

Legacy

Each game cost a dollar and I watched Zeb pay Wally and get his card. Maxie also gave Wally a dollar, but Wally reached into his pouch and began counting back change for a twenty. So that was their scheme. In ten seconds they had each made eighteen dollars, and I was sure their counting game would be repeated many more times before the weekend was finished. I stayed in the background and continued to watch the trio. Maxie and Zeb only played one game of bingo and then rose from their seats, never once letting on to anyone that they even knew Wally at all. Rock had told me they were all sneaky, and I had just seen my first evidence that he was right.

I kept hearing a unique bell sound, accompanied by cheers, and when I turned around I saw where the noise was coming from. In the southwest corner of the park, near the shelter house, there was a dunking booth, and the man on the platform had a microphone so he could taunt any prospective throwers and raise more money. When I got closer I could see that it was Crusher who was in the booth, and the cheers had risen each time the target had been hit and Crusher had fallen into the water. I laughed as he got out of the water time after time, took his seat and resumed verbally baiting whoever was throwing the baseballs at the small red target. This was a money maker for the Jaycees and Crusher was certainly doing his part.

I walked around the park for a total of two hours and the only money I spent was on a glass of Coke. Rock eventually showed up, which made me happy. A Gowrie 4th of July was a party on his home turf, and I looked forward to him being my guide. If there was anything else going on, he would know what it was. As we talked, Crusher's turn in the dunking booth came to an end, and he was replaced by Arch, a Jaycee in his late twenties who was even better at riling up the crowd than Crusher had been. The people were lined up several deep to take their shots at hitting the target and getting him wet.

Rock suggested we ride around for a while, so we got into his car and hit the road. He drove slowly through town and I reached into the back seat and grabbed his 8-track of *Frampton Comes Alive*. Once the music began we sang along and I also kept the rhythm on

Legacy

my air guitar. The noise of the park was in stark contrast with the quiet of the east end of town. Frampton's guitar rang out clearly when we turned around at the funeral home, but our music could barely be heard whenever we got near the park.

Eventually we left the main drag and drove around on the side streets of town and I decided to tell Rock what I had seen at the bingo tent. "You were right about Maxie and his buddies stealing and being good at it," I began.

Rock looked at me curiously. "Why? What do you mean by that?"

"I saw them in action. Watched them stealing from the Carnies," I continued.

He laughed a little. "No way. How did they do that?"

"It's pretty slick really. Wally somehow got a job working at the bingo tent. I watched them. Maxie and Zeb sat down in his area and acted like they didn't know him. They paid their dollar each for the bingo game, and Wally gave each of them back change for a twenty. Easy money and no chance of getting caught. They played one game and then got up and left with more money than they had when they sat down."

"Wow!" Rock exclaimed. "Wonder which one of those clowns came up with that idea. Are you sure that's what they were doing?"

"Yeah, I'm sure. I stood a ways behind them and watched the whole deal. I'll bet Maxie and Zeb play lots of games of bingo this weekend."

"Oh, I bet they do too," agreed Rock. "Those guys are just bad news all around, but that's pretty brave even for them."

"Wanna get them busted?" I asked out of the blue. "I think I know a way to do it without them having any idea we were a part of it."

"Go on," said Rock with great interest.

"All we have to do is find the guy in charge of the carnival and explain their scam to him and have him watch them just like I did."

"Yeah, I like that. And we could have the cops standing there ready to pounce on them along with the manager of the carnival."

"Good idea," I continued. "Let's wait until the 4th though so we can totally embarrass them in front of tons of people. It's more fun to bring down guys like that in big flames." We shook hands in the car, sealing the deal, and then drove around a while longer as Frampton continued rocking on the 8-track player.

CHAPTER 17

The 3rd of July was a much busier day in town than the 2nd was. The carnival opened at noon and there were several other activities throughout the day. A ladies' group in town put on a game called "Cow Patty Bingo" as a fundraiser, and that was definitely not something I had ever seen in the city. They marked a pen with a hundred squares, similar to a checker board, then raffled off each square for twenty dollars. If the cow pooped in your square you were the winner. There was also a talent show in the park, so would-be stars sang and danced on the stage all afternoon. The demolition derby was that night, and I was both anxious and curious to see that. At the same time, I was nervous to see Kathy again, but I knew she would be there.

Later that afternoon Rock and I were walking through the park when Kathy and Cheri walked up to us. Rock hugged Cheri, and I smiled at Kathy. "Hi," I began weakly.

"Hi," responded Kathy. "We didn't get lost this time, so our trip down here was a lot shorter than last time!"

That broke any remaining tension as all four of us laughed out loud. "That's good," I added. "So what's new?"

"Not much," continued Kathy. "Just ready to see a Gowrie 4th of July. How about you?"

I had given her an opening to tell me she was no longer engaged, but she had not taken it, so I didn't press any further. "Same here," I stated.

"Anybody wanna ride some rides?" asked Rock.

I spoke up quickly. "Not really. I'm good with just watching."

"We do, we do!" exclaimed Cheri. "Come on. You guys gotta ride with us."

Legacy

Rock looked at me with pleading eyes. "Come on Eli. Can't let the girls down."

I could feel the unspoken pressure of the snare I suddenly found myself in, and I quickly realized the easiest path was to just go along. "Okay, which ones?" I asked.

"We like the Scrambler and the Ferris Wheel," stated Kathy. "Let's ride those two."

"Let's go," instructed Rock as he took Cheri's hand and started walking toward the Scrambler.

I walked beside Kathy but did not take her hand. I was still unsure of what she was thinking and feeling about me, about us. It didn't take much longer to get my questions answered, however, for when we got onto the ride she was pressed tightly against me every time our car changed directions and she held tightly onto my leg. I put my arm around her and she smiled each time the ride brought her up against me.

The Ferris Wheel was more of the same, especially when our car got stopped at the top of the ride. The view was great, but I didn't admire it for long. Kathy slid herself close to me again, looked into my eyes, and quietly said, "Hi." I laughed at her but I understood. I put my arm around her again and we were still kissing when we reached the bottom of the ride. Several people in line began cheering us on, which embarrassed us both a little, but not enough to stop kissing.

After the two rides we grabbed some corndogs and walked toward the bingo tent. Both Rock and I had seen Maxie and Zeb in the park, and if they were going to run their money scam again we both wanted to see it. We told the girls we would pay for them to play a couple games, and they liked that idea. We sat at an angle from Wally's area, close enough to see but far enough away to be able to act nonchalantly.

Kathy and Cheri instantly got into their first game of bingo, and they got really excited each time they were able to place a kernel of corn on one of their numbers. Cheri got nervous when she was one number away from two different bingos, but someone else won before her numbers were called. Before the second game started both Maxie and Zeb sat down, and again they were apart

Legacy

and each acted like he was all by himself. Rock watched them as intently as I did, while still acting like the girls' cards held our attention. Zeb was first. We watched him give Wally a dollar then watched Wally count out several bills and hand them back to Zeb. Wally walked ten feet or so and repeated the same process with Maxie.

Rock looked at me and grinned. "Slick," he said to me quietly.

"Told ya," I answered.

Kathy looked up from her card. "What's slick?"

"Oh, nothing," answered Rock. "Just a little inside joke."

"Okay, she smiled and returned her attention to her bingo card.

Neither girl won the second game either, and it was time to head toward the demolition derby, so we left the park and headed that direction. Rock drove all of us there with Kathy and me in the back seat. There was already a crowd gathering at the derby arena and a third of the bleachers were full. We found seats in the front row and watched the rest of the people file in, which they did in a steady stream. At 6:30 the first group of cars was driven into the arena. My excitement level rose as I heard each engine rev up. I still couldn't fully imagine what I was about to see, but there were eight cars along the outside of the dirt circle, each facing outward with the trunks toward the middle.

Suddenly a booming voice sounded on the loud speaker and the announcer welcomed everyone to this year's edition of the Gowrie demolition derby. He then went on to introduce the first heat of drivers who sat anxiously in their cars. The announcer had something humorous to say about each driver and each car, and most of the cars had been uniquely painted to match the driver's personality. One car was all black with a white skull and crossbones on the hood. Another was a checkerboard of red and black and was named The Lumberjack. The car that amused me the most was painted bright green and had yellow question marks of all sizes covering the car's body. Across the trunk was a face of the Riddler from the Batman TV series.

Shortly after the introductions, the actual derby began and the cars were maneuvering around the dirt arena, attempting to crash into their opponents as hard as possible. Each car had a small flag

Legacy

on its hood and judges stood nearby monitoring the crashes. If a car was put out of commission its flag was lowered, and the other drivers knew not to crash that driver any more.

I was impressed with the violence of some of the collisions, and I was glad the drivers all wore helmets and were strapped into their seats. Eventually, after twenty minutes, the first heat was down to its two final cars, a 1967 Chevy Impala and the Riddler car, a 1972 Plymouth Fury III. Both had sustained a lot of damage but were still drivable. Those two went at each other to see who would emerge the winner, a process that was made tougher because they both had to work around the other dead cars in order to get to each other.

I was thirsty and I knew I could still watch the finish during my walk to the concession stand. "Anybody else want anything?" I asked. "I'm gonna go get a drink." Rock and Cheri both said they were fine, but Kathy asked me to bring her back a glass of lemonade. "Will do," I smiled as I walked away.

When I got to the drink line I heard a violent crash and I saw it had happened right in front of our seats. The crowd cheered loudly and I thought the first heat was probably over, but I was wrong. The driver sitting directly in front of Rock and the girls was trying everything he could think of to do in order to make his car move again. The driver of the Riddler car positioned himself at an angle where he could deliver the final, winning blow to the other car.

Everyone in the audience roared with anticipation. They knew the end was near and the excitement level of the final crash built to a fever pitch. I was still three deep in the drink line, so I had to watch from a distance. The driver of the Riddler car began what he hoped would be his final trip across the arena. His target was clearly in sight and he moved directly toward it, with nothing in his way. The other driver sat helplessly, still trying to make his car move in order to avoid the impending crash he could see coming his way. As the Riddler car closed in, the crowd collectively held its breath, waiting for the final cheer, but that cheer never came.

In its place came shrieks and screams and panic. At the last second the seemingly stalled car lurched backward just far enough for the Riddler to miss it, and the Riddler had just kept going over

Legacy

the barriers, through the picket fence, and into the bleachers. I watched in horror and disbelief as the people tried their best to scatter and avoid being hit by the car. Rock reacted quickly and I saw him literally throw both Cheri and Kathy higher into the bleachers. They landed awkwardly but were safe. Rock, however, did not have time to get himself out of the way and I heard him cry out as the trunk of the Riddler car ran into him. I ran as quickly as I could toward my friend, hoping for the best but fearing the worst.

The paramedics reached Rock a few seconds before I did. The collision had knocked him to the ground and he lay there screaming and pounding the ground with both his fists. The girls cried uncontrollably as they watched Rock being tended to. The other people who were nearby stood silently and those farther away strained for a look that would tell them what had actually happened. Bruce, the driver of the Riddler car, stood as closely as he could, wearing a look of both sorrow and fear. Sweat ran down his cheeks but he stood motionless and watched the medics work.

The ambulance sirens jolted everyone back to some level of consciousness, and when I realized there was nothing I could do to help Rock, I turned my attention toward the girls.

Cheri was still sobbing and her entire body shook as she stared at Rock lying on the ground in pain. Kathy had calmed down a little bit but still seemed to be in shock to some degree. She had a scrape on her left arm and it bled, but it appeared to be relatively minor. "Are you okay?" I asked when I reached the girls.

Kathy answered first in an extremely soft but almost hysterical voice. "I'm fine, but what are they doing to Rock?"

I held Kathy's bleeding arm and tried my best to determine how bad her injury actually was. "What about this?" I asked.

She looked at her arm and noticed her wound for the first time. "Oh," she said. "I don't know. I guess that happened when I hit the bleachers. I'm okay, really."

A lady I didn't know handed me a towel to clean Kathy's arm with, and Kathy winced as I began wiping the blood, but she sat still as I got the wound as clean as I could. Another paramedic noticed what I was doing and he looked at Kathy's arm. After he examined her, he put a bandage on it and then turned back to Rock.

Legacy

Cheri seemed to be fine physically, but emotionally she was a wreck. Kathy hugged her and tried her best to calm Cheri down, but she didn't have much success. I thought Kathy had succeeded until the ambulance crew rushed a stretcher to the area and carefully lifted Rock onto it and strapped him down. When Cheri watched that, she broke into tears again.

I heard one of the medics say he thought that Rock had a broken leg and perhaps some bruised or cracked ribs and I was thankful that his injuries were no more severe than that. He was still in obvious pain as we watched him disappear into the ambulance, but I felt certain that he would be all right. The ambulance drove quickly out of sight which left everyone else standing in the area both trying to absorb what had happened and trying to figure out what to do next. The general sentiment was to cancel the rest of the demolition derby, and those in charge were meeting to make the final decision when the girls and I left. We were headed to the hospital, but we had to go back to the park first to get my car.

It didn't take long for us to walk the five blocks back to my car. I had no idea where we were going, but the girls knew. The hospital was in their town, so I drove and they gave me the directions as we went along. It only took twenty minutes to get there then we had to find out where they had taken our friend. Not exactly the 4th of July adventure I had looked forward to.

It took another thirty minutes to find the right area of the hospital, and then another ten minutes before we got any word at all on Rock's condition. We sat helplessly in a waiting room until a smiling nurse came to talk with us. "He's going to be fine," she began in a practiced, comforting tone. "The doctor is setting his leg and he'll have to wear a cast for a while. He also has some bruised ribs, so he'll be quite sore, but none of them are broken. It was a bad break on his leg but he's in good hands."

The three of us collectively sighed in relief and I immediately felt better. The looks on the girls' faces told me they were equally relieved to hear the news. "He'll be out for a while and we will have to keep him overnight. Visiting hours are already over, so there's really nothing you can do to help him tonight. I'll sure tell him you were here though. What are your names?"

I spoke up. "Tell him Eli, Cheri, and Kathy were here."

"None of you are immediate family are you?" she asked.

"No. Just good friends."

Just then Rock's parents walked up to us wearing a grim look of uncertainty and concern. Once the nurse was sure the two were indeed his parents she led them through some doors and back to another part of the hospital where we three were not allowed to go.

The girls had to ride back to Gowrie with me because their car was still there, but we all felt great relief and the drive back to Gowrie was a lot more relaxed than the trip to the hospital. Both of them took turns retelling what had happened at the demolition derby, at least as much of it as they could remember, and as the events were retold we all agreed that everyone had been incredibly lucky. It easily could have been much, much worse.

CHAPTER 18

The girls wanted no more of Gowrie that night and drove straight home. I drove uptown and was somewhat surprised to learn that the demolition derby had continued, though I was told only a few people sat in any of the lower bleacher seats after Rock's accident. I soon found myself again in the park, and walked around with no real plan or purpose. I just needed to unwind, and that seemed like a good place for me to do that. Word of the accident had spread quickly and I had to give updates on Rock's condition at least a dozen times before I eventually walked back to my car and drove home.

Grandpa was watching television when I walked in. I was surprised he was still awake and was even more surprised to see that he was watching an old movie called "The Fly." Once I started telling him about the events of the night he lost all interest in the movie and gave me his full attention. He let me tell the entire story without interruption, and when I had finished it was his turn.

"That must have been really scary," he began.

"It was," I answered. "And I felt so helpless. I watched it all happen and couldn't do a damn thing to stop it. Rock was amazing though. He didn't hesitate for a second and just threw both girls out of the way of the car. I don't know if I would have thought to do that or not. He saved them first and then he thought about getting himself out of the way."

"We all would like to believe we would do what Rock did, and fortunately most of us never have to find out what we would really do," continued Grandpa.

"Why is that fortunate?" I inquired.

"Well, I'll tell ya," he explained. "How many others there tonight took care of someone else before they got themselves out of the way?"

I thought for a minute, reliving the scene one more time, trying to recall the details of the chaos. "None that I can remember. Everybody else pretty much just ran."

"That's what most people do. We talk the talk about taking care of others, but when we are threatened we usually worry about self-preservation first, ahead of worrying about others. Some people are exceptional though, and what Rock did was heroic. You pick good friends."

I smiled. "Mom might have a hard time believing that. She hated my friends back home."

"Let's think about that for a minute. It's a fact that the people we attract to us we attract because of the person we are. Are you the same person you were before you got here?"

"Well, I'm still me, so I guess I am the same person," I stated.

Grandpa shook his head. "Think a little harder. Are the friends you have here the same kind of friends you had before?"

"No, not even close to the same," I replied.

"Why do you think that is?" he asked.

"I guess I'm not the same person I was when I got here am I? I've changed."

"Right," he smiled. "As you said, not even close to the same. Your Mom wouldn't recognize you, but once she did I'm sure she would be extremely happy with the new you."

"You really think I've changed that much?" I asked, half fishing for more compliments.

"I remember when you got off the plane. I could see the anger in your eyes and in your walk. You hated everything, including me, and you didn't even know me."

"I'm not sure I hated you exactly," I sighed, "but I definitely wasn't happy to be on a plane to Iowa."

"Maybe that's more accurate," Grandpa continued. "Remember when I asked you about that *Go Your Own Way* song?"

"Yeah, I do."

"That song doesn't fit you so well now, does it?"

"No," I answered. "Well, at least I hope it doesn't. But if changing can happen as quickly as it did for me, then why doesn't everyone who's angry or unhappy change? Or am I a unique case because you were here to help me?"

"Anybody can do it if he wants to. That has always been true," explained Grandpa, "but most never do, and there is a variety of reasons why they choose to stay as they are. You understand that it really is a choice, right?"

"I do now. Not sure I would have thought that way back in the city. People I know there who struggle kind of see that as their destiny or something. It's like their fate was decided early, and since they don't really believe they can change it, they just give up and accept where they are in life."

"Did you ever think that maybe nobody ever told them or showed them that they could be more and have more, and that being happy and productive was much more within their reach than they thought?"

"Nobody ever told me. Well, Mom did, but nobody else, and I guess I believed my friends more than I believed her. Does who a guy runs around with really make that much difference in how a person thinks?"

Grandpa suddenly wore a really serious look. "It makes all the difference in the world, for everyone. We think like the people we are around the most. We talk like them, dress like them, take on a lot of their values, and really begin to act like them in many ways.

Think about your buddies back home. Isn't that how it was for you?"

I thought back to how I dressed in the city, how I talked and thought and acted. "That's exactly how it was."

"Here's something for you to try and remember about all of this. At any point in your life, you will by far be the most influenced by the five closest people to you, for good or for bad. Those five will either keep you down or help you soar. It all depends on who you choose to spend your time with. Whoever that ends up being will make all the difference."

"I guess that answers my earlier question about why people don't change when they could," I stated knowingly. "They hang around with other people who are negative and don't want to change."

"That's a big part of it for sure," Grandpa agreed. "Family legacy and lack of ambition are not just found in the city. There are a lot of good people around here, but I'm sure you've seen examples of people keeping each other down too. Some even do that on purpose and that may be the saddest and most selfish thing of all. People with no goals or desire to change will kill their friends' dreams too, so those friends with goals won't change and leave them behind which would make them look bad."

"I never thought about that," I replied.

"Everybody you've been around here has encouraged you and been nice to you haven't they?" he continued.

"Yeah, pretty much."

"It doesn't take long for our friends to affect us, and they always will. Do you think your friends back home have thought about what you're doing here in Iowa? Do you think they would like you as much now as they did before?"

"I doubt it," I concluded. "They are probably doing the same things we were doing before I left, and I don't think their routines have changed too much. They never do."

"Probably so, and does spending your time like that still sound fun to you?"

"No, it doesn't," I stated confidently. "It sounds like a huge waste of time."

"I'm glad to hear you say that, and your Mom will be glad to hear it too. Life really isn't as complicated as we make it sometimes. Once a person understands that everything we do and say is a choice, then we should never complain about the results. Sometimes things happen that are out of our control, but most things in our lives are there because of our choices. We put them there. If you are smart enough to know right from wrong and still choose the wrong way on something, then you shouldn't complain or act shocked when some trouble comes your way. You chose it."

"Right and wrong," I mumbled, more to myself than to Grandpa. "There's something along those lines that I need to take care of tomorrow."

"Wanna talk about it? Can I help?" he asked sincerely.

"No thanks. I think I can handle it by myself. Yeah, I know I can."

Grandpa gave me a somewhat concerned look but he didn't ask me any more questions about it. It was getting late and I was tired from everything that had happened, so I excused myself, walked upstairs to bed, and tried to get some sleep. Tomorrow was the actual 4th of July and I wanted to experience it all.

CHAPTER 19

People began arriving for the parade shortly after daybreak, even though the actual parade didn't start until 10:00 am. Many parked their vehicles in favorite spots along the parade route so they would have a trunk or a tailgate to sit on as the procession passed them. I got to town around 8:30 and I drove down Main Street. I was a bit surprised to find hundreds of people already there just talking and waiting for the parade. Grandpa told me he would get to town between 9:00 and 9:30 and he planned to bring a lawn chair and sit in front of the bowling alley in the middle of town.

I had no real idea where I would be during the parade, but at the moment I was more concerned about Rock so I went to his house in hopes of getting an update from his parents. Luckily they were

Legacy

home and the news was good. Rock's leg was in a full cast so he would have to use crutches for a few weeks, but he was going to be released at noon and then he would be home. He had told his parents that if they saw me, he wanted me to come pick him up after he got home, and I quickly told his parents I would be happy to do that.

Since Rock's house was less than a block from Main Street, I just left my car where it was and walked up to the parade route. The crowd had increased dramatically just in the short time I had spent at Rock's house, and people were still pouring into town. Maybe the 12,000 number I had been told wasn't unrealistic after all. The start of the parade was still a few minutes away so I stood and watched the people around me. Most had some type of patriotic clothing on, such as a red, white, and blue shirt, and the excitement was genuine. Many waved small flags up and down the street and people of every shape and size hustled to claim their spots close to the street.

The canon shot caught me totally by surprise and made me jump. A man standing next to me laughed and told me that was the ceremonial start of the parade. I looked to the east and saw the local police car driving toward me, leading the way as the first entry in the parade. The flashing red lights circled as he slowly drove along. The bowling alley was just three blocks away from where I was, so I decided to walk there and look for Grandpa.

I found him sitting next to Kenny and Herman, each in a lawn chair right next to the street. The only one missing from their lunch group was Captain, and I was sure he was sharing his vast knowledge with someone else along the parade route. When I got near them, Kenny saw me first. "Carl, it looks like you didn't hide well enough," he laughed. "Your grandson found you."

"Ha ha," I replied. "Since this is my first Gowrie parade I wanted to see how you long time veterans did things."

Herman chimed in. "You can sit on the tailgate if you want to Eli. That brown Ford right behind you is mine."

"Great!" I replied and I hopped up into the back of Herman's pickup. It took a few more minutes for the police car to reach us, but after that the parade was a steady stream of things that lasted a little more than an hour. There were old tractors and brand new ones, and it seemed to me that each one's engine made its own unique sound. Two huge combines were next, followed by the local school's marching band. There were several patriotic floats that portrayed celebrations of Independence Day and many of them had themes that showed the USA from Colonial days to modern times. The 1st place float was sponsored by the local elevator.

Several other bands performed, and there was a group of men on small motorcycles. They drove in fancy patterns along the street and were quite entertaining. Multiple fire trucks filled the street, and their sirens were deafening. Two people rode by on unicycles, and since it was an election year there were at least a dozen politicians in the parade, some waving from the seats of convertibles and others walking the route shaking hands and smiling a lot.

Bringing up the rear of the parade were the horses. There were over a hundred of them in all, both individual riders and area rodeo clubs. I had not seen many parades in my life, but it didn't take me long to understand why the horses were last in the lineup. There were countless reminders left in the street that would undoubtedly end up on someone's car tires later.

Grandpa, Kenny, and Herman seemed to have a good time during the parade, and their biggest laughs came from watching the kids wrestle each other for all the candy that was thrown their way. When the parade ended the crowd immediately began to disperse and move on to whatever was next in their day. For some it was home for a barbeque but most headed toward the park and the carnival. Grandpa, Kenny, and Herman remained in their chairs and watched the people hurrying around them. None of them had anywhere else to be so they just sat and relaxed. Herman reached into his pocket, brought out his can of Prince Albert tobacco, and rolled a cigarette for himself.

Well, how was that?" Grandpa asked me. "Did you like the parade?"

I jumped off the tailgate and stood beside the trio. "Yeah, I did. It was really long."

Legacy

"There were some extra things this year because of the elections this fall," added Kenny. "The politicians never miss a chance to try and get a few more votes."

"Ain't that the truth," stated Herman.

I didn't have any definite plans either, so I was unsure of what to do. I sat with Grandpa and his friends for another fifteen minutes, as the crowd continued to thin out, and then I walked back toward the park. Ironically, one of the first people I ran into in the park was Maxie, and it didn't take long for him to make me angry.

"Hey, city boy, what are you doing?" he asked sarcastically.

"Just walking around. Why?" I replied.

"No reason," he continued. "Heck of a deal with your buddy last night. When I saw the car hit him I thought he was dead. Oh well, can't win 'em all."

"What's that supposed to mean?" I asked loudly.

"Oh, nothing," he smirked. "I just never liked ol' Rock boy too much. It would have been kinda cool to see him really get popped."

I was certain my face turned instantly red with rage, but I let the comment go. I had to force myself to remember that I had a little surprise for Maxie and his friends, and now I was even more motivated to see that through. Finally I just uttered to him, "Whatever," and walked away as he stood there laughing.

I strolled over to the Jaycees' dunking booth to watch the good natured teasing over the microphone. The line of people ready to throw baseballs was long and I was glad to see the Jaycees were making money. I walked up to a small group of guys I knew and found myself in the middle of a conversation that troubled me. Josh, Lennie, and Crusher all wore concerned looks as they spoke to each other.

"What all did they get?" asked Lennie.

"Well, I'm not totally sure yet," answered Crusher, "but as far as I know we're missing both kids' bikes, three guns, and our stereo."

"Damn," replied Lennie. "So you think there might be more?"

Crusher looked down and shuffled his feet angrily. "Could be. Just don't know yet."

Lennie then looked at Josh. "What about at your place?"

Legacy

"They broke into my big shed and stole my motorcycle," began Josh. "Then they broke the glass out of the back door of my house and got into all kinds of stuff. Some antiques I had stored away, two of my guns, and worst of all a lot of cash. I'm gonna tear somebody's head off!"

Lennie's look of concern grew even more. "How much cash?"

Josh replied quickly. "Two thousand dollars. I was getting ready to buy some more pigs right after the 4th so I had it all in a money box. Never thought I had any reason to hide it, but I guess I did."

I just stood and listened quietly but I was thinking about what they said had happened. "Do you guys think your stuff is here in the park in one of the Carnie trailers?"

Crusher didn't hesitate at all. "Yeah, I do. I've never had any trouble like this before, and now the Carnies are in town and two of us get broken into. Makes sense that it was them doesn't it? Seems logical to me."

"It does to me too," added Josh.

"Does to me too," agreed Lennie.

"Maybe it makes too much sense," I interjected. "Sorry for jumping into the middle of your conversation, but from what I heard I'm not sure you guys are thinking about the right thieves."

"What are you talking about?" asked Crusher with a confused look on his face. "You know something about this? If you do, you better tell us."

"No, I don't," I continued, "but I have a hunch about something. Have either of you told the police yet?"

Josh stated emphatically, "We both did."

"Good," I said. "If all this is on the record already that will help. That is if my hunch is right."

"What hunch? What is it that you think you know about this stuff?" demanded Josh. "If you know who stole our stuff I want to know now."

"That's just it," I continued. "I don't know for sure, but I don't think the Carnies did it. I think they are just being used as convenient scapegoats. Give me a little time and let me see what I can do about getting all your stuff back." They looked at me apprehensively, desperately wanting to know what I thought I knew. "I may be way off base here, and you may be right about the Carnies, but I think I know a way to find out as soon as today."

"How much time?" asked Crusher, still angry but equally intrigued by the possibility of finding out who had robbed him.

"Just hang on for a while," I continued. "If I'm right, you'll have your answer very soon. I'll let you know as soon as I know something, either way." With that I left and walked toward my car. It was time to see if Rock was home. I needed his help in order to put my plan into motion, and I had no doubt he would be eager to help me.

It took only a couple minutes to walk to Rock's house and he was sitting on the porch when I reached his driveway. We both smiled as I bounded up the three steps and onto his porch, and I shook my head as I looked at his cast. It covered his entire leg, from his foot clear up to his hip, and all that was visible were his toes.

"How ya doin?" I began.

"I've been better," he answered, "but overall not too bad. I'm still sore as hell though."

"I bet you are. Got those crutches figured out yet?"

"Oh yeah, no worries there," he explained. "I've had to use them before. The only part that sucks is going up and down steps. I can motor pretty good on flat ground."

I grinned at him. "You ready to get out of here? You're the local hero now and your public awaits."

"Hell yes, I'm ready to go," he stated. "I don't think I'm much of a hero though. I just did what anybody else would do."

"Maybe," I stated, "but don't be surprised if you get treated like a celebrity today."

"Yeah, right. Let's go," he said as he awkwardly rose to his feet and grabbed his crutches. "Man, six weeks of these things."

Before we walked down the steps I began telling him about Josh and Crusher being robbed and my ideas about who had done it. I also started telling him about my plan for solving the mystery and how he could help. "Are you up for being a hero twice in two days?"

He laughed at that thought. "Of course I am." He pointed to his t-shirt and said, "It's high time everyone knew that I have a big "S" here on my chest! So you have a plan, huh?"

"Yeah I do, and you're a big part of it," I explained. "Hop in and I'll tell you about it as we ride around a little bit. We have to get started on it right away if we're going to make it all work."

Rock gave me a funny look. "Hop in. That's a good one." It was far more complicated getting Rock into my car than I had imagined, but we got him in, and as I drove around town I told him my suspicions as well as my ideas for making things right.

We needed the help of the local police chief, Jim Johnson, whom Rock knew well, so we drove around until we found him. I knew the 4th of July was an exceptionally busy day for him, but I hoped he would be willing to listen to my plan and then be willing to help us with it. Chief Johnson was even more receptive to my ideas than I had imagined he could be, and once he listened to all of them our next stop was the park. We needed to talk to the carnival owner, and with the police chief by our side, that conversation would be much easier to have than if it had been just Rock and I.

CHAPTER 20

Chief Johnson had little trouble arranging a meeting with Carlos, the owner of the carnival, and the four of us talked privately in Carlos's trailer, seemingly a world away from the overflow crowd not far from the trailer door. Chief Johnson and Carlos both seemed to think my plan had some merit and were willing to give it a try. Carlos told us that he often had to face situations similar to this one, where his people were falsely accused of crimes that locals actually committed, and he was extremely eager to turn the tables for once and prove his own people innocent if he could.

Carlos voiced his frustration. "People in my line of work seem to always have to deal with this kind of crap. We're the outsiders, the gypsies, the dirty people who come to town for a few days then disappear. We're easy targets. Most of us are actually just like the people here in Gowrie. We're pretty much all from small towns

Legacy

and we work our butts off for seven months so we can live and survive just like everybody else. We know what we're getting into when we sign on for this, but we do it anyway because we like what we do. I can almost guarantee that none of my people broke into anyone's home or stole anything, and you'll have all the help and cooperation from me that you need. Just tell me exactly what you want me to do."

I shook hands with Carlos and thanked him in advance, and then I laid out my entire plan for all of them. It wasn't complicated but Chief Johnson and Carlos both had to be near enough to witness everything. If everything went like I thought it would, then they would be close by and able to swoop in quickly and take control of the situation at the appropriate time. When we were all on the same page, Rock and I left Carlos's trailer and slowly made our way to the bingo tent.

There were thousands of people in the park. The rides were continually full and people kept trying to win the stuffed animals at all the games of chance throughout the midway. People carried corn dogs, sno-cones, and cotton candy like treasures. It seemed that everything tasted better on a sunny 4th of July afternoon. Rock stood out from the crowd because of his cast and his crutches, and as is usually the case with a small town, almost everyone knew what had happened at the demolition derby. On our way to the bingo tent several people stopped us to see how he was doing and to tell him how proud they were of him for what he had done.

"Told ya," I grinned. "Hero."

"Whatever," he blushed. "Let's get this plan of yours in gear."

"I'm ready," I stated confidently, and we walked closer to the bingo tent. I wasn't surprised to see that nearly all of the seats were full, but I didn't see Maxie or Zeb among the players. Wally was busy working, but we would have to wait a little longer before we could begin.

Our wait was a short one, which made me happy. Maxie and Zeb walked around the corner of a concession stand and strutted confidently toward Wally and the bingo tent. I looked around and made sure Chief Johnson and Carlos were also in place. They were. It was time.

Maxie and Zeb took their seats on Wally's side of the tent as expected, and I could tell they had no idea that at least four other sets of eyes were carefully watching their every move. They seemed only to be aware of the people sitting near them, and they tried their best to make sure none of the nearby players saw how they worked their private money game. Both Maxie and Zeb, unwittingly did exactly as I suspected they would do, and I again made sure Chief Johnson and Carlos had seen their criminal transactions. They both nodded their heads to me, and the next step was about to start.

"Ready?" I asked Rock.

"More than ready," he smiled. "This should be fun."

I then took out the small cassette recorder and turned it on. Rock tucked it under his shirt. It was important to also capture Maxie's own words as well as seeing his actions. "Go get 'em hero," I said as I patted Rock on the back.

"Whatever," he replied and he went as quickly as he could toward the bingo tent. I could see the excitement in both his face and his steps as he maneuvered through the crowd using his crutches.

The caller had just called the second number of the game when Rock reached the tent. When he got there he stood directly behind Maxie and Zeb, close enough that his shadow covered both their cards. Maxie turned around first, and when he saw that the person behind him was Rock he laughed. "What the hell do you want?"

"Hmm, let's see. What do I want?" began Rock. "How about half the money Wally just gave you two. That might be a good starting place."

Maxie's face turned red and his eyes narrowed. "I don't know what you're talking about. I'm just playing a game of bingo."

Rock laughed at Maxie's weak attempt at an innocent explanation. "Yeah, right. You're a big bingo fan huh? Big tough guy like you just having fun, trying to win a stuffed animal by playing bingo. Nice try."

"Watch your mouth crip or you'll have casts on both legs," replied Maxie. "You're messin' where you don't belong. You've been warned."

Legacy

"You don't scare me Maxie. You're just a big mouth who thinks he's somebody. I hear you wish the car would have hit me harder than it did or maybe even killed me. Kinda curious if you have the guts to say that to my face."

Maxie began to squirm in his seat and seemed unsure of exactly how to proceed. In the past his intimidation methods had usually worked, and he was certainly not used to being directly challenged face to face. Carlos and I had inched closer and could hear the entire conversation. Zeb was also sitting close to Rock and Maxie but remained silent, apparently waiting to follow Maxie's lead, whatever direction that might take everyone. His eyes were locked intently on Maxie and Rock and he seemed oblivious to the rest of us.

Finally Maxie answered. "I never said that. You're full of crap, man. I've never seen a cast on a leg make somebody so brave before. What do you want from me anyway?"

Rock smiled. "Me? I don't want anything, but there are a few other people who do. The owner of the carnival isn't too happy about how you three have been ripping him off and I know a whole group of Jaycees who are ready to tear your heads off for robbing their friends' houses."

I listened intently as Rock threw out our hunch on the robberies, knowing that we really had no actual proof. I hoped that Rock had succeeded in pushing Maxie hard enough that he would react and admit what his trio had done.

"You thought you were so smart," continued Rock. "Did you really think nobody saw you trading your dollar bills here for change for a twenty? The people who have been watching you guys figure you've stolen at least a couple hundred dollars so far. That sound about right?"

N-32 was called over the loudspeaker but Maxie and Zeb were no longer paying any attention to their cards. "Who's watching us? Nobody saw us. You're nuts."

"Nobody saw you what Maxie? Nobody saw you ripping off the Carnies? Is that what you mean? If that's true, then how is it I know what you've been doing?"

Legacy

Maxie angrily grabbed Rock's shirt. "I don't know how you found out. What do you want? Some of the money?"

"How much have you ripped off here?" asked Rock, knowing he was about to hit pay dirt with his questioning.

"Over three hundred, but we've already spent some of it, so we don't have it all. Wait a minute. You were in the hospital. You couldn't have seen anything. What do you want, really? What's this all about?"

Rock continued. "I told you already. I don't want anything, but the same people who saw you boys stealing here also know it was you who broke into Josh's and Crusher's houses and robbed them. Those are the guys you should really be worried about."

Zeb slid closer to Maxie and looked really worried. "Maxie, you said all this was foolproof. What the hell? He knows everything we did. How can that be?"

Maxie replied confidently. "I don't know how he found out, but I'm about to beat some answers out of this one-legged punk and find out."

I watched with great satisfaction all that happened next. Carlos gave a wave, some sort of signal, then walked and stood directly behind Maxie. "I wouldn't if I were you," he began, placing his hands firmly on both Maxie's and Zeb's shoulders. Within seconds a group of at least fifteen Carnies had engulfed the two, and they, along with Wally, were roughly walked away from the bingo tent and taken back toward Carlos's trailer.

Chief Johnson approached Rock and me wearing a satisfied look. "Nice job guys. We'll take it from here. Those three are in deep shit."

"Thanks Chief," I smiled. "I'm glad it all worked out. Can you get them for the robberies too?"

"I think so. Right now in the middle of all those pissed off Carnies I'm thinking they'll lead me right to wherever they hid all the stuff they stole. Guess I should get back there. Can I have the tape recorder Rock?"

Rock reached into his shirt and handed the recorder to Chief Johnson. "Absolutely."

Chief Johnson started walking away from us, then he stopped momentarily and turned around. "Was all that really based on a hunch?"

I looked him directly in the eye. "Part of it was."

He shook his head and resumed walking. "Hell of a hunch."

I slapped Rock on the shoulder and congratulated him. "You were excellent. I thought he was gonna punch you."

"So did I," he replied, "but man, that was fun."

"Come on hero," I continued. Grab your crutches and lets go find Josh and Crusher and tell them the news.

CHAPTER 21

The only major event remaining on the 4th was the fireworks later that night, so Rock and I had several hours to just float around and goof off, which we did. Rock didn't mind walking around for a while, but then his leg and his armpits got sore and he needed to sit and rest. We stopped and ate Maid-Rites at the shelter house near the dunking booth and stayed there for about an hour, just talking to people and watching all the activity in the park. We were both still excited about the two mysteries we had helped solve.

Crusher walked back into the park with his wife and two small sons. He wore a swimsuit, so I assumed he was about to take another turn in the dunking booth, and his boys showed their excitement, anticipating all the joys and the thrills that a carnival can bring to a small child. Rock and I were both anxious to tell him our news so we left our seats and met him near the dunking booth.

"Hey Crusher," I began. "Your turn again?"

He looked at us and gave us his childlike grin. "Yeah, my fifth shift. Just can't get enough I guess." He noticed Rock and studied his cast with a very serious look. "How are you doing? Nice to see you up and around so fast."

Rock shook Crusher's hand. "I'm as good as I can be. I think you're about to be better too."

He looked at us curiously. "Huh?"

"Tell him Eli," stated Rock.

"Tell me what?" asked Crusher.

"Well, you remember when I said I might have a way to get your stuff back? Yours and Josh's both?" Pretty sure we got that done."

Crusher's excitement level instantly rose. "No way! Really? Already? How? Who? What did you do?"

"I told you I had a hunch. I overheard something a couple weeks ago and just set up a few dominos. With the help of Chief Johnson, the owner of the carnival, and ol' Rock here, the dominos all fell in the right direction. I think I can safely say both you and Josh are gonna get all your stuff back very soon."

Neither Crusher nor his wife could contain their smiles. "That's awesome! So who was it?"

"Can't you guess?" asked Rock.

"Maxie," he said with a scowl. We both nodded our heads. "I should have known. Those dirtbags. How did you catch them?"

"That will all come out soon enough," I responded. "Then you'll know the whole story." I leaned down to Crusher's oldest son, Brady and said, "The good news for now is that it looks like this guy is going to get his bike back."

Brady was five and had just finished kindergarten. He looked like both his mom and dad and was perceptive enough to have followed the conversation. "I get my bike back? Yeah! I need my bike."

"A guy's gotta have his bike doesn't he?" I asked.

"Yeah, I need it so I can ride with Charlene," continued Brady.

"Charlene?"

"My girlfriend," he stated as a matter of fact. "I don't like school being out cause I can't see her too much. She's pretty."

"I bet she is," I agreed.

"Yeah. The teacher yells at me sometimes cause when we were supposed to be napping, I slide my mat over to Charlene so we can talk. We don't get nap time in the summer though. I miss her."

Crusher and his wife grinned at their son's kindergarten exploits and then turned their attention once again to Rock and me. "Thanks guys. Well, thank you isn't enough, but we're mighty grateful. Josh will be too."

Legacy

"Our pleasure," said Rock. "It was actually a lot of fun."

"I'm sure it was," continued Crusher. "You can tell me all about it soon, but my shift is about to begin at the booth so I'd better get over there."

"Later," said Rock, as Crusher and his family walked away from us, each stepping with much livelier steps than they had taken just minutes earlier.

The rest of our afternoon was spent walking around the park and riding around town in my car. Around 7:00 Rock and I drove out to the farm to see what Grandpa was up to and to get away from the crowd of people for a while. It had been an extremely hot and sunny day and the early evening breeze felt good as we walked from my car to the door of the house. We found Grandpa in his recliner pretending to be interested in whatever was on television. I was mostly sure the sound of us opening and closing the door had awakened him. He was rubbing his eyes when we walked into the living room and joined him.

"Good show on?" I asked with a small hint of sarcasm.

"Sure," he answered without much conviction.

"What's it about?"

"Hard to explain," he smiled.

"Uh huh. You do love your naps don't you?"

"I do indeed," he confirmed. "What are you two doing out here? Too much excitement in town?"

"Just taking a little break," I explained. "We did have a bit of excitement though."

"Oh?" he asked. "I would think you'd want to avoid excitement for a while Rock. What happened?"

I asked, "You want the whole story?"

"What good is hearing half a story?" he began. "That just leads to questions and you'll end up telling the whole story anyway.'

"Okay. You wanna tell it Rock, or should I?"

Rock declared, "Go for it."

I began at the start, from the conversation I had overheard near the keg at Josh's party, to Maxie's comment in the tavern about having more money soon, to his arrogant comment about wishing the car had hit Rock even harder, to Josh and Crusher being robbed

Legacy

and the timing of using the Carnies as the scapegoats, the bingo money rip off, to Chief Johnson and Carlos, all the way to the trio being surrounded by Carnies and taken away to be placed in the hands of the law. It took me several minutes to recite the entire adventure to Grandpa, but his prior drowsiness had left him and he was paying complete attention as I talked.

Everyone in town knew the stories surrounding Maxie and his alleged activities, and Grandpa was no exception. He had never had any personal run ins with Maxie but he shared the suspicions of many in the area whenever things turned up missing. A part of him seemed pleased both that Maxie had finally been caught in the act and that Rock and I had played such a key role in making that happen.

"I guess it was a matter of time for Maxie. If he really has done all the things people say he has done then it's not surprising that he kept getting bolder and bolder. It's the same for all of us. Each time we do something and we're rewarded for it, we believe we can do it even bigger and better the next time, and if that works we continue to go for more. When a person does that with positive things the results can be amazing, but when he does it with negative things, like Maxie did, the results are never good. Eli, you were quite clever piecing all that together. A little lucky too. I'm impressed."

"Thanks," I replied, unable to contain my pride. "But I couldn't have ever gotten it done by myself."

"That's true," continued Grandpa, "and there's a big lesson in that too. The bigger and more complicated a project is, the more important it is to have good people helping you. The best things in life are hardly ever accomplished alone. They are almost always a shared effort. Just another reminder of why it's so important to make sure you spend your time with good people. How do you think today would have gone if you still thought like you did back in the city?"

"Good question," I stated, pausing slightly to consider it fully. "I probably would have been impressed with Maxie and his buddies and been mad that I didn't think of it first."

"There ya go," was his only response.

I looked at my watch and decided it was time to head back into town. "We're going to go watch the fireworks. You wanna come with us?"

"No thanks. I think I'll turn in before long. You and I will be in the bean field early in the morning, so use your head with how late you stay out tonight."

"Oh yeah, my first taste of walking beans. The next Iowa adventure! You should join us Rock!"

"Funny guy," laughed Rock as he grabbed his crutches and we started toward the door.

I patted Grandpa on the shoulder as I passed him. "I'll be home early."

CHAPTER 22

The fireworks were well worth waiting for and Rock and I watched them from the hood of my car in the parking lot near the swimming pool. The traffic jam at the conclusion of the fireworks was terrible as everyone inched his way home at the same time, and my first Gowrie 4th of July came to a close. It took nearly twenty minutes to drive from the swimming pool back to Rock's house, and from there I drove back to the farm and went to bed.

The morning came early, as it sometimes did, and when I didn't respond to Grandpa's call up the stairs he began to serenade me with his favorite wakeup words…

It's nice to get up in the morning,
It's nice to get up in the morning,
It's nice to get up in the morning....
So get your butt up now!

His method was short on creativity but long on effectiveness. I think he counted on the fact that I never wanted to hear a second verse of his song, if there even was one.

Legacy

When I got downstairs I could tell he had been up for a while. Breakfast was made and several jugs that were already filled with ice water sat on the counter. It was bean walking day, whatever that meant, and I was in for another Iowa first. After breakfast we went outside and he led me to the grindstone. I saw several things which I mistook for weapons that were leaning next to the garage, right next to the grindstone.

"Who are we attacking with those?" I asked.

"Not who. What. Those are our bean walking tools."

"Bean walking tools," I replied. "Interesting." I looked them over and studied my choices. There was a hoe, a long metal curved hook, and what looked like a short machete, something he called a corn knife. "Which one works best?"

"Oh, they all work just fine after we get them sharpened up. It's like most tools. Their effectiveness usually comes down to the operator and not the tool. You can try out each one and see which one you like best."

"Terrific," I responded as the wheel of the grindstone began to spin at a very high rate of speed. "I think I like the look of the hook the best. Seems like less bending over to me."

"Like I said," he continued, "they all work, even the dull ones."

"The dull ones work?" I asked, feeling there was more to follow.

"Of course they work. Just not as well as the sharpened ones. A guy could take the dullest ax ever and eventually chop down a large tree, but a little time spent here at the grindstone can make everything in the bean field easier. Same with people and the stuff we get into. Nearly always, if people took a little time to think things through, and do even a small bit of preparation, I think they'd have a lot more success and a lot less stress. Remember when you first got here and you wondered why I was spending so much time making sure everything about the tractor and the planter was in good shape?"

"Yeah, I remember," I stated, easily seeing his parallel between then and now, "and I get it. Crank that grindstone up and let's get these babies sharp!"

Grandpa just grinned. I could tell he enjoyed it when he knew I grasped his subtle lessons. Ten minutes later all the implements

Legacy

were sharpened, and shortly after that a truck pulled into the driveway. When the people got out of the truck and walked toward us I looked at their faces, but I didn't recognize any of them. They slowly walked in our direction, water jugs in hand, and even though I knew first impressions could often be wrong, I didn't see a lot of extra ambition in any of them. I hoped I was wrong. There were three of them, all brothers who wanted to make some extra money. Evidently I was the only bean walking rookie in the group, as each of them loped directly toward the implements and chose the one he would use when we began.

The oldest of the brothers chose first, as if there were some form of unspoken family seniority rule at work with the selection process. He looked to be a year or two older than I but our similarities seemed to end there. He wore a dirty green hat that was soft and misshapen. It was early in the morning, yet his jeans showed the spots and stains from a previous day's activities. The others called him Teaser, which both puzzled me and intrigued me, though I didn't ask anyone about it. The design on his white t-shirt belied his disinterested face since it showed the smiling yellow face outline made famous by inviting people to "have a nice day." He chose a corn knife.

The middle brother, Andy, shorter and heavier than Teaser, chose a hoe, and the youngest of the three, TJ, who appeared to be around fifteen, also selected a corn knife. As lethargic as the other two brothers appeared to be, TJ looked like he had even less energy than either of them. They all showed an attitude I had seen many times in the city, and I continued to watch them closely as we prepared to begin.

Grandpa had known them all since they were small boys, and he stood and watched them quietly, just taking them in stride as they got ready to head to the field. "Let's go boys," he stated. "The first field is the one by the house, so we'll just walk to it. Grab your water jugs."

It was a short walk across the yard to the bean field and we each took our positions, taking four rows apiece. The rows were half a mile long, but to me, a complete novice, they looked longer. I had been given the simple instructions of removing everything from my rows that wasn't a bean! I had no idea what I was getting into but it had begun.

The first round was fairly easy and took roughly an hour to complete. The morning sun was bright but it wasn't too hot and the conversation was pleasant and friendly. There were plenty of things to get rid of in my rows, and I tended to lag behind the rest of the group. I learned a quick lesson in bean walking etiquette and protocol as I watched the others finish their rows ahead of me and then just stand and rest rather than coming back to help me finish my rows. Apparently what was yours was yours, good rows or bad ones.

Following a short water break we began our second round, and nearly halfway to the far end of the field everything suddenly changed. I was so lost in my own thoughts and cleaning up my rows that I was caught unaware when Grandpa exploded in anger. When I looked up it didn't take me long to sort out the cause of what had made him so mad.

"Teaser, you need to come back," yelled Grandpa.

Teaser, who was quite a ways ahead of the rest of us, stopped and looked back. "Come back for what?" he asked cynically.

"Your rows aren't clean," observed Grandpa. "Look at all those milkweeds you skipped."

"Milkweeds?" laughed Teaser. "I ain't choppin' them today."

Grandpa stopped his steps immediately and stood tall and straight. I knew Teaser had just given a really bad answer. "You're not chopping them today huh? Did I hear you right?"

Teaser laughed again. "You heard it right. It's a no milkweed day today."

The rest of us could see the impending explosion and we only had to wait a few seconds for it to happen. Grandpa spoke in a tone I didn't know he was even capable of. He spoke loudly, quickly, and with an anger level that made me immensely happy his words were not directed toward me.

"You lazy little shit," he screamed. "If you're not chopping them, then you're not chopping anything. Get the hell out of my field. You can walk back to town and you can get started right now. Get out of here!"

Legacy

Andy, TJ, and I stood silently, as we awaited Teaser's response. The extent of Grandpa's instant anger had surprised him, but he knew that the man who had just fired him was not one given to idle threats. Grandpa's stare seemed to cut straight through Teaser's previous arrogant attitude, because Teaser angrily tossed his corn knife onto the ground and began his three mile walk back to town. Grandpa stared at Teaser's back for what seemed to me to be several minutes, and Teaser must have sensed that because he never looked back once. He just walked through the field until he reached the highway and eventually he disappeared from our sight.

The rest of us quietly got back to our business and neither Andy nor TJ said anything to defend their brother's behavior. They knew he had messed up with both his words and his attitude toward Grandpa Carl, and they had no intention of joining him. All they wanted to do was walk some beans and make some money, so they put their heads down and made sure everything in their rows was clean. The rest of that round remained relatively quiet, and then things got back to normal, which made everyone happy. It didn't take long for Grandpa to find his smile and his humor once again.

Teaser was not mentioned by any of us the rest of the day as we made our way up and down the rows and slowly across the field. I knew he could have returned and apologized but he was too proud and immature to do that, so our bean crew stayed at four people instead of five. It took most of the week to complete all three of Grandpa's fields, but even a city boy like me could understand the difference in the before and after once we finished. The fields now looked like smooth, soft green blankets fluttering in unison as the breeze rocked the top leaves back and forth.

Grandpa and I stood together and looked at the final, completed field. "It looks good, doesn't it? I asked with a smile.

"Yeah, it does," he agreed, "and it's important to have it done well. Protecting the garden, you know!"

I patted him on the back and grinned broadly. "I know."

CHAPTER 23

I wasn't in town much during our bean walking week, but I did go in once, on Thursday night, and got Rock out of his house for a while. He was moving a lot better with his crutches than he had in the park on the 4th, but nothing about his movements would qualify as quick. Gowrie had settled down from its 4th of July energy and things seemed to have returned to their normal routines. The streamers and decorations had been stored away until they resurfaced again next summer, and the only traces of the carnival even being in the park were the matted down areas where the rides and the trailers had been for four days.

Rock and I shagged the drag for two hours and Main Street was fairly full of others doing the same thing. The summer sun still stayed up late and the temperature was seasonably pleasant, which made it seem much earlier in the day than it actually was, but time didn't really matter to either of us. The pace of the evening was slow and relaxed, and after what seemed to be our fortieth trip down Main Street we decided to head out of town and cruise the gravel a while.

This time we drove east on the gravel, slowly making our aimless journey away from the sunset and the other people in town. We passed Coon Mound, which did not look as intimidating as I had been told it was. It seemed to me to just be a small hill covered with grass, that looked empty and harmless. It did not appear to be the enormous mountain monster that I had heard about, one that struck fear into the eyes and hearts of everyone who dared go down it on sleds or toboggans in the winter. I said as much aloud and Rock was quick to contradict me.

"Oh, yeah, you gotta go down that thing in the snow!" exclaimed Rock. "Doesn't look like much now, but covered in snow it's a whole different deal. Plus, at the bottom there's a creek, so if you're going too fast at the bottom and overshoot the ending, you end up down at the bottom of that. Guy broke his ribs there last winter."

"Good times," I replied half-heartedly. "That's just what you need, something else broken. Besides, I'll be back in the city by then. You'll have to send me some pictures."

Rock looked away from me and stared out the window at nothing in particular. "Back to the city, huh? What for? Can you really say you miss being there?"

"I don't know," I answered thoughtfully. "It's where I'm from. Home, ya know. Just like this place is home for you. I guess I miss parts of it, but honestly not as much as I thought I would when I first left. Small town Iowa is still weird to me in lots of ways, but it's good here. Good people and this tiny little town is so alive. There's always something going on. When I first got here I thought it would be like a ghost town or something."

Rock laughed. "So we've kind of grown on you."

"Yeah, I guess so. I don't know how to explain it, really. It's comfortable here."

At that point we reached a stop sign and realized we had gone clear to the next town, which caught us both by surprise. "Harcourt," explained Rock. "Been here yet?"

"No," I answered. "What have I missed?"

"Not a thing," he laughed. "Not a thing. Ready to head back?"

"I guess so," I stated and as I made a U-turn and pointed my car back toward Gowrie I decided to change the topic. "I've been in the beans all week. Have you seen Cheri?"

"Haven't seen her, but we've talked a couple times on the phone. The calls can't be too long, cause my folks holler about the long distance charges, but we talk when we can. Have you called Kathy?"

I turned and gave him an unsure look. "No, I haven't. Was I supposed to?"

"That's up to you partner," he said coyly. "You like her don't you?"

"Yeah, I like her, but this engagement thing of hers bothers me. Besides, I don't even have her phone number."

"You gotta get over her giving her ring back. From what I hear she was ready to do that before she met you. You just helped speed it up a little. Just think of all the fun double dates we can go on. Of

Legacy

course you'll have to do all the driving for a while yet," he smiled as he patted his cast. "I can get her number from Cheri if you want me to."

I didn't answer immediately and just drove on in silence, staring blankly into the deep red July sunset. "Okay. I'm only gonna be here for another month or two though, so I don't know how serious we should get."

"Just take it as it comes, man. It'll all work out like it's supposed to."

I took a different gravel road back, this one a mile farther north than the one we had been on going east, just because I wanted to see new things and continue to learn my way around. A mile or so from Gowrie we came upon what looked to be a totally deserted farmyard. There was a two-story house, unpainted and untended, that stood in the center of two other buildings, in equally bad condition. The weeds grew tall in what could have been the yard, and the paint on the two buildings showed signs that they had once been red. Each acreage I had seen so far had been well maintained and full of life, so I was immediately intrigued by what I saw. "What's this place all about?" I asked Rock. "Looks totally deserted."

"It is," he replied and I thought I saw a small shiver run through his entire body. "Go faster man. This is our haunted house, the Nordquist place. Gives me the creeps just to be this close to it. Keep driving."

"What? Are you kidding me?" I laughed. "A haunted house in Gowrie, Iowa? No way!"

"Yes, way," he continued. "Nobody has lived there for twenty years and probably never will. I wish they'd tear the damn thing down."

"What makes it haunted?" I inquired, a little more interested because I could now tell that Rock was serious.

"A long time ago a guy who lived there went nuts. Killed his wife and two kids. Didn't shoot them either. Used an axe. Very gruesome stuff. Then he went out and stood in his front yard and waited for a car to come by. No idea how long he waited, and can't imagine what the hell he was thinking while he waited, but finally

Legacy

an older couple drove by. He ran into the road and flagged them down, acting like he needed their help, so of course they stopped. I guess he laughed some weird laugh at them, told them that he had just killed his family, then stepped back away from the couple's car, put a gun to his head, pulled the trigger and died right where we just drove. Just keep driving man."

"That's awful," I commented. "Still doesn't make it haunted though. Just a really sad story."

"Well, over time people have driven by on this road and claimed to have seen lights on upstairs and have claimed to have heard the wild laugh of somebody, but no person has ever been seen there. I guess we all just kind of leave it alone and stay away. Don't wanna tempt whatever spirits are running around on that place. Maybe that's why it's still up and hasn't been torn down yet. I don't know"

"Wow. The Nordquist place. So Gowrie has a haunted house."

We arrived back in Gowrie and cruised the drag one more time before I took Rock home. "I've got one more day left in the beans, so I'd better call it a night." I waited until I saw that Rock was safely up his porch stairs and then I drove away, once again alone with my thoughts. I thought about returning to the city and the things that awaited me there. I thought about Gowrie and the new things I had found here. Suddenly the equation in my mind didn't add up like it always had before, and that surprised me. This little town had indeed grown on me, like Rock said, and for the first time ever I actually considered what a life here might be like, and I didn't hate the idea. I thought back to my first ride to the farm from the airport, and it slightly irritated me to acknowledge that Grandpa had been right yet again. I had asked him how anyone could want to live in a small town like Gowrie, and he had told me that in time I would know the answer and would never have to ask the question again.

I pulled into the farm, parked my car, and sat for a moment taking everything in. The sun was just below the horizon, but it wasn't totally dark yet, and as I looked around in every direction I felt an inner calm that I could never remember feeling before. This place definitely had grown on me. As I walked toward the house I spoke out loud to Grandpa, even though I knew he couldn't hear me. "You were right again. I get it."

CHAPTER 24

Grandpa paid Andy, TJ, and me $4.00 an hour each for our time in the beans, and I was happy to receive my $152.00 check at the end of the week. With gas over fifty cents a gallon and my desire to add to my wardrobe, the money came in handy. It wasn't often that I had extra money in my pocket when I was in the city, and it felt good, mainly because I knew I had worked to earn it.

Rock called on Saturday morning and told me he wanted me to come pick him up around noon. He sounded unusually excited about something, which got me intrigued, but he shrugged off my observation and just told me to be there. Grandpa's day was going to be spent with the carpenters who were finally ready to begin rebuilding the garage. Something had initially delayed them after the tornado, and then the holiday got in the way, but I could hear them in the yard and I knew their work was about to begin. Grandpa would be busy with them all day in his roles both as socializer and supervisor, so I was free to do whatever I wanted. A day with Rock sounded like fun.

Rock was waiting for me on his porch and he was down the steps before I had even pulled into his driveway. He wore a mysterious smile as he greeted me and climbed into my car. "Hey, man," he started. "So your days in the bean field are done for this year, huh?"

"Yes, they are," I smiled. "It wasn't so bad. After Teaser's stupidity the first day we actually found ways to make it fun. We told jokes and of course listened to Grandpa's stories."

"Oh, I'm sure Carl had no shortage of stories to pass on to you guys."

"You got that right," I continued. "Amazing all the things running around in his head. He's always so understated too. You never know he's teaching ya something while he's doing it, but then something comes up and you realize that what he told you was right."

"Best kind of teaching," added Rock. "I used to just tune out the teachers who tried to tell me how to think in school. Carl's been passing on his stories for as long as I can remember. Let's go."

I just shook my head as I backed out of Rock's driveway and began to drive. "It's funny how my Mom tried to tell me some of these same things back home, but I just mostly tuned her out. I don't know if I didn't believe her or if I just didn't wanna hear it."

"Maybe you just weren't ready yet. Took a change of scenery to get you thinkin' better," concluded Rock.

"Maybe so. So what's going on today? You look like you're all pumped about something."

Rock adjusted his cast leg and gazed through the windshield. "I am pumped. I got a call from Crusher this morning and he told me that he and Josh got all their stuff back. Maxie and the boys are still in jail and they're gonna be charged with all kinds of things. Josh even got his wad of cash back. They had it stashed and hadn't spent any of it yet, because they were too busy stealing from the carnival. Idiots. Crusher said the cops found things from other robberies too, so there's no telling how much trouble those three are in."

"That's cool," I commented with a smile. "I haven't been here long, but long enough to not like those guys."

"Yeah, they're easy not to like. Guess it took a fresh set of eyes and ideas to catch 'em. People around here have been trying to catch them for a long time. Your bingo plan was brilliant!"

"I was just lucky that I saw them switching the money that first time and then remembered all their talk about the 4th being a good time to make money. Just put two and two together and it worked out."

"So, you ready for some more fun tonight? Rock asked, randomly changing the subject.

"Fun is always good," I laughed, "but what is it? Your last idea was a blind date."

"Are you sorry about me doing that?" he asked, pretending to be serious.

"No, not sorry. Just still a little nervous. Not quite sure where all this is headed."

Rock continued, "Nobody's ever sure. Stop thinking so much and just enjoy the moment. So are you ready for some fun or do I have to go alone?"

I looked at his leg and laughed. "If you're going alone, whatever it is better be close You still can't drive."

"Oh, yeah. I forgot! Guess you'll have to come along then won't you?"

"Guess so. So where are we going for all this mysterious fun?"

"Dodge. There's a new disco and the girls want us to check it out with them. Not sure how much dancing I can do just yet, but it will still be a good time."

"A disco, huh? My boys and I went to a couple of those back in the city, and we had a pretty good time. Could be fun seeing how you Iowa folks shake it. So we're going there tonight?"

"Yeah, let's head up there around 8:00. Maybe you'll even be brave enough to get Kathy's phone number tonight," he laughed. "Can't believe you haven't done that yet."

"Haven't needed to. You seem to always have things arranged. I may need some new clothes though. I didn't think I'd need any fancy duds here, but now I might."

"Just wear something casual but nice. It doesn't have to be fancy. We're not trying to be Travolta."

"Okay, the disco it is!. Another Iowa first for me!"

Legacy

CHAPTER 25

The building was fairly large but unassuming, and without the huge neon HANGAR sign out front it could easily have been mistaken for a warehouse. The parking lot was large and square but when we arrived it was only half full, perhaps because it was still early. Rock looked for Cheri's car but didn't see it, so I parked and we got out. Rock put his crutches under his arms and we made our way to the front door. We were both in good humor and were filled with the anticipation of what we would find on the other side of the door. Once inside, we were immediately met with a ticket window where we had to pay our $4.00 cover charge, so our enthusiasm faded a little, but only a little, for the night ahead held great promise and we knew that a lot of fun was waiting at the end of the long, curved hallway.

The music was already playing but it was more like background music rather than dancing music. When we reached the end of the long hallway we saw an incredibly long bar to our left and the dance floor to the right. The entire place was dimly lit, but we could see the size of the room, and it was bigger than I had imagined it could be. The dance floor was directly in the center and it was surrounded by dozens of tables and chairs. Rock and I smiled at each other and continued on farther into the disco. Through a wide arched doorway directly behind the dance floor there was a large game room filled with pool tables, arcade games, and pinball machines. The pool tables were already full with players who wore serious looks when their cues were in their hands and who grabbed their beer bottles when their opponents shot. The noise of the arcade games rang out loudly and I watched the players move their hands and bodies in sync, doing their best to make their quarters last as long as possible.

Rock and I went back through the open archway and returned to the dimly lit dancing area. To our left, in the back of the building, we could see even more tables on the main floor. There were also a couple steps that led to an area somewhat separated from the main floor by a metal railing and slightly above the other tables. Rock navigated the steps slowly and we claimed one of those tables.

Once we sat down, I began the conversation. "This place is nice. Hard to tell from the outside, but I like it."

"Yeah, this will be a big deal for this town. Most of the bars uptown are either really small and cramped or have strippers. This place is huge."

"So who all is coming?" I asked. "Just Kathy and Cheri?"

"I don't know for sure," replied Rock. "I think some other friends of theirs will be with them too. You know how girls have to be in groups. Guess we'll see before too long."

A tall, pretty waitress with an empty tray in one hand approached us. She wore a stewardess outfit that included a navy blue skirt and a white blouse that kept with the airline theme of the disco. Rock and I both grinned at her and we ordered our first beers. We couldn't help but follow her with our eyes as she walked away to get our drinks.

Suddenly, seemingly out of nowhere, multi-colored strobe lights began flashing everywhere and the sound of a large jet engine drowned out every other sound in the building. It was as though a jumbo jet was taking off right beside us. The lights flashed faster and faster as the engine noise reached its highest pitch, and as the imaginary plane took off the DJ began the music. Rock and I were both caught off guard by the opening show, but we looked at each other and grinned. "Damn. Wasn't ready for that!" I exclaimed.

"Me either," he added. "About jumped out of my seat. Pretty cool though."

People immediately found their way onto the dance floor, as if they had been waiting for a gate to open that allowed them to begin dancing, and the night was officially underway. Some of the guys wore white pants and white leisure suits. They wore colorful, shiny shirts that I guessed were silk or satin, and had on shoes with thick raised heels. Apparently *Saturday Night Fever* had enough reach to make it to central Iowa, because counterfeit Travoltas were everywhere. The girls' outfits varied widely. Some wore long, tight dresses that made complicated dance moves impossible, but most wore short summer skirts that bounced as they moved and twirled. Each person made his own fashion statement, and I suddenly felt somewhat underdressed in my khaki pants, pullover shirt, and tennis shoes.

The stream of people filing into the Hangar was now steady. From where we sat we could see the movements of many distant silhouettes, but we could not distinguish specific faces or identities. As we continued our people watching, the stewardess returned with our beers. We gave her a nice tip, and she smiled broadly and hurried to her other tables, promising to return to us often.

Fifteen minutes later the girls found us. Cheri waved at Rock when she finally saw him, and she and the others gleefully bounded up the stairs and joined us. Suddenly our peaceful table for two was loud and filled as the six of us said our greetings. Rock extended his arm and Cheri slid in closely to him. The others, whom I didn't know, took seats across from us, and Kathy sat next to me. It seemed like all the girls talked at once, bubbling with the excitement of the new disco and the possibilities of the night that lay ahead. I watched as they fluttered constantly in their chairs like hummingbirds, and it seemed to me that they were already involved in multiple conversations at the same time and mostly oblivious to both Rock and me. The music was loud which caused their voices to rise even more, and I sat and silently wondered if any of them was actually doing any listening.

The waitress returned, which broke up the chattering, and the girls each ordered their drinks. Rock and I also ordered refills and the busy stewardess hurried to get each of us what we wanted. Kathy saw me staring at the waitress as she left to fill our orders, and she lightly punched me in the shoulder. "Hey!" I uttered, turning to face her. "What was that for?"

"Jeez," she scoffed. "Could you be more obvious?"

"I just wanted to make sure she didn't trip on those steps. Just tryin' to be a good guy," I explained unconvincingly.

"Right. Whatever," responded Kathy.

In order to quickly change the subject, I leaned forward, clapped my hands together, and spoke to the entire table. "So why aren't you girls out there dancing already?" Kathy scowled at me but I pretended not to see it.

"Oh, we'll get there," replied Jacie, one of the other girls. She was taller than the others and had a warming smile and shoulder length blonde hair. "We just need to have that first drink first."

"Gotcha," I answered. I began tapping the table to the beat of the song. One corner of the dance floor was filled with girls dancing enthusiastically with no one in particular. "Girls in the city do that too. Doesn't matter if they have a partner or not. They just like the shaking and the dancing.

Kathy responded first. "Oh, we do that too once in a while. Sometimes it's frustrating waiting for you guys to ask us, so we just get up and go ourselves. Are you a dancer or just a drinker?"

I took a long drink from my beer bottle and looked at the dance floor. "I've been known to dance a little. I don't know any of those fancy line dancing steps though. Just kinda regular dancing."

Kathy smiled a little, raising one corner of her mouth, and replied, "Same here. Guess we'll have to see what moves you've got pretty soon."

"We can do that," I stated. I then turned and tapped Rock's cast. "Maybe Rock can show us some one-legged steps too."

"Oh, yeah," smirked Rock. "You know it." He began to pretend to dance in his chair. "I got the moves buddy, but for now I think I'll just watch. You can go shake a leg though. Kinda curious to see those city boy moves of yours."

Ten minutes later Kathy and I made our way to the dance floor. I didn't recognize the song that was playing, but that didn't matter. It was crowded but we found some room in a corner and let the music take us away. We stayed for three fast songs and then held each other closely during a slow one. Holding her felt as good as it had felt at Josh's party the first night I met her, but no matter how hard I tried, I could not get her previous engagement out of my thoughts. When the pace of the music picked up again we returned to the table. "Not bad partner," commented Rock. "Don't think you'll win any contests but not bad."

"Yeah, yeah," I responded. "That was just the warm up. After a few more beers I'll be really good!"

"Ha. You'll just think you're good."

"Probably true," I laughed, "but that's all that matters isn't it? Thinking you're good and having fun."

"I guess so," stated Rock as he raised his beer to mine for a toast. "Here's to fun!"

We walked to the exit around 1:00AM. The night had been extremely enjoyable, a mix of dancing, laughing, and strengthening still infant friendships. The six of us walked out together, verbally reliving the evening's highlights, and promising to return soon and often. Kathy and I had danced to at least a dozen songs, both fast and slow, and I know we had given the appearance that we were together as a couple, though neither of us had said anything to each other that confirmed or denied that. Our cars were on opposite sides of the parking lot, so we parted just outside the door of the disco. I gave Kathy a quick goodnight kiss, then Rock and I slowly walked to my car and headed back to Gowrie.

CHAPTER 26

The next two days were spent on the farm. The garden looked great, but Grandpa reminded me that it still needed a lot of attention and care. Our vegetables were all growing and some were even ready to eat, but the weeds were relentless. It was early afternoon on Sunday, and once again I found myself on my knees in the dirt pulling weeds that seemed perpetually intent on choking out all the good in our garden. Grandpa stood nearby, evidently in a supervisory role, and while he watched me work he inspected all the rows we had planted.

"Does this process ever end? I asked hopefully.

"Nope," he responded without looking at me. "I thought you had already learned that. If you ever slack off on tending your garden, whether it's this one or your life, the weeds will instantly move in and take over. We can stop temporarily with this garden in the fall, after all the vegetables have ripened and been eaten, but next spring it starts all over again. With our lives, we can't ever afford to take even temporary breaks. If we do, the weeds and thistles will get us every time."

"I guess I'll keep pulling weeds then," I said with a wry smile. "I want to be able to eat all this stuff."

"There's nothing better." He then walked toward the new garage to do some more organizing. The carpenters had worked two long days and had nearly completed the rebuilding, and I could see the excitement in Grandpa's eyes whenever he looked at it or talked about it. New is fun no matter what age a person is.

I joined him in the garage after I had subdued the garden weeds and he immediately put me to work. There were numerous new shelves and drawers that he couldn't stand to see empty, so we found new homes for all his wrenches and tools and hoses and bolts. We stacked countless cans of oil and transmission fluid as well as various tires and boards that might be used someday for something. Since the new garage was larger than the old one, there was more space to store and stack things, and Grandpa seemed intent on putting as much in there as possible while still leaving room for his truck.

Legacy

We placed and piled and arranged things for two hours before Grandpa declared himself satisfied and was ready for something else. He suggested we go for a drive, which didn't interest me much, but I could sense he had something more on his mind, so I consented. The July sun was still powerful and the cab of Grandpa's pickup was sweltering. We were both already sweating from the garden and the garage, but the temperature in the truck caused my sweat to run even more freely than before. We both rolled our windows down, but that didn't help much since any breeze that we felt was also extremely warm.

He drove slowly on the gravel, so we didn't stir up any large clouds of dust behind us, and for the first mile or so there was no conversation. He just silently looked at the fields we passed, but I knew the conversation was coming, though I wasn't sure what direction it would take. Three miles away from the farm he finally spoke. "So the dancin' joint was all right?" he began.

I smiled at his first words and the memory of the previous night's activity. "Yeah, it was fun. It's a really nice place too. Pretty sure we'll be going there a lot."

"Good. Good. A guy needs a place like that where he can let loose a bit. Probably loud too, huh?"

"Oh, it was loud, but that's part of the fun," I explained. "Gotta have it loud."

He shook his head. "The new generation I guess. Sometimes I miss that kind of stuff, but my time for that has passed. It's your time now."

"You used to go dancing a lot?" I inquired, now interested in hearing more about Grandpa's past.

"Sure, but we didn't have any discos. I'm a polka man myself. You probably don't even know what that kind of music is do you?"

"Umm, not really," I confessed, "but I guess every age group has its own thing. I wonder what will come after disco."

He turned to me and with a sarcastic half smile stated, "I don't know, but it will more than likely be louder and even harder on my ears." We both shared a laugh as the truck reached another intersection. Before turning the corner he pointed to a farm house just off the road. "See that place over there?"

"Yeah," I replied. "Nice looking acreage. What about it?"

"Well, I'll tell ya," he continued. There was no other traffic on the road, so we sat where we were as he began his story. "The guy who lives there is named Roy Dale Erickson. I've known him for a very long time. He's been on his farm even longer than I've been on mine. He's almost seventy, and it's getting harder for him to keep up just because he's getting up there in years. He raised his family there, two boys and a girl. He told me once that it was his dream and wish to turn his farm over to his kids one day so they could carry on what he had built and worked on and created for so many years. Didn't work out though."

I was mildly intrigued so I asked for more details. "Why not? What happened?"

"His daughter was the oldest and she never really liked being on a farm. She went off to college and married a lawyer. I think they live in Denver now. She's not back much. The boys were lazy and totally without ambition. They were always in trouble and doing stupid things, wrecking their cars, smoking pot, vandalism, things like that. They embarrassed Roy Dale terribly and he eventually basically kicked them out. I think he gave each of them some money and wished them luck, but he told them not to come back to him for any more because he was done with them. He said to me that when he turned them out he told them that since they had all the answers to everything they wouldn't need his help anymore, and they could get out into the world and find out they had been asking the wrong questions. Sound familiar?"

I stared intently at the motionless farm yard in front of me. It was neat and clean, but it suddenly seemed to me to be a really lonely place. "So this whole story was really about me? Am I the sons with all the wrong answers?"

Grandpa began to slowly drive down the road again. "You used to be."

He surprised me with his answer. "Used to be?"

"Yes, and not very long ago either. Remember our first few hours together coming back from the airport? You were so cocky and angry. Mad at your mom. Mad at me. Mad at the whole world because the world hadn't made you a star yet. Hadn't even noticed

Legacy

you. You had it all figured out, but you knew nothing. Remember?"

"I remember," I answered softly and with great humility. "You said used to be. You don't think that's me now?"

"You're not the same young man today, no. Do you have it all figured out yet? No." He then looked at me with an unusually serious look. "But I like the progress I've seen. You're getting there. Something tells me that back in the city you didn't spend much time relaxing or having actual conversations, just kicking back and enjoying and appreciating this amazing world we live in. You never did that did you?"

"No, I didn't," I agreed. "We always had to hurry up and be somewhere, even though we didn't do anything once we got there, wherever it was. I don't think it ever occurred to me even one time to relax."

"From what I understand you didn't listen too well either. Did you ever have a real conversation with your mom? I know without even being there that she tried to have them with you."

"Not really. I think she wanted to talk to me a lot but I always just blew it off for some reason. I feel bad about all that now. I can only imagine how frustrated I must have made her."

"You should feel bad, but that's all part of growing up. We all fall and stumble when we're young. She could see how fast you were falling and she knew, or at least hoped, that being here could be the net you needed to catch you. I think you can now see that her plan to send you here was a good one."

"I do," I answered, nodding in agreement. "So what is Roy Dale going to do?"

"I don't know, but it makes me sad to think about it. A man needs a legacy and I know how disappointed he is with the prospect of his legacy not being what he wanted it to be. He has told me that several times. I can't explain why, but lots of people will let you down, and many times it will be those closest to us, the ones we tend to count on the most."

I added, "That's a depressing statement. You're usually more optimistic than that."

Legacy

He drove on. "It is a little depressing isn't it? It's the truth though. Okay, enough of that kind of talk," he stated as his familiar grin returned to his face.

We were quiet for the next couple miles and then finally my curiosity got the better of me. "So do you think about your legacy too? I mean you're working the farm by yourself and you're in your sixties. Mom obviously chose the city instead of staying here, so when you told me about Roy Dale it got me thinking about what you want to do with your place eventually. You are thinking about stuff all the time, so I'm sure you've got something in mind don't you?"

Without looking at me he quietly responded. "I've given it a little thought."

I waited for his next statement, but he said no more, so I prodded further. "Well, care to share or is it a secret?"

He thought for a few more seconds and then responded. "I've given it a little thought. For now that's probably enough."

"All right," I stated, though I was disappointed with his lack of answer.

We neared the northwest edge of Gowrie, passing the cemetery which was on our right, and Grandpa looked at me. "You up for some ice cream? My treat!"

"Sounds good," I answered.

"Then off to the Dairy Queen we go."

CHAPTER 27

August arrived and brought with it some oppressive heat mixed with periodic, necessary rain showers. The 4th of July was a distant memory and normal summer activities were in full swing. The swimming pool was crowded every day, and when Grandpa didn't have work for me to do, I often joined the crowds there. The Jaycees were in the middle of their softball season, and I spent several nights watching them compete in their maroon uniforms, as they played against other area teams. The thing I enjoyed the most about those nights was the post game fun at Sherm's tavern, which was where the team usually congregated after the games were over.

Rock and I had met the girls at the disco several more times, and a comfortable routine seemed to be developing there. It appeared to me that meeting them there kept everything simple and uncomplicated, and that helped keep me at ease with Kathy. I was still unsure how much longer I would remain in Iowa, and I knew she was leaving for college before too long, so any type of serious commitment to her or anyone made me nervous. Simple and casual was a much better answer for me, though I was never totally sure Kathy felt the same way. I really liked her. Truth be told, I didn't have a clue what to do with her, and therefore I tended to do nothing, even though I knew there were many times I should have and could have stepped up and told her the things I was thinking.

Grandpa and I still found our way to Hazel's quite often for lunch, and I was happy to no longer be the new guy or the outsider. I didn't think I'd ever make the fashion conversion to overalls like many of the men in town wore, but my boots and my jeans suggested that I belonged, which was far different than when I had first arrived in town. There is no substitute for familiarity in regard to how a person is treated. Even Captain had stopped making "city boy" jokes about me and frequently had actual conversations with me, which was a sure sign of my acceptance. His conversations were usually aimed at enlightening me about something he was sure I needed to know, but I remembered Grandpa at the elevator saying it was best to just take Captain in stride and let him feel important, so that was what I usually did.

Kenny continued to be excited about the progress of his new house, and he regularly gave us updates on its construction. Herman never seemed to run out of jokes to tell, but he continued to struggle whenever he reached his punch lines because he made himself laugh so easily. In all the time I had known Herman he had never once been without his smile, and I enjoyed being around him. I could easily see why Kenny, Herman, and Grandpa were close friends. Captain, though, I still couldn't figure out.

The Jaycess had been excessively excited for a couple weeks as they prepared for a huge fundraiser night that would provide them with money they would need to continue all the things they did for the community. They had been selling ten dollar tickets that paid for a night of dancing and a dinner that featured huge Iowa pork chops. I had been asked at least a dozen times if I had bought my ticket, and like everything I had heard before the 4th of July, I hoped the evening lived up to its hype. This little town continued to surprise me. There was always something big going on that seemed to find ways to get as many people as possible involved. That would have never happened back in the city.

Rock and I bought our dinner tickets and also bought tickets for Kathy and Cheri who planned to meet us there. Oddly, the dinner and dance were to be held in Harcourt, six miles east of Gowrie, and when I asked about that Lennie told me that Gowrie didn't have a community center or a building large enough to handle the expected crowd. We were confident that the girls could find Harcourt, even though they had never been there before, because from Dodge all they had to do was get on a highway and drive south. No turns. Even Grandpa had bought a ticket to the dinner. He didn't care about the dancing, but he had a real passion for good food, and the delicious, huge, Iowa chops were too much for him to resist. Josh had promised him that the meal would be excellent, and Grandpa also enjoyed supporting the Jaycees because over the years he had seen the countless good things they did for the area.

Legacy

On the night of the event Rock got delayed doing some things for his parents and we arrived later than we had planned. The meal and the music were already underway when we got there, and one of the first things I saw inside the building was Grandpa and his group voraciously devouring their chops and beans and coleslaw. I tapped Grandpa on the shoulder and began, "Must be good. Usually at least one of you guys is talking while you eat at Hazel's."

"It is good, replied Captain in between bites. "Hell of a lot better than Hazel's too. You better get in line sport. Don't want them to run out before you get yours."

"Thanks Captain," I replied, "but I'm pretty sure they know how many tickets they sold and I imagine they have enough. You guys have a good time."

Rock had left me, and when I turned away from Grandpa's group I saw him waving his arms at me. He had found Cheri and Kathy, who had gotten there before us and saved us some seats. When I joined them we didn't stay at the table very long, because Captain was right. The food line was getting longer by the minute and we were all hungry. The Jaycees were all smiles as they piled the food onto everyone's plate and I was thanked numerous times for being there. The food was amazing and I ate every bite, as did the others in our group. The girls, who were usually somewhat shy about eating in front of us, put their shyness away and just dug in. All the while, in the background, the band played and helped keep the energy level of the room very high.

After we finished our pork chops and had thrown our plates away, the real socializing began. The dance floor was crowded and I could see that Kathy really wanted to get out of her seat and join them. Before I could get her out there though, Crusher came by and asked me to go outside with him for a little while. He didn't give a reason, but I excused myself and went with him. I gave Kathy an apologetic look and said, "I guess I'll be back after while. No idea what he wants but it must be important. Maybe you can find another dance partner while I'm gone."

Kathy gave me a semi-frustrated look and replied, "I may just do that."

Legacy

I walked away with Crusher but turned back once to look again at Kathy, somewhat unsure as to why she appeared angry with me. He led me outside to where Josh and Lennie were waiting, standing together under a shade tree. I greeted them then waited patiently to hear whatever it was they wanted me to know. Crusher began. "We didn't want to talk about this in front of everyone, but there are some things you should probably know about. It's about Maxie."

"Maxie?" I inquired. "I thought that whole deal was taken care of."

"It was. It is," added Josh, "but there's more. With guys like him nothing is ever totally over, especially when he thinks he was wronged."

"I don't understand. He did the stealing. How was he wronged?" I asked curiously.

Lennie tried to explain. "You have to think like those guys think. First of all, they will never think that anything they do is wrong, even if it's illegal. Once you understand that, you can sort of see what might be in their heads. They know they were set up on the 4th and I guess they've decided you did it, and well, you can imagine the rest. They want to even the score with you."

"I see," I replied quietly. "How do you know this?"

Josh chimed in to answer my question. "One of the deputies at the county jail is a friend of mine and he overheard a conversation Maxie had with one of his visitors. They talked about taking out the city boy and the crip, and he asked me to warn whoever that was, if I knew who they meant. So here we are. We figured you could get Rock up to speed on all this."

"Maxie gets out in a couple weeks," continued Lennie, "and he's stupid enough to act on his threat right away, even if it means getting put back into jail."

Suddenly I was extremely interested in what I was hearing. "So what do you guys suggest?"

Josh continued, "Well, we've been talking about that and we're not sure. They're all sneaky as hell so we think it's a bad plan to just sit around and wait for him and his buddies to do whatever they come up with to do."

Legacy

"I agree," I responded, "but what does that mean? Go after them first?""

"We're not sure yet what's best," added Crusher. "You did pretty good setting up the bingo thing to get him caught and get our stuff back on the 4th. We were thinkin' that maybe if you knew about their intentions you could start thinkin' up something like that again."

"Boy, I don't know," I sighed. "Have Maxie and his buddies ever been violent before? I thought they just stole stuff."

Lennie thought hard for a second then responded. "No, I don't remember them ever getting into a fight. They talk tough and I guess they've just bluffed their way through with their image and their reputation."

"Yeah, that's right," expressed Crusher. "I've never heard of any of them fighting anyone either. Guess I've never thought about that before."

The conversation continued for another ten or fifteen minutes before I remembered that Kathy was probably waiting for me inside. If she was mad before, when I left the table, she was more than likely steaming by now. I had been gone much longer than I had anticipated, but this information was definitely something I needed to know. When I returned to our table, I immediately noticed that Kathy was not sitting there with Rock and Cheri, who were unusually quiet. I could sense that something was going on, but I was unaware of what exactly it was.

"That took longer than I thought," I began, "but it was important. You and I have some things we need to talk about and figure out Rock."

"We do?" he asked, totally unaware of what he was unwittingly involved with.

"Yeah, we do," I continued. "More Maxie crap. We can talk about it later though. Time for fun tonight. Where's Kathy? The bathroom?"

Rock and Cheri looked at each other sheepishly, then Cheri answered softly. "Uh, no. She's dancing."

We all simultaneously turned our heads to face the dance floor, and I saw that Cheri was right. The band was playing their version of Chicago's *25 or 6 to 4*, and Kathy looked like she was having a good time moving to the music. I didn't know the guy with whom she was dancing. I had seen him around town but had never met him. "That's cool," I said with a phony smile. "Who's the guy she's dancing with?"

Rock tried his best to answer without any emotion. "His name is Dennis. Pretty good guy. He does construction. I guess he saw Kathy sitting here by herself and he asked her to dance. She looked once at the doorway and then just got up and went with him."

I took a long drink from my cup of beer and tried not to watch the pair dancing. It wasn't as easy as I thought though to act disinterested, and I found myself stealing glances quite often. During one of my peeks, Kathy's eyes met mine, so I knew that she had seen me back at the table. I smiled at her but did not get a smile in return, which made me a bit uncomfortable. I turned to Cheri and asked, "Is she mad at me because I went outside for a while?"

"You'll have to ask her that," Cheri replied. "She did come down here to see you, and you've hardly said two words to her."

I shook my head in disbelief. "Really? I'm here now. I didn't know those guys would pull me outside for half an hour. She really is mad?"

Rock joined in then. "I don't know man. You two will have to figure that out. Can't help you with this one."

The song ended and the dance floor tempo changed. The band went into a rendition of Bread's *Baby I'm a Want You*, a slow, romantic ballad which prompted many people to leave their seats and get close to each other as they danced. Ten or fifteen seconds into the song I surveyed the dance floor and saw Kathy and Dennis locked in a tight embrace, turning a very slow circle and talking to each other. Rock and Cheri saw it too. "Not so cool," I stated.

Rock consolingly tapped my shoulder. "Yeah."

I feigned disinterest when the song finished. I looked behind me to where the food clean up had begun. The Jaycees were busy washing, wiping, and putting things away, but even as I watched them work, my thoughts were on the dance floor. Less than a minute into the next song my attention was quickly returned to our table. Kathy and Dennis stood beside Cheri, standing very closely to each other, and Kathy spoke simply and directly. "Hey guys, we're going for a little walk. Be back after while."

Kathy did not wait for a reply from any of us, though she did give me a sideways look as she and Dennis neared the doorway. After they left, Rock, Cheri, and I sat in silence for what seemed like several minutes, though I know it wasn't nearly that long. Eventually I spoke first. "Well, this night is turning out to be all kinds of fun."

"Wow, sorry man," replied Rock. "I don't even know what to say."

"Me either," added Cheri.

I tried my best to smile at both of them. "No need to say anything. She's free to do what she wants with who she wants. I'm sure they'll have a nice walk."

"Right," interjected Rock. "A nice walk. Who are you trying to kid?"

I looked at him for a moment. "Just myself I guess. I know this is a big night and all, and I'm sure there's a lot more fun to be had, but I think I'll take off. I don't think I need to be here when they return and hear about all the fun they had on their walk. Can you catch a ride home with somebody else?"

"Yeah, I'm fine," stated Rock with a knowing nod of his head. "I'll get home. Catch up with you soon."

"Yeah. Hey, at least the food was good!" I stood up and slowly prepared to leave, looking once at the doorway to make sure Kathy wasn't there. "You and I have some big things to talk about, some things we need to get on pretty quick."

"Whenever you want," he stated.

"See ya. I'm out. You two have fun," and with that I turned and walked out of the community center, wondering if Kathy was taking a walk out of my life.

CHAPTER 28

Rock's cast came off two days after the pork chop dinner, and when I talked with him on the phone he sounded more excited than I had ever heard him sound. His freedom had returned to him and I could hear his enthusiasm. He told me the first thing he did was hop into his car and remind himself how much more he enjoyed driving than riding in the passenger seat. He made his way out to our farm early Monday afternoon, and I was glad to see him. I had just finished weed eating the yard when he showed up, and he joined me in the garage. While we talked, Grandpa suddenly appeared out of nowhere.

"Hey Carl," began Rock.

"Well look at you," replied Grandpa. "Must feel good to have both your legs working again. Good for you. Eli, I gotta go to Dodge for a while. I should be back for supper but you might have to fend for yourself."

"Okay," I responded. "What are you doing in Dodge?"

"Oh, it's nothing. Doctor's appointment. Time for the annual physical. He's pretty thorough, so I never get out of there as fast as I'd like to. I'll see you guys later."

"Okay," I answered.

With that Grandpa got into his pickup and drove away, and I put the weed eater back where it belonged. I really liked the new garage because everything had its proper place and was easy to find. Rock fumbled with some tools lying on top of the work bench, then picked up a hammer just to have something to hold. "So what's the Maxie news we need to talk about? You've had me curious since you mentioned it the other night."

"Ah yes, the other night. We can talk about Maxie in a minute. You all have a good time after I left?"

"You know I had fun," he replied. "Always do. But I don't think that's really what you're asking about is it?"

"Of course I meant you," I grinned. "Who else?"

"You're pitiful. Their walk lasted about forty-five minutes and she was really surprised to find out you had gone home. Not sure that was what she intended and I don't know exactly what she read into that move of yours."

"She can read whatever she wants into it. So did she have Dennis take her home too?"

"No. The girls went home by themselves. Dennis hung around with us for a while, but I guess we were too boring for him or something because he took off and went back to his other buddies."

"Sounds like everybody lost," I concluded.

"Maybe so," Rock added. "I don't know why she did all that. Maybe to see your reaction or see what you were thinking about her. To see if you'd get jealous and fight for her or something. I don't know. Who can figure women out?"

"What am I thinking? Same as before. She's heading to college in a week or so, and I'm heading back to the city before long. I like her, like her a lot, but I'm not ready for anything serious, especially long distance."

"Okay," said Rock. "I guess it'll all work out somehow. You should at least call her before she goes off to school though. Can't leave it just hangin' out there like it is now.

"I'll call her. No idea what I'll say, but I'll call her. That should be interesting."

"Okay, Romeo, talk to me. Maxie," Rock demanded.

"Come on. Let's sit under a tree and I'll tell you what I know. Hope you're feeling clever and creative." We walked over to the row of poplar trees and found a comfortable, shady spot, and I began telling Rock what Crusher, Josh, and Lennie had told me.

The August sun was radiating brightly but the gentle breeze made the afternoon mostly comfortable, and it felt good to sit under the trees. "Okay, apparently Maxie and the other two get out of jail shortly and they're mad at both of us. I guess Maxie sat and thought during his jail time and decided that you and I set them up at the carnival, and now he wants his revenge. Josh and the others gave me the heads up the other night in Harcourt. That's what took me so long outside."

"Maxie's a dandy isn't he?" Rock stated more than asked.

"What's he supposed to be going to do to us?"

"Who knows, but a deputy Josh knows overheard him talking about getting both of us, and evidently the deputy thought he was serious."

"Unbelievable. So what are you thinking?"

I gazed blankly at the bean field next to the yard, and watched the beans swaying in unison to the breeze. "I don't have a plan yet. I've thought about a couple things but wanted to see if you had any ideas. "Whatever we come up with, we need to be quick about it, cause he gets out in a couple weeks. You guys have all known him longer than I have, but they told me the other night he'd probably try to get us back right away."

"Yeah, I'd say that's more than likely true," added Rock. "I can see him sitting and stewing in his cell, getting madder at us by the minute."

"So, any thoughts?"

"Not right off hand, but we've got a little time. We can work on it. They really think he's mad enough to actually come after us?"

"Yeah, they do," I answered sincerely. "Nothing they talked to me about had any kind of joking to it."

"It's kinda funny in a way.. He must really think he's above everything. He and his boys have ripped off so many people, and now he thinks he's entitled to get even with us because we helped him get caught once."

I turned quickly toward Rock. "Wait a minute How many people do you know of that have had things stolen? I mean, how many that think Maxie did the stealing?"

"Oh, man, let me think. The Hadens, the Gustafsons, the Vinchattles. Those three I know of for sure. We can ask some of the other Jaycees. I'm sure they'll know more. You look like you have an idea."

I grinned a little. "Maybe the start of one."

Rock smiled back at me. "Care to share?"

"No, not yet. Let's talk to the guys and see who else they can add to your list." With that I stood up and brushed the dirt off my pants. "Wanna go swimming?"

Legacy

"Nah," replied Rock "I look goofy with one tan leg and the other one totally white. There's a softball game in town tonight though. Thought I'd go to that. I think it starts around six."

"Sounds like a plan. I've got to pick some things out of the garden. It's all getting ripe faster than I can keep up with it. It all tastes pretty good though."

Rock nodded in agreement. "Nothing's as good as fresh stuff right out of the garden. Ours isn't as big as this one but the beans and the tomatoes taste just as good I'm sure."

I walked into a row of beans, crouched down, and began picking everything that was ready to be cooked and eaten. "There's so many," I laughed. "I need to go get a bowl or something to put them all in."

"I'm outa here. See ya later at the game."

"Okay. Enjoy your driving!"

"Oh, I am," he replied as he walked toward his car, got in, and drove away.

I returned to the garden with my bowl and continued to pick the beans. I also found numerous onions and radishes that were ready, and it was finally time for me to get to taste some kohlrabi. We had far more sweet corn than we could ever eat by ourselves, and we had eaten tomatoes at every meal for the past two weeks.

5:45 rolled around and Grandpa had not gotten home yet. I figured either the doctor's appointment had taken a long time, like he thought it might, or he was grabbing some food in Dodge before he returned home. I left him a note and then drove into town to watch the softball game. Both teams were finishing their warm-ups when I took my place behind the Jaycees' dugout. The summer sun still shone brightly on the field and it was hot enough to make me sweat just standing still. All the players were sweating profusely.

Throughout the game I talked with several of the players and asked them the same thing I had asked Rock earlier. Several of them knew families who had been robbed in the past couple years, and the general consensus was that Maxie and his buddies were behind all or most of the crimes. In addition to the names Rock had given me, I was able to add the Magnussons, Ericksons, Borers, Patricks, and Nettletons to the list, eight families in all.

After the game, which the Jaycees won 14-8, we once again made our way to Sherm's for a beer. Even a few players from the other team joined us, which I thought was good, an example of rivals competing yet remaining friendly and respecting each other. The air conditioning felt good and for a week night Sherm's was fairly crowded. I was hungry so I ordered a sandwich with my beer, and when the food arrived I ate heartily. The conversation in our group was loud and random until Crusher found a moment to get more specific with me. "Eli," he asked, "have you thought about what we talked about?"

"I have, and I may have an idea. It's fairly elaborate though and would take some doing to pull off," I replied. "Could be fun though."

He gave me a look that showed he was extremely intrigued and curious. "How elaborate?"

"Well, if I can get some details worked out, it could take about thirty people and some really good timing."

"Thirty people? Gonna gang up on 'em and beat the hell out of 'em?"

I laughed. "Not exactly, but we could probably find at least that many people willing to help out couldn't we?"

Crusher nodded at me. "Around here? That many and a whole lot more. So what's the plan?"

"Not yet. But tell me this. Do the Jaycees or some other groups around here have any fancy costumes that might be scary? I don't mean just masks but the whole deal."

"Sure," he answered. "We do. For several years we've been running a Halloween haunted house as a fund raiser. We've got all kinds of stuff."

"Excellent. Start rounding all that up will ya? Is it pretty much the softball team guys who have the costumes?"

He looked around, taking mental inventory, and stated, "Yeah, pretty much. There are a few others, but mostly it's this group here, the softball guys."

"When is the next Jaycee meeting?" I inquired.

Crusher could see where I was going with my question. "When do you want it to be?"

"How about Thursday night? It won't take long to lay everything out for all of you, but the things we talk about need to stay secret."

"No worries there," he exclaimed with confidence. Then he stood and addressed the whole group loudly. "Hey, guys. Jaycee meeting Thursday at the softball field. 6:00. It'll take less than an hour. Be there."

CHAPTER 29

I began to notice that Grandpa was now allowing both of us to wake up later than he did earlier in the summer. It was a rare occasion that I heard the "It's nice to get up in the morning" song, and I couldn't figure out why he was doing that, but I really didn't mind. It wasn't that there was any less to do. He just seemed less rushed to do anything, and a lot of the physical tasks around the farm had become my jobs, under his direction of course. He seemed to walk more slowly too, and when I thought about it, I realized that he had begun to talk less and smile less than usual.

The day after the ball game I wanted to have a talk with him. Several things were on my mind, ranging from Kathy and her heading to college to Maxie and his desire for revenge to me heading back to the city, and I wanted to hear his thoughts and suggestions. I went outside and found him underneath his pickup changing the oil. He always obsessed about the oil in his machines, and it made me think back to our planting days and how thorough he had been with the oil and the grease on his tractor. I saw again how he lived the lessons he tried to pass on to me.

"Getting her changed?" I spoke to his boots, which was the only part of him that could be completely seen. I could hear the wrench turning and heard the filter drop into the pan he had placed on the ground.

"Workin' at it," he replied with a mild strain in his voice. "What are you up to?"

"Nothing much," I replied as I shuffled my feet in the gravel. "Just got a few things on my mind that I wanted to run by you."

"Be with you in a minute. The oil is almost done draining out."

"No hurry."

A few seconds later Grandpa slowly slid himself out from under the pickup and sat up on the ground. His hands were covered in oil and he looked at me as he grabbed a rag and started to clean himself. "Got some things on your mind huh? Fire away. I'll sure help you if I can." He walked around to the front of the pickup and began pouring quarts of oil into the truck.

"Well," I laughed. "Where to start. You know I've sort of been seeing Kathy right? It has gotten a little complicated and I'm not sure what to do."

He gave me a large grin as he reached for the next quart of oil. "Woman trouble? It won't take long for me to tell you all I know about women. What is it that you think is complicated?"

"I really like her and we always have fun, but we've reached the point where we won't be just twenty miles apart any more. She's leaving soon for college and will be three hours from here and I'll eventually be heading back to the city and will be halfway across the country. I just don't see how anything like that can work."

"I see," he replied with a thoughtful look. "Geography can be a big hurdle in a relationship. It's also not an impossible hurdle to handle. Sometimes it's just an excuse."

I looked at him blankly. "An excuse for what?"

"For anything," he explained. "For not committing. For walking away. Relationships are tough in the same room, and they're tough thousands of miles apart. It takes work no matter what, and if somebody is unsure then geography can be a convenient out."

"Hadn't thought of it quite that way. This is all new to me and I hate to admit it, but I feel lost. Like a little kid. It's like there's stuff I think I should know but I don't, so I guess I pull away from her even when I don't really want to."

"So now we're getting closer to the real reason you think it's complicated aren't we? It's not the miles. Insecurity can also cause a lot of grief and frustration."

"I don't know what exactly it is. Something is stopping me from really being with her. At first I thought it was because she was short and I'm tall, but that was stupid. When we met she was engaged and then she ended that, so that made me a little jumpy. Now she's going away to college. I don't know if it's all that put together or just me not being ready for something serious."

He took the empty quart bottles of oil, gathered them up and walked toward the garage. "Come on. Let's go sit on some buckets and really think this through." I followed and the talk continued. "You obviously like her a lot, and apparently she likes you too."

"Yeah, I like her," I agreed. "She even went out of her way over in Harcourt to try and get me mad or jealous, but I don't think I handled that right either."

"What do you mean?" he asked curiously.

"Well, I just left. Walked away. Didn't stick around to let her see any reaction or give an explanation."

"That might have been the smart thing to do. Also might have been cowardly. Hard to say. Have you talked to her about that?"

"No."

"So you really don't know what all she's thinking do you?"

"No."

"No wonder you think all this is complicated. You've made it that way. Knowing the answers is always better than not knowing, even if you don't like the answers you hear. You spend a lot of time wondering what she's thinking don't you?"

"Yeah, I do," I replied.

"Then why are you so naïve to not understand that she's probably wondering what you're thinking too. Seems to me you've done a poor job of communicating what you're feeling."

"Maybe," I added.

"One of the worst words in our language is maybe. You just spin your wheels with that word."

"You're right. It's like I'm almost always where I want to be with her, but I can never quite get all the way there. She and I need to have a real talk don't we?"

He gave me a look that suggested I had just asked an incredibly obvious question and in his understated way uttered a one-word reply. "Maybe."

"You're funny," I replied, and we both shared a good laugh.

"So, that's one. What else did you want to talk about?"

My thoughts were so focused on Kathy that it took me a minute to remember. "The other thing? Oh yeah. It's Maxie."

"Maxie? I thought he was still in jail. What do you want to know about him?"

"It's not really knowing anything about him. It's more like people with his mentality in general. I've dealt with a lot of Maxies in the city, so I have a bit more of a head start on this one. Handling bullies is more familiar territory than dealing with girls."

"So what's to handle?" he asked. "I still don't know what you mean."

"Okay, I'll try and explain at least part of it. He gets out of jail soon and he's pissed off at Rock and me. Evidently he's out for his revenge with both of us and I think it would be better to go on offense with him rather than wait and wonder what he might do."

"Go on. What are you thinking?"

"I've got an idea, a pretty elaborate one actually, but if it works right, then maybe nobody around here will have to worry about Maxie and his crap any more."

"With guys like him you have to go all in. They will always believe they are right, so whatever you're planning it had better be good. Is it as elaborate as the bingo thing on the 4th of July?"

I laughed a little at the question. "The bingo thing looks like a kindergarten idea compared to this one."

"I won't ask any more, and you can tell me as much or as little as you want to. I'd say go for it and try for an ending with him. If you don't then he'll be a burr in your saddle for as long as you're here. With Maxie, you need something definite. 'Maybe' will always be to his advantage."

"That's what I was thinking too," I added. "I may take you up on the offer to help. I'll let you know after I get a few other things lined up."

"Okay. I wish your Mom could have heard this conversation. You're finally using your head for some actual thinking. Pretty sure she would like that."

I smiled at him and all I could think to say was, "Yeah, I think she would too."

CHAPTER 30

Later that evening I summoned the courage to call Kathy. I knew we had to talk but I still didn't really know what to say to her. Her mom answered the phone which made me even more uneasy, but I pressed on. After a couple minutes of general small talk we eventually arrived at some substance. "So you leave in a couple days for school. Doing anything special for your last weekend at home?

"I think we're going to the disco," she replied without any extra emotion. "What are you doing?"

"Nothing planned yet but the disco sounds fun. We can make it sort of a send off party for you."

"That's kind of what we were thinking too. You and Rock are welcome to join us."

I swallowed hard and found the words somehow. "Might be a good idea if you and I had a long talk." After that I waited for her response. For several seconds all I heard on the other end of the line was silence.

"You think so?" she finally said. "We've had all summer and now when I'm leaving you think it's time to talk? I've thought that for two months. Man, you are a tough guy to figure out."

I felt like I had just been scolded but went with it. "I know. Maybe I can help with some of that Saturday night. I'll try to anyway."

Legacy

"Okay, I guess we'll see," she responded. I could hear the positive reluctance in her voice. "See ya Saturday."

The next night at 6:00 the Jaycees gathered at the softball field just as Crusher had instructed them to do. Once everyone was assembled, Crusher got their full attention. He looked over the group one more time just to make sure that only those trustworthy enough to be part of the plan were there to hear it. He understood how critical it was to keep whatever we were going to do secret.

"Okay guys, here's the deal," he began. "You all remember right before the 4th when Josh and I had our places broken into. Well, we all suspected it was Maxie and his boys, but as usual with them, we had no proof. The part that a lot of you don't know about that whole deal is that Eli and Rock here made it possible to get all our stuff back, even Josh's cash. The details aren't important now, but these two set Maxie up in a trap which he walked right into, and that's how he ended up in jail."

With that revelation there was a general murmur of approval among the group, and then Crusher continued. "That's the first half of the story. Now here's the rest. Maxie somehow found out that Eli and Rock set him up, and as you can imagine, he's pissed. He gets out of jail pretty soon and we know that he plans to get some kind of revenge on both of them. Josh and I are pretty grateful for what they did for us, and Eli and I have talked about it and we think that just sitting around and waiting for Maxie to do something like that is stupid. We thought going on offense was a better move, and Eli has some sort of plan to do that. I don't know what the plan is yet either, but he needs our help. That's why I had all of you show up here tonight. Maxie has been a pain in this town's butt for a long time and Eli thinks he might have an idea that can change that, right Eli?"

I stepped forward and stood next to Crusher, facing the entire group. "I think so. I hope so anyway. There's a lot to it though, and it's gonna take some preparation." I then gave them a sneaky grin. "Could be a lot of fun, but I have to say that if there is not total secrecy it won't work, so if you're in I need you to be all the way in."

Crusher added, "Anybody not wanting part of this? If not, now's the time to go." We all looked around at each other, but nobody moved. Everybody was in. "Good," he stated. "So Eli, what's the plan?"

I took the next fifteen minutes and laid it all out for them. Several of them were given specific things to do as part of the preparation and each promised to get those things done quickly. The others had parts to play as well but would just need to show up when it was time to put the plan into action. The plan seemed to meet with everyone's approval and when the meeting was over most of the group headed home. A few of us went to Sherm's for a beer and some relaxing. The juke box played non-stop as we sat and talked in our booth. Once in a while one of the guys would mention something about the plan, and I would have to remind him of the need for secrecy. There were many moving parts and loose ends to the plan, and I knew we would only get one shot at it, but the almost immediate extra talking in our booth made me only cautiously optimistic that it would all come together the way I wanted to. It was my plan, and I had to believe in it to make it work, but I had to admit to myself that I wasn't totally sure.

CHAPTER 31

Saturday night arrived and Rock and I headed north to Dodge and the disco. I was both excited and apprehensive about the conversation that I knew Kathy and I would have, and I tried hard to let the excited emotion win the battle inside my head. Driving was still new and fun to Rock after his weeks in his cast, so he drove and I stretched out in the passenger seat. He had the radio cranked up and tuned in to Dodge's new FM station, and the Doobie Brothers kept us company on the highway.

The August heat was still radiating its excessive warmth, even as the sun dipped into the horizon, and I was glad that Rock's car had air conditioning. Dodge seemed unusually busy, as if others had the same idea we did of getting out to observe an unofficial end of the summer. I figured there were going to be a lot of area people like Kathy who wanted one last summer party before they left for whatever college destination they were headed to. It seemed liked a really fun night to be out and I would have been completely excited except for my inner apprehension about my talk with Kathy. I didn't know where that talk would go, but I had a gut feeling that my sitting on the fence and keeping things superficial was about to come to an end one way or the other.

There was a line to get inside the disco. It wasn't horribly long, but it took us a few extra minutes to get through the door, into where the party was already well underway. The colored laser lights flashed in every direction and the music was loud and lively. I watched the dancers as Rock and I walked through the building, weaving our way through the crowd to the back and up the stairs to our regular table where the girls were already waiting for us. Besides Kathy and Cheri, there were several others whom I didn't know sitting at the table, and when we approached they all greeted us warmly. Rock took a chair next to Cheri and I found a spot directly across the table from Kathy. Through the noise of the music and the clatter at the table our eyes met and we silently smiled at each other. She looked especially good in her summer outfit, and a part of me thought that was a bit unfair. If had to let her go tonight she was not going to make it easy for me. It was difficult for us to have an immediate conversation, but I knew that as the night went on it always turned into a game of rotating chairs as people came and went. We would have our chance.

Rock was not much of a dancer, even without his cast on, but Cheri persuaded him to leave his seat for a few slow songs. I looked across the table and extended my hand toward Kathy. "Like to join them?" I asked.

"Sure," she replied with a smile on her face. We both rose from the table and walked down the steps together.

Barry Manilow serenaded us with his song *Even Now* as we embraced for the first time in several weeks, and it felt good to hold her. Rather than putting her head on my shoulder, which she usually did when we danced, she looked directly into my eyes, giving me an extremely confident, yet sincere look. We danced two consecutive slow songs then a fast one before we returned to the table. This time, however, we sat next to each other. We had been up close to one another for almost fifteen straight minutes and yet had spoken only a few words. I knew that would change drastically before the night ended.

"Big crowd," I observed in an attempt to start some sort of conversation. "More people than I've ever seen in here before."

Kathy looked around, mostly unimpressed, and replied, "Lots of college people I suppose. Who knows? Just a good night to party."

"I guess so," I stated. "Kind of an end of summer for lots of you."

"We have a lot of warm weather left, but we'll be tanning at school and not here."

"That's true. I keep thinking about what's going on back home. I'd probably be working in a shop somewhere or being a delivery guy. I never dreamed I'd be a farmer, even for a little while."

"Is it bad being a farmer?" she asked very seriously.

"No, it's not bad. It's just not something I ever even thought about doing. I didn't see too many fields or small towns growing up."

"So you're going back home?"

I paused there and noticed that several others at our table had begun eavesdropping on our conversation. I smiled politely at them then turned back to Kathy and leaned in closely to her. "Would you prefer to continue this outside? I think we both have a lot to say, and I'd rather tell you in private."

She took a long drink from her glass and nodded in agreement. We both rose again from our chairs and I spoke to Rock directly, and to the others indirectly. "We're gonna go out for some air. Be back in a while. Rock, can I have your keys?"

He tossed them to me and Kathy and I walked outside together. It instantly got easier to talk when we could no longer hear the music. The sun was down and the streetlights now shone brightly everywhere. Activity in the parking lot was minimal and I suggested that we go sit in Rock's car, which we did. The moment

I had thought about, worried about, and wondered about had finally arrived.

The console that separated the bucket seats acted like a wall between us, at least for the first few silent seconds in the car. After a minute or so I finally said something. "So are you excited about leaving or nervous?"

She looked at me innocently. "A little of both I guess. Everything is going to be new, so that part is a little scary, but it's also kind of exciting."

"Sounds like me when I first got to Iowa. It's so different here than anything I have ever known my whole life. It took a while to learn all the rules here."

"And now you think you have us figured out?" she asked with a hint of a smile.

"No, not figured out totally," I responded, "but a least I know some things. It will take more than a few months to get it all. You should understand that since you already told me you've had trouble trying to figure me out in that same amount of time."

"That's true. You are tough to figure out. When we talked on the phone you said you'd help me understand you better. Well, here we are. I'm listening."

I sighed heavily. "Yeah, you're here and I do remember saying that. I'll do my best but be aware ahead of time that not all of this is going to be easy for me to say. I may fumble it a bit."

"Okay," she stated in an understanding tone. "Let's just start and see where it goes."

"Just start huh? I actually tried to plan out how I'd say all this, but I forgot all the stuff I thought about. Face to face is a lot different than pretend and practice." I tried to laugh a bit but her eyes looked through me and I knew it was time to begin. "Back in the city I never had a real girlfriend. Ever. I mean I liked a few girls and they liked me, but it never amounted to anything. Hate to admit it but all this is new to me and sometimes I feel pretty lost. That makes me uncomfortable."

She stopped me there. "What do you mean lost? I don't understand."

"Maybe lost is the wrong word. I don't know. Maybe in over my head describes it better. I feel like I'm about five years behind the rest of you and I don't know how to catch up."

"Behind how?" she asked with a curious look on her face.

"Behind with everything. I had buddies back home but never real friends. I haven't even talked to them once since I've been here and I don't miss them at all. We hung out every day. I watch you and Cheri and you're as close as family, which is very cool, and Rock and I get along great and I like that too, but it's routine and normal for all of you. I've never let myself open up before and all of you do it so easily. I want to do that, but I'm just not there yet, not like you are."

"Do you mean opening up to Rock or me?"

"Both. It seems so natural and easy for you to say what you're feeling. I wish I could do that, and I'm trying to get better at it, but I'm just not as ready for something serious in a relationship as you are."

"You mean you're not ready for anything with me. Is that what you're saying?" She asked the question and suddenly wore a look as if she were sorry she had spoken the words. I know it took courage for her to ask because somewhere inside her, she had to know the possible answer could hurt a lot.

I tried to find a smile. "Believe this okay? I have never met a girl I liked more than I like you, but again, you're ahead of me. I think you know exactly who you are and what you want in life, and part of me is jealous of that. I don't know who I am or what I want. Back home I never even thought about it, but here I think about it a lot. I need to find out. Does that make sense?"

She breathed heavily and turned in her seat to face me directly. "I guess so. Are you saying you want me to wait for you until you figure all this out?"

I took her hand in mine. "That's a great offer, but no. I don't want you to wait. One thing I have learned here is how selfish I used to be back home, and asking you to do that would be terribly selfish. That's also what makes this so hard. I know I have to let you go."

"You don't have to," she responded quickly.

"Yeah, I do," I explained. "Nothing about me is conventional or orderly. You've got future goals all lined up and you're ready to get them started. I think trying to fit me into all that, whether it's from three hours away or a thousand miles away, would be a problem. Trust me, there's a big part of me that wants to just grab you and say let's go live happily ever after somewhere, but I know that can't just magically happen. I may wander around for years trying to figure all this out, and that would definitely not be fair to you. In fact, you'd probably end up hating me. So I know I have to let you go. You'll get to college and find your doctor or something, and you'll start working on those dreams of yours with him. That's how it should be."

"Wow," she said, "you hardly say anything for two months, but when you turn the spout on it comes pouring out. Does it bother you to think that we'll always wonder how it could have been?"

"You mean twenty or thirty years from now will I be kicking myself thinking of the one who got away?"

"Something like that."

"Yeah, I'm sure I'll wonder, but that's down the road. I think you're very special, but right now I can't give you what I think you want me to give you. I really wish I could. Can I have you the rest of tonight or would that be selfish too?"

She leaned in and kissed me deeply. "You're not selfish at all. Let's go in and dance some more."

CHAPTER 32

For the next week, while I did anything, I found myself wondering about Kathy. I felt a sense of loss that I couldn't actually define. Part of it was sad but not all of it. I wondered if she and I would ever again share a tight embrace. I wondered if she was settled in at college, and I wondered if any of her thoughts were about me. I still believed that letting her go to chase her dreams without the sense of obligation to me was the right thing to do, but sometimes it made my stomach hurt.

Grandpa and I did small jobs around the farm. We mended some fence, continued to eat the fruits or our garden, and he insisted that we paint the garage. He had bought several gallons of barn red paint and I laughed at him for his lack of originality. He took my mocking in stride and eventually even agreed with me that his color choice was very predictable for a farmer. We started on the back, with me climbing the ladder and him supervising.

The peak of the roof was fifteen feet high and I was more than a little uncomfortable up there. I got the top boards done as fast as I could so that I could drop a couple steps on the ladder and feel a bit more secure. Once I got everything up high covered in red he grabbed his brush and joined in. I could see how the process would go on each of the sides of the garage, and we found plenty to talk about while we painted. "You haven't said much about Kathy," he stated. "Did you two have your talk?"

"We did. It was both good and bad at the same time."

"So what happened? Where do you two go from here?"

I paused my brush stroke for a moment but did not look at him directly. "Nowhere. I let her go." Only then did I turn to see his reaction.

He put his brush down and stepped toward me. When he was close enough to reach me he gently slapped the top of my head, which really caught me by surprise. "What's the matter with you? You give up way too easily. When you find a woman who's worth having you fight to keep her no matter what. I wanted to tell you that before, but you had to decide for yourself. Being miles apart is a poor reason to surrender without a fight."

"You hit me!" I laughed. "What the hell?"

"Trying to knock some sense into you."

"Too late," I replied.

He shook his head, picked his paint brush up again and continued. "Apparently so. Let me tell you something. You're not a kid any more, and you're going to have to do something you've never done before. You're going to have to figure out what's actually important to you. If I asked you to tell me your philosophy of life could you do it?"

"My philosophy?"

"That's what I thought. You'd better figure out what it is. We all have one, whether we know it or not. Your philosophy is everything that matters to you. The words you use, how you treat others, the behavior you use and tolerate in others. The things you'll fight for and the things you won't. The things you spend your money on. All of it and more, when you put it together, is your philosophy, and my advice to you is to go sit under the sparrow trees sometime and figure yours out."

"Hmmm," I stated. "Philosophy. I'll work on that."

"What about the plan with Maxie?" he asked. "Someone uptown said he had heard that Maxie is about to get out of jail. Are you ready for whatever you have cooked up for him?"

"I think so. If it all goes down like I want it to, it will be quite a night, one that Maxie and the others will not soon forget."

Grandpa flipped over a bucket and took a seat. I watched him rub his legs as our conversation continued. "Are you going to tell me any of the details or do I just have to read about it in the paper after you're finished?"

"I don't think any of this will make its way into the newspaper," I responded. "You want some details huh? Let's see. I've seen what you can do with a shotgun into some trees. How good are you with a rifle?"

He tilted his head toward me in an odd fashion. "You want me to shoot him?"

"No," I laughed. "Give me a little bit of credit. We're going to try and scare the hell out of them though, and if the first part of my

Legacy

plan doesn't work right then a couple well placed, near missing rifle shots could be very effective."

"I don't know about that," he responded in an extremely serious tone. "Guns are not toys to play games with. Are you sure you know what you're doing here? Are there other guns in your plans? I don't like that idea at all."

"No there aren't," I answered. "What's the matter with your legs? They seem to be bothering you a lot lately."

He suddenly became aware that I had seen him rubbing his legs and he immediately stopped. "Oh, nothing. Just a little stiff," he said as he rose from his bucket. "Let's get this baby painted. And if you have any other plans for Maxie that involve guns you need to change them. Too many things can go bad or wrong there, and if that happened there would be some really serious and lasting consequences. Don't go there."

"You can relax, okay? I told you it was fairly elaborate but nobody is going to get hurt. We're just going to give them an early trick or treat and let a few people they've ripped off and robbed over the years show them what they really think of them. It should leave a lasting impression on Maxie and Wally and Zeb and let them know without a doubt that everyone is wise to them and their crap and nobody is going to take any more of it."

"No guns?" he asked again, as if to receive final confirmation of my earlier answer.

"No guns. I promise. Just a good old-fashioned awakening to a new set of realities for them."

He looked at me for a moment. "Uh huh," he grunted. "Just be careful."

"Don't worry," I assured him. "I won't be alone. Trust me, the trio of the hour will be seriously outnumbered, and any thoughts they might have of getting even with anyone, including Rock and me, will leave them for good."

"I hope you're right. Come on, we've got one more side to paint."

I carried the ladder around to the east side of the garage and was glad to be in some afternoon shade and out of the direct sunlight. When I returned for the paint and my paint brush I noticed Grandpa once again rubbing his legs but this time I didn't say anything about it. When we finished painting we walked completely around the garage, inspecting our work, and though I was still not a fan of his color choice I had to admit the garage looked a lot better now that it was fully painted. I could tell Grandpa agreed when I saw his smile of satisfaction.

We had everything cleaned up and put away before sundown, and by then we were both hungry. I suggested that we head to town and get some food at Sherm's and Grandpa liked my idea. I even volunteered to drive, partly because I wanted to and partly because I didn't know what was going on with his legs and I suspected that he would be glad to just sit as a passenger for a change, even on a short trip to town and back.

There were about twenty people in the front room at Sherm's when we arrived, so we had no trouble finding a booth to sit in. Grandpa hadn't been inside the tavern for quite a while, a couple years he told me, and he observed that everything was pretty much just as he remembered it. "Some things in this town never change," he noticed as he maneuvered himself into his seat. We both ordered beers, salads, and steak sandwiches, and then basically sat quietly for a couple minutes and enjoyed both the air conditioning and the juke box.

"Yeah, but some things do change," I replied. "The last time you were in here I had never even heard of this place, or for that matter, anything else in Gowrie. That's a change."

"That's true," he smiled. "I guess it takes the eyes of someone new to see things clearly sometimes. Staying in one place year after year brings us feelings of security but it also dulls our vision and our senses to the things around us every day, and even if something new appears we might not notice it. We just stay in our routines and do what we do. Sometimes it takes fresh eyes to show us what we've been missing, even when it's sitting right under our noses."

I looked around the tavern then turned back to Grandpa. "What do you think you've missed in here in the past two years?"

Before he could answer, the waitress arrived with our food, and we put our talk on hold so that we could devour our steak sandwiches. In between songs we could hear the loud voices in the

Legacy

back room and it sounded like a card game had suddenly gotten quite intense. At least two men were arguing with each other about something, though we couldn't hear the exact specifics. Grandpa shook his head and stated, "Those guys back there. If the best you can do is sit in the back of a bar and fight and argue, then you don't have much. Don't even know who they are, but if they're married I feel sorry for their wives and kids."

"Really?" I asked, a little surprised by his unusually quick judgmental comments.

"Yes, really.. Think about it. If they'll talk and act like that in public where people can see and hear them, how much worse do you think they are capable of at home in private? Acting like children," he concluded.

The arguing in the back room stopped and several people appeared in the doorway, some guys I knew and some I didn't know. Teaser was one of the first to walk through the doorway and when he saw Grandpa Carl he turned and went in the other direction, evidently still looking for those milkweeds to chop. Another slender twenty-something man emerged from the card game and his eyes met mine. I had seen him before but we had never spoken and I didn't know his name. He walked with a bounce, a strut that professed a misplaced arrogance that his lack of size should not have allowed him to possess. He struck me as the type of guy I had seen countless times in the city, a mouthpiece not afraid to instigate things because he always believed he had bigger and tougher guys watching his back.

He took a seat on a stool directly across the aisle from our booth and kept his back to us while he sipped his beer. After we finished our food Grandpa and I remained in our booth and talked a while longer, and then I rose to pay our bill. I stood about three feet away from the guy on the stool, and I had not really paid any attention to him until he spoke to me. "You ready?" he asked out of the blue with a slight chuckle in his voice. "Almost time."

I turned and faced him with a curious look on my face. "Excuse me? Ready for what? Do I know you?"

"Nope, but I know you," he replied. "Not that it matters all that much but I'm Wally's cousin Stewart." He paused as if to let that revelation fully sink in to me. Apparently it was supposed to scare or intimidate me. It didn't.

"Okay," I stated as I received my change from the waitress. "Same question. Am I ready for what?"

"Maxie will be back in two days and he's anxious to get together with you and your buddy Rock. In fact, so are Zeb and Wally, and when they told me about you two I thought it sounded like fun, so you can count me in too."

My grin evidently surprised him. "Excellent. The more the merrier for that kind of party. I'm looking forward to seeing them too. Shall we say Saturday night around 9:00?"

His face showed the disappointment he must have felt when he realized his initial threat had not scared me like he had intended it to, so he made another attempt. "Maybe you don't understand what I mean. The four of us are going to have some real fun with you two, and if Saturday night at 9:00 is when it happens, that sounds good to me. I'll let them know."

Grandpa slid out of the booth and had begun walking toward the door. Before I joined him I spoke one more time to Stewart. "Oh, trust me pal, I understand what you mean. I'm just not scared by it. We'll be uptown Saturday night." Then I did something that I knew for certain would make him incredibly angry. I slapped him lightly on his knee as I walked by and said, "I can see why the other three want to have you join them. You're so big and tough you could probably handle us by yourself. See ya Saturday big man." With that I walked out the door and got into my car.

Grandpa sat comfortably in the passenger seat and gleefully rubbed his stomach. "That hit the spot!" he exclaimed. "The food has always been good there. I remember that. And you even paid for it. Made it all taste even better! Who was that joker at the bar on the way out?"

"Stewart somebody," I answered as I turned south and headed out of town. "Wally's cousin. Looks like he wants in on our fun with Maxie, which is fine with me." I then laughed out loud. "I wanted to tell him to stay out of it and that he had no idea what all he was stepping into, but I knew it wouldn't do any good. Besides, he made me mad sounding so tough and trying to be a big shot. Can't wait to see his face Saturday night."

CHAPTER 33

Friday morning I called Rock and told him it was time to get some things ready for what we had come to call Maxie Night. He was more than ready. We both were. I knew it would take us a while to prepare everything and I wanted to get started early in case there needed to be any changes in the plan. "Gather up your stuff and call Lennie. I'll get my things and I'll call Crusher. I'll be at your place in twenty minutes," I instructed.

Rock replied with a great excitement in his voice. "I'll be ready and waiting for you."

As soon as I hung up the phone with Rock I called Crusher and he said he would meet us. Grandpa overheard me on the phone with both Rock and Crusher and was still curious about what we had planned. "What's up? Sounds like you two are finally going to put this mysterious plan into action.

I smiled at him. "I guess so. Looks like it's finally time for the showdown with Maxie. Before we do that though, we've got a few details to get lined up. I want everything to be perfect.

He thought for a minute and then spoke again. "Need any help?"

His question told me a lot. It said that he not only supported me but he trusted that I had thought things through and he was mostly sure that our end result would be a good one. "Thanks, but I think we're good for now. I'll need lots of help tomorrow night. Might still take you up on it then."

Before I left I gathered up the things I had already set aside to use in the plan. I had a long piece of rope, three of our bean walking corn knives, every candle I could find in the house, and three long extension cords. Once I had all that in my trunk I drove to town, concentrating more on the next few hours than the three miles I had to drive. Rock was waiting for me outside, standing beside

Legacy

several folding chairs. He also had several candles in a box and a life-sized stuffed dummy.

It was mid morning and it was already hot. I felt an interesting mix of excitement and nervousness as we left town and made our way to the Nordquist house. I went over my plan in my head for the hundredth time, trying once again to convince myself that it would all work out like I thought it would. Evidently Rock could sense what I was thinking because he began to tap the dash of my car and exclaimed, "This is gonna be so good!"

We pulled into the Nordquist driveway and Crusher was already there waiting for us. "Unload your stuff here and then park behind the shed by my truck so we don't get any extra attention on ourselves," he told us.

We did as he suggested, and when I got back into my car to move it, Lennie pulled into the driveway. He unloaded his things and parked his pickup beside my car. Crusher had been friends for a long time with cousins of the Nordquist family who had died in the house. The cousins also knew about all the rumors of Maxie's stealing and they were more than happy to play a silent part in ending that, so they had willingly given us permission to be on their place and had given Crusher the keys to the house.

None of us had ever been inside the house before, so initially we just walked around and examined all that we had to work with there. Everything had a thick layer of dust over it, and large cobwebs adorned nearly every corner of the house. There were five rooms and two large closets downstairs, and an eerie looking stairway which led to the upstairs. Surprisingly the steps didn't creak when we walked up them, but I was glad, and once upstairs we found four more rooms and two more closets. There was also a back porch just off the kitchen and a doorway in the middle of the downstairs that opened up to steps leading down to the basement. After exploring the upstairs and the main floor we looked at each other, trying to decide if we wanted to go down to the basement or not. Daylight had stunted the history and the legend of the house, but the thought of what might lie in the basement placed just a hint of apprehension in everyone. The safety in numbers theory kicked in and we walked down the steps together, a trip that proved to be completely uneventful. All we found was more dust and more cobwebs.

Now that we understood the layout of the house we could begin our preparations in earnest. We placed numerous candles all over the house, especially on the steps leading to the top floor. Rock's chairs were placed in the master bedroom, which faced away from the road. The six corn knives were hidden inside a downstairs closet, and Lennie tied the end of my long rope into a proper noose, which he then placed around the neck of the dummy that was tied to an open beam in the master bedroom.

For the next hour or so I walked the others through all the details of what I wanted to take place, explaining how we would get Maxie's group maneuvered upstairs and completely inside our trap. It would be up to Crusher and Lennie to have everyone in place before 9:00, and fill the others in on the specifics of what they should do once everything began. It would still be somewhat tricky getting Maxie and the others to follow us out to this house, but I was counting on their egos and their overconfidence. I calculated that if they saw Rock and me by ourselves in a car they would believe they had the upper hand and that they had us right where they wanted us. I believed that once they thought that, they would follow us willingly and eagerly.

Lennie and Crusher convinced me that they understood everything and assured me they would be ready on time, so we locked up the house and returned to town. I had high hopes that the following night would go well and that nobody would get hurt, but there were still a lot of moving pieces in the puzzle and a lot of ways things could go wrong. If everything went right, all of Maxie's power in the area would be gone. If things went wrong, it would be a huge mess.

Legacy

CHAPTER 34

Saturday morning was spent mowing the yard and tending to the garden. I was amazed at the amount of food our garden continued to produce. We had eaten from it for a month, and still there were new beans, potatoes, and onions that were ready to eat every day. We had given away all the excess sweet corn and the tomatoes we were unable to eat by ourselves, and I enjoyed seeing the pride and the joy in Grandpa's face as we shared that food with his friends.

We also spent an hour doing a little touch up painting on the garage, filling in some of the thin spots with what was left of the barn red paint. After that he insisted that I change the oil in my car. I was glad to be busy, and I appreciated all the diversions he created, for I knew that if I had nothing to keep my mind busy I would have had too many thoughts of the night ahead and how things could go wrong.

We went to Hazel's for lunch and the only member of Grandpa's normal group who was there was Kenny. He beamed when he spoke about the progress on his new house. The carpenters and plumbers had been there all summer and it wouldn't be long until he and his family could fully move in and begin life in a brand new home. "They've about got it done," Kenny stated with a smile. "Well, the main parts anyway. Seems like there's always detail things that take longer, but the women are so excited. We're all ready to get out of that little trailer we've been living in all summer."

"Good for you Kenny," responded Grandpa. "I've driven by several times and it all looks great. They got your sheds and garage up really fast didn't they?"

"Boy, did they! Not quite so quick with the barn, but since I got to start from scratch I had some things I wanted different than in the old one, and it's going to be bigger than the other one too."

"Is all your milking equipment set up and ready to go?" Grandpa asked.

"Mostly," continued Kenny. "Not sure how to operate all that new fangled stuff yet though. Maybe I'm getting too old to start over with milking fifty cows and farming all these acres. I don't know sometimes."

Grandpa nodded his head with understanding. "I think that every morning when I roll out of bed. Wonder how much longer I wanna do this. But then I think and wonder what else I'd do. Dirt and crops are all I know and everybody knows farmers never actually retire."

"Sometimes I think about selling it all and just relaxing," explained Kenny. "I know Denise doesn't want the place. She wants to find a husband and have a house in a town somewhere, so I don't know. Now everything here is new again, and that's exciting, but sometimes I just get really tired."

We were all quiet for a moment, and didn't speak until the waitress placed our sandwiches in front of us. Grandpa turned to me and spoke softly. "You see Eli, when you get our age that legacy question just keeps popping up. Guys your age think about the future and we know we have a lot less future left than we used to have. We want to know that we did it right our whole life and that we made a difference, and we also like to believe that a part of us will live on somehow after we're done and gone. Sometimes we have our doubts, but believe it or not, we still think long term, just in a different way than you do."

"Just like Roy Dale," I stated in between bites.

"Yes, just like Roy Dale," he replied.

The remainder of the meal was casual and light hearted and when we finished, Grandpa and I walked outside to his truck. He walked ahead of me and I noticed him favoring his left leg with each step he took. "You okay?" I asked.

He seemed surprised that I had noticed, and his limp suddenly disappeared. "Fine. Just got a little stoved up from the chair I guess."

"Right," I answered, mostly sure I had not just heard the truth.

The rest of the afternoon lasted a hundred years. I tried to watch some TV but nothing on any of the three channels held my attention for long, and I got tired of getting up so often to change the stations. I took a nap, but it was a short, restless sleep. The seconds on the clock ticked away, at times too slowly, but most

Legacy

often far too quickly. I recalled Grandpa's lesson with our previous bird problem. "Meet it head on," he had told me. I knew if I just sat around and waited for Maxie to exact his revenge it would change everything for me, and I couldn't do that. I had no desire to allow him inside my head for even one minute longer than necessary, and I believed that taking the offense and meeting the challenge head on was the right course of action to take. It made me feel a lot better knowing that Rock and I would be far from alone when we did that.

At 7:30 I lifted myself up off the couch and I knew it was time to go. Grandpa had been in his recliner for a while, periodically losing his battles with trying to keep his eyes open, but he sat up in his chair when he heard me stirring around.

"I guess it's time," he spoke without emotion or judgment.

"Yeah, it is," I replied. "Time to go to town."

"I still don't know everything you're going to do," he continued, "but I know you've thought it through and you need to trust that. You've been jumpy all day, and I know how waiting for something can be the hardest thing. This is one of those times you need to believe in yourself. Good luck with it."

I smiled back at him. "Thanks."

As I began to walk out he added one more bit of advice. "Don't do it half way. Once you start you see it through completely, and whatever happens you have to make Maxie believe it's exactly what you had planned, whether it really is or not."

"Okay," I replied. "Meet it head on."

"Always," he spoke with an affirmative nod of his head.

"Later," I said and I walked out the door.

I'm sure my heart raced faster than usual as I got closer and closer to town. Was Maxie already there waiting for me? If he showed up early and started trouble ahead of schedule then everything could be ruined. When I thought about that, I determined that we needed to avoid that possibility, and Rock and I should stay out of sight until it got closer to 9:00. I pulled into Rock's driveway and when he heard my car he bounded through his front door and began shadow boxing on his front porch. I

Legacy

watched him for a few seconds then got out of my car, pretending to quiver with fear.

"Boy, I'm glad you're on my side!" I exclaimed.

"You better know it," he grinned. "Just like Ali."

"Let's try not to do much boxing tonight okay?" I requested.

Rock stopped his dancing around and replied. "I'll try, but if any of those clowns wanna go a couple rounds, I'll go with 'em."

"I know you will, but something tells me they'll all be good little boys once we get everything started."

He punched the air a few more times. "Well, they'd better be good, but I'm ready just in case."

"Yeah, yeah, you're a bad dude. Got me shakin' just watching you. We need to hang out here a while just in case they show up early. We don't want to blow everything before the other guys are ready."

"Okay," he agreed. "Hadn't thought of that. Come on in."

We sat in Rock's room for an hour and mostly talked about nothing. I was somewhat surprised at how casual and at ease we both appeared to be, with each of us knowing that some potential danger lay only minutes away. When 8:45 arrived we looked at each other, and without a word we rose and walked out to my car. It was time to go.

The first thing we did was go to Casey's and put four dollars worth of gas into the car. I had forgotten to do that earlier, and I wanted to make sure I had enough gas in case we had to cruise the town for a long time waiting for Maxie to appear. As I walked out of Casey's I saw that we wouldn't have to wait at all. The black pickup drove by slowly and all four guys were inside. Stewart had been true to his word and had decided to join the others. When they saw Rock and me at Casey's they sped to the Dairy Queen corner and then turned around quickly and came back. They stopped the pickup in the middle of the street, directly in front of Casey's and immediately began to taunt us verbally. Wally and Zeb each also flashed baseball bats to try and intimidate us.

"Hey boys," yelled Wally through the passenger window. "Didn't think you'd show. Thought we'd probably have to go hunt you down. Sure glad you're here though. How does it feel to know you're about to have your asses kicked? Where do you want it to happen? Right here?"

I took the opening Wally had given me. "Uh, give us a few minutes to think of a good place and we'll be there. We'll stay on the drag and stop you when we've decided. That work for you?"

"Yeah it works just fine," yelled Zeb. "Almost time for some batting practice." They all yelled at us in unison and drove away.

I got into my car and Rock looked at me. "Almost time buddy. Looks like everybody showed up for the party."

"Everybody on the other team. Let's just hope all of our guys are waiting when we get there."

Rock shivered at the thought of what I had just said. "Hadn't even considered that. That would be really bad wouldn't it?"

I tried to grin but didn't do a very good job of it. "Yeah, that would be bad."

Legacy

CHAPTER 35

We shagged the drag a few times and acted like we were nervous each time we met their black pickup. Eventually 9:00 arrived and we were ready to go. We met Maxie's truck in front of the theater and I stopped and held my arm out the window, indicating I wanted to talk. When Maxie stopped opposite me the others in the pickup again showed us their bats again and yelled wildly, bouncing up and down on the seat with great enthusiasm, and I wondered if they were surprised by the contrast of calm we displayed in my car.

"Let's do this!" bellowed Maxie. "I'm tired of waiting and tired of driving around."

I responded quickly. "I agree. Nordquist place in ten minutes."

Maxie's face showed his surprise. "Nordquist place? Why there? You wanna fight us at a haunted house?"

"Got a problem with that big shot?" asked Rock from the passenger seat. "It's nice and private. Unless you guys are afraid of going out there at night. I think it sounds fun. Never know what we might come across out there."

"We're not scared of nothin'," stated Wally. "I like the idea of somewhere private like that. No witnesses."

I grinned broadly and calmly replied, "So do I boys. So do I." With that we drove off and made a direct path to the Nordquist house. It was crucial that we arrived before they did, so I drove faster than normal. Even in the limited starlight I could see the long trail of dust rising behind my car as we raced along the gravel road to the north, turned east and then arrived at the Nordquist house.

Rock and I hopped out of the car quickly and ran to the front door. Once he saw it was us, Crusher opened the door and we hurried inside. "Everything set?" I asked. "They'll be here in a minute."

Crusher grinned broadly. "Everything is ready." He then yelled loudly. "Okay everybody. Showtime. Let's do this right. People in costume, no talking at all. Remember that."

Legacy

We left the front door a few inches open intentionally and the candles on the steps leading upstairs were lit, showing a path we wanted them to follow. Rock and I watched from the second bedroom window upstairs, and when I saw Maxie's headlights approaching we looked at each other and shook hands. "Here we go," I stated. It was all finally happening, and I believed we were ready.

Maxie parked directly behind my car, and they all got out. The candles on the stairway showed the open door, but the group stood outside and looked around before making any kind of move toward the house. Zeb and Wally held their baseball bats up and appeared nervous and ready to strike at any unusual things that might appear. Everything inside the house and out in the yard was quiet, so we could hear their conversation.

"Where are they?" began Stewart. "I thought they meant we'd be outside."

Zeb looked at the house carefully and spoke next. "The door's open. I guess that's for us."

Maxie spit angrily on the ground and then yelled loudly into the darkness. "I didn't come out here to play games. Show yourselves!"

I gently wrapped on the window which caused them all to jump slightly. I shined a flashlight directly into Maxie's eyes and replied. "We're upstairs. Come on up. Or don't you tough guys like haunted houses? Be careful of the blood stains on the steps though." After I said that, Rock and I retreated from the window and went into the master bedroom where we sat in two of the folding chairs and waited. Four more chairs were against the wall opposite us. The only light in the room was what shone from six candles we had lit, and they gave off a reasonably eerie glow. I was glad that I knew what was about to happen instead of just walking into the unknowns that surely faced Maxie and his group. Otherwise, in this particular house, I might have been somewhat jumpy too.

I still didn't hear any movement on the steps so I decided that a bit more incentive was needed to get them upstairs with us. I hollered loudly in a taunting tone, "Are you guys coming up or not? We don't have all night." With that, Maxie's group had to press on and continue up the stairs, and it was then that I yelled out the phrase that would spring everyone else into action and hopefully cause enough confusion and perhaps enough fear in Maxie's group that they could be easily overtaken. I yelled with all the feigned fright I could muster. "Oh, no! What's that? Bats! Hundreds of them! Bats! Look out!"

I heard the movement on the steps and in the other parts of the house, and it all happened with great speed and efficiency. Six figures appeared together at the top of the stairs, all in complete Halloween costumes. They said nothing but while Maxie's group's attention was directed their way, fifteen more costumed figured emerged from various parts of the main floor and the group of four was surrounded on the stairs. Two men, whom I later found out were Arch and Woody, advanced up the stairs fearlessly, directly at Zeb and Wally, and took the baseball bats from them without incident.

The wave of costumed men pushed the group up the stairs, all without speaking a word, though I could hear some whimpering from Stewart. They physically led them to where Rock and I sat in the master bedroom and ushered them to the four chairs we had placed along the wall for them. The group of twenty-one men blocked any possible path of escape, and a genuine look of fear and surprise showed in all their eyes.

"What the hell is this?" asked Maxie with the toughest sounding voice he could find inside himself.

I rose from my seat and walked closer to him. "Shut up Maxie," I began. "For once in your life just shut up. You wanna know what this is? This is a small collection of people from around here who have had enough of you. And here's the part that's going to drive you crazy. You're never going to know exactly who these guys are. We do have some others here though who wanted to say a few things directly to you."

The wall of costumes parted and the eight men who had agreed to face down the group entered the room, each wearing his own look of personal anger. Danny Haden, Craig Nettleton, and Alex Borer each carried corn knives. The eight stood as a unit, facing the group, and I could only imagine the terror and helplessness the four in the chairs must have felt.

Ted Erickson got right next to Maxie's face. "Remember when you broke into my house you lousy punk?"

Maxie nodded his head slightly.

"You changed our lives and I'll never forget that. My wife is always scared now and my little girl never feels safe, even at home. You took that from us and I'd like to knock your damn head off." When he finished, his finger was an inch from Maxie's face, which caused Maxie to visibly squirm.

Josh stepped up next. "You come to my party, eat my food, drink my beer, and then break into my house and rip me off? We should have had this little party two years ago. What were you guys gonna use those bats for?"

Zeb whimpered weakly. "Nothin'."

Josh laughed at Zeb. "Nothin' huh? Maybe we'll use your own bats for some nothin' on you."

Craig Nettleton and Danny Haden stepped forward with their corn knives. "Forget the bats. We've got these," stated Danny. "Nobody ever comes in this house so some new blood stains wouldn't even be noticed for a very long time. How deep is that hole out back that we dug?"

Crusher moved forward and answered quickly. "I used my backhoe so it's good and deep. Plenty wide for four guys too."

"Excellent," replied Danny with a smile.

That was too much for Stewart and Wally and they both began to cry. "Please, no!" begged Stewart. "I wasn't with them on any of that stuff."

Josh got in Stewart's face immediately. "Then why are you with them tonight? You're just as stupid as they are. I understand you were talking pretty big the other night at Sherm's. Couldn't wait for this party could you?" He stood back and gestured to all the guys in the room. "Here we are tough guy. Let's party."

Stewart could only shake his head, indicating that he did not want any part of what Josh was offering. Josh bent over and lightly slapped Stewart on both cheeks. "Getting smarter already, aren't you?"

Maxie's eyes darted all over the room, looking like a caged animal desperately searching for any path of escape, but who couldn't find one. It was obvious that he knew he was beaten, and he finally spoke. "So now what? You gonna chop us up and bury us?"

Josh looked at the costumed men and then looked back at Maxie. "Haven't completely decided yet, but we'd rather not. Eventually we'd have to explain something to somebody. But here's the deal boys and you'd better take it to heart. You're done. Finished. Completely. Do you understand?"

Wally, Zeb, and Stewart shook their heads in understanding humility, but Maxie hadn't fully gotten the message yet. He answered, "Yeah, I understand," but his tone suggested otherwise. Josh picked up on Maxie's sarcasm and motioned for several of the costumed men to come nearer.

"I don't think Maxie fully gets what we mean, and I think he needs some more convincing. Two of you grab his arms and four of you hold his legs. Let's show him what corn knives can really do when they are as sharp as these are."

The men advanced and Stewart let out a loud gasp. The men held Maxie tightly and any remaining sarcasm he might have possessed left him quickly. "Okay, okay, I'm sorry," pleaded Maxie. "I'm done. What do you want? Don't use the knives! Please!"

"Are you sure you understand Maxie?" asked Josh. "You're about an inch from bleeding all over this room."

Zeb's face had turned pale and I thought he was going to pass out.

"Yes, I understand!" exclaimed Maxie.

"What is it that you understand?" continued Josh. "Tell us, and remember, you only get one chance to get this right. Guys, let him go for the moment, but stay close. Okay Maxie, tell us."

"We're done," Maxie explained. "No more stealing."

Josh nodded. "So far so good. You also think you're tough. I've seen you bullying weaker guys before and then thinkin' that's funny. That ends too. As far as your earlier plans for tonight, even you geniuses should have already figured out that Rock and Eli have lots and lots of friends, far more than you do. If you ever try and pull anything against either of them, you'll meet this group again and there will be a lot less talking. Know what I mean?"

"I got it," replied Maxie sincerely.

Josh continued, trying to really reinforce the message. "See this group? We'll always be around. Nobody in here likes you and with a few phone calls we could easily triple the number of people we have here now. Remember that. You're done. Finished. Completely. For good. You're going to walk out of here tonight, but if any of us ever gets wind of you stealing anything from anyone or doing the things you've done in the past you can forget any hope of mercy. We'll hurt all of you bad. Time for you boys to find a new hobby."

Crusher spoke up. "I want to hear from each of them that they really understand. I still wonder if they know how easily they got off tonight. Do you understand the new rules Stewart?"

"Yes."

"Wally?"

"Yeah."

"Zeb?"

"Yes, and thank you."

"And Maxie, you piece of shit. I'd still like to knock your teeth in. What did you need my little boy's bicycle for? You for sure better understand what we're telling you tonight. Tell me you do and make me believe it."

Maxie looked as directly at Crusher as he dared. "I understand."

Crusher stepped back and Josh motioned for the remaining men in the doorway to part and make an opening. "Never forget this night and what it could have turned into for all of you. Now get the hell out of here and consider yourselves very, very lucky."

The group didn't have to be told twice. They rose quickly from their chairs but walked carefully through the gauntlet of men. Once they reached the stairway they ran to the bottom of the steps and out the door. Maxie started his pickup and he sped away from what he thought would be a totally different night than he got.

CHAPTER 36

No one in the house said much until we saw Maxie's tail lights turn south and disappear into the other lights of the town. Only then did the masks come off and the hand shaking begin. From our point of view the night had gone perfectly and had been a total success. "Thank you everybody," I shouted. "You were all outstanding!"

Crusher beamed with satisfaction. "That was fun. How did you ever dream something like that up? I would have never thought to do that."

Several of the men patted Rock and me on our shoulders and offered their congratulations. "I don't know," I replied. "Sometimes I just think differently. Glad it worked out like it did. I think we scared them all enough to hold their attention for quite a while. Hope so anyway."

Ted Erickson added, "I think so too. It was really hard not actually hitting Maxie, and I didn't know how far you were going to go with those corn knives once you started that bit. Thought we might see a little blood."

"It was pretty believable to me," stated Rock, "but that's what it took to finally get Maxie's attention. Did you see the others' faces when you did that? They looked like they knew they were next."

I raised my hands and got everyone's attention. "Okay, we got this done and half of making this work forever is Maxie never finding out who the masked guys were. He has to wonder every time he meets someone on the street. It has to be ongoing so we have to make a vow of secrecy here. That's tough with this many guys, but all of you kept the setup for this night secret, and I believe we can keep it quiet going forward too. We made a lot of people around here safer tonight, but nobody can ever know what we did. Maybe someday we can relive tonight over some beers but we need to agree that we never talk about any of this around town. Ever. Agreed?"

"Agreed," answered the group in unison.

"Let's get out of here," insisted Crusher. "Get everything you brought and let's get all of you back over to my place so you can get your vehicles and get home."

It took less than five minutes to gather up the candles, chairs, and everything else. Crusher locked the door behind us and we were out of the Nordquist house. Josh and Crusher brought their pickups out from behind the shed and all the guys piled into the truck beds. Rock and I stood beside my car as they all drove away, and I gave them all a final thumbs up.

Rock stood by the passenger door and looked at me over the car. "That was wild," he laughed. "Completely wild. A hell of a lot of fun too."

I smiled in return. "Everybody did great. Let's just hope the message sticks with all of them."

He opened his car door and stated assuredly, "It did. I've known them my whole life and never saw them that scared. Wally and Zeb thought they were going to die. They got it."

I took the back roads to Rock's house and stayed away from Main Street, simply to avoid being seen uptown by anyone. We were both going directly home, just like all the other guys who had been with us. This night had never happened.

I got back to the farm a little after ten and surprisingly Grandpa was wide awake in his recliner. I walked in and sat on the couch, pretending to watch the news with him. It only took a couple minutes for his curiosity to get the best of him. "Well," he began, "you made it back in one piece. Guess it went well?"

"Perfectly," I replied.

He rose from his recliner and in his understated method said, "That's good. I'm tired and think I'll hit the hay. See you at breakfast."

While I sat alone on the couch I realized he had stayed up out of concern for me and what might have happened with Maxie. He didn't show affection often, but I felt good when I understood he had just done that in his own unique way. I still didn't fully understand all the Iowa ways but I had come to understand the people here were solid and had real substance to them. It was fun to be a part of that.

Legacy

***   ***   ***   ***   ***   ***   ***

August faded into September though the weather could not be used to evidence that. Most days were still quite warm. Grandpa took me to another traditional area event on Labor Day, and I witnessed my first rodeo. I couldn't decide whether I liked everything I watched, and I knew it was not something I would ever take part in personally, but parts of the rodeo were extremely entertaining. The grass in the yard at home was still growing and needed attention, and our garden was bearing the last bits of food for the year.

In the middle of September Grandpa told me that it was time to plow up the garden. He brought out the tiller, filled it with gas, and of course checked the oil. I pulled the starting rope until the engine roared. I then began churning the dirt and slowly grinding up all the plants that had fed us so well throughout the summer. Row after row of carrots and onions and radishes disappeared and were forever mixed with the rich, black soil, and while I continued to work Grandpa stood nearby and watched my progress. More than once I caught glimpses of him rubbing his leg, though he attempted to do that nonchalantly.

I thought about returning to the city far less than I had ever imagined I would. I had not talked to any of my friends since I arrived in Iowa, and I found that I really didn't miss them at all. My only contact with home had been a few phone calls to Mom, and I did find that I missed seeing her. There had never been a specific date set for me to leave Gowrie and return home, and to my surprise, I realized that I was in no real hurry to leave.

Rock and Cheri were still together and I joined them often at the disco. Kathy and I had not talked since she left for college, and I had resigned myself to the idea that she would find someone there who could better give her what she wanted in a relationship. I thought of her often but I knew that she and I would not be a couple at this point in our lives. Maybe someday, knowing the curves and twists that life can present, but not now.

Legacy

At Hazel's, most of the talk now revolved around harvest plans and preparations for bringing the crops in successfully. Kenny, Dorothy, and Denise were now in their new house, and Kenny's bounce was fully back in his walk and his words. Herman and Grandpa spoke mostly about getting the corn pickers and the combines all lined up and ready to go. The weather had been good most of the summer so they were all very optimistic about high yields from their fields. Grandpa couldn't resist reminding Captain of the advice Captain had given him the day Grandpa and I went to the elevator to contract his beans. As it turned out, Grandpa had timed it perfectly and the $6.71 per bushel he had locked in was as high as the price ever got. Captain, of course, could still not admit he had been wrong, and he pretended that he didn't remember ever giving Grandpa any advice on his beans.

School was back in session everywhere and on Friday nights most of the people in town could be found at the football field, watching and supporting the local high school team. I learned that the team was quite good and had been good for over a decade, and there was no doubt in my mind that the entire town was behind them.

Grandpa's legs still troubled me, though he would never admit there was any real problem. He moved more slowly now than when I had first arrived and he had gone to see the doctor again. Whenever I brought the subject up he passed it off as age or fatigue or just being stiff, but I didn't buy his excuses. I didn't know anything about muscles or veins or arteries, but even I could see that something was wrong. Time after time he told me there was nothing to worry about, but he never convinced me that was true.

The Jaycees' softball season had come to an end and they celebrated with a cookout that I was invited to attend. Arch told me their record was something like 68 wins and only 18 losses, and I was surprised to learn they had played that many games. Most of the players on the team were farmers, and now that it was almost harvest time, softball was no longer a priority. After a summer of playing, relaxing, and tending the fields they had planted, it was once again time for the farmers to get back to work and do what they did best.

Legacy

Before the crops were brought in, however, Gowrie found one more reason to bring the town together and party, the Firemen's Ball. Every year on a late September Saturday night the people of this area gathered to dance and drink and show their support for the local volunteer fire department. Even Grandpa got excited about the Firemens' Ball. He didn't dance but all his buddies would be there and it would be a good excuse to cut loose and have some fun before the grind of the harvest fully took over. I was skeptical, especially since I didn't have a date, but this town had not let me down with anything yet, so I went.

The Ball got underway at 9:00 and went until 1:00 A.M., and the band that played was very good. I was obviously one of the youngest people there, but finding dance partners was much easier than at the disco. There were plenty of other singles there, both men and women, and everyone seemed to come with the intention of having a great time. Throughout the night I hardly sat out a song, and had fun with a variety of dance partners. As usual, the wives and single women wanted to dance far more than most of the men, and the men were generally more than happy to turn their wives over to me to dance while they stood and talked with their friends. The biggest portion of my Firemens' Ball night was spent dancing with Penny Marie Petit, an attractive blonde who was nine years my senior. She loved to dance and had come there by herself. I had seen her around town several times throughout the summer, and we had spoken briefly once or twice, but I didn't really know much about her. During one of my short dancing intermissions, she had walked up, taken me by the hand, and simply led me to the dance floor.

From that point on, for the rest of the night, until the band stopped playing, we were a couple. We got creative together during the fast songs, showing off our moves and trying some new ones. I had never been close that like with a woman older than I, but as the songs continued the age gap became irrelevant. She had made my first Firemens' Ball a memorable one, and I didn't know if there would be more with Penny in the future, but I hoped there would be. At the end of the night I even walked her to her truck and before she got in to go home she leaned into me and gave me a deep, passionate kiss.

I didn't sleep much that night as thoughts of Penny, our dances and our kiss, ran laps around my mind. Eventually my eyes closed and the night came to an end. So many things had happened to me here in Gowrie that had never happened to me back home in the city, and I tried to absorb everything. There had been so many firsts for me here that I could not even begin to count them, but the most surprising things to me were how involved the whole community got with any event and how easily I seemed to fit in here. I still thought of Kathy often and wondered if she was doing well at college, and now there was Penny. Could I have a relationship with a woman nine years older than I was?

I was at times frustrated by the life I had lived growing up in the city. It was only now that I had begun to understand how limited a person's point of view can be on everything, simply based on his environment and lack of variety of experiences. There were so many people I had met here who had opened my eyes in countless ways. Grandpa, Rock, Kathy and the Jaycees had all shown me how much I had previously missed out on in regard to relationships as well as how unselfish people could be with each other. The people of this area had amazed me over and over from the tornado to the 4th of July and the pork chop dinner to the Firemen's Ball. These people looked for excuses to come together and enjoy each other as a community, something totally foreign to me in the city.

Even something as seemingly simple as Josh's hog roast had left a huge impression on me. The innate kindness and willingness to share and give were uncommon back home and unfamiliar to me, but I had been shown many times all the good that can result from living that way. These people had accepted me without hesitation, perhaps initially because I was Carl's grandson, but his credibility surely had only lasted a short amount of time. When that wore off, any friendships I had fostered, and there were many, had developed because of my actions, and that made me feel good.

So where did I go from here? I had no desire to ever return to the life I had left just a few months earlier but I didn't have any real plan in mind for anything else. Grandpa had once asked me if I had any goals, and I now realized that it was time I really thought about my future. I wasn't even sure how to begin doing that but it was time to do something. I had never before thought about leaving any kind of legacy, but now things like that popped into my mind fairly regularly. I knew for sure I didn't want to have the legacy of a guy who just hung out on the corner with his shiftless buddies and spent a lifetime accomplishing nothing. Five months ago that might have worked for me, but not any more.

CHAPTER 37

Harvest time in Iowa. The culmination of months and months of tending enormous gardens that were capable of feeding the world. If a farmer had done well with his planting and cultivating, and if the mix of sunshine, rain, and temperature had been good, he could look forward to a rewarding crop that would carry his family through the upcoming winter and beyond. Grandpa had stressed to me how important it was in life to respect the process of things. Results did not always instantly appear but the ground work still needed to be done correctly. I now realized how naïve my response had been on planting day when I said how easy farming was. "Just plant and wait and then harvest it." I had no clue.

One morning in late September Grandpa and I sat together at the breakfast table. He had mixed up some batter and we were having pancakes. While the pancakes cooked on one burner the bacon and sausage sizzled on another, and the entire kitchen had an aroma that made my mouth water. I had never been a part of combining beans or picking corn before, so there were things about which I was curious.

"The fields look good to me," I began, "but I have nothing to compare them to. You think we took care of them all right?"

He grabbed the spatula and slid two pancakes onto my plate with a grin. "I think so," he replied. "Funny how different a guy talks once he feels like he has some ownership in something isn't it?

They look good to me too. Remember your first day of planting? Spilling the seed all over the ground. Hating where you were and what you were doing. Feeling so sorry for yourself. Remember that?"

I looked into the distance, recalling the details of that day, and I almost couldn't recognize the Eli I saw in my mind. "I vaguely remember," I stated with a knowing smile. "Seems like a long time ago doesn't it?"

He put the spatula on the counter and poured some more batter onto the griddle. "Sometimes it does. Sometimes it still feels like you just got here."

"I know what you mean. It's hard for me to believe I've been here for almost five months. Wasn't this supposed to just be a summer thing?"

Without facing me he asked bluntly, "You ready to go back to the city?"

"I didn't say that," I responded defensively. "Just making an observation. When I got on the plane to come here I was told that the plan was for me to be here all summer."

"And you were. You know it's entirely up to you. You can stay or we can put you back on a plane tomorrow. Just say the word and you can go back to your other buddies and all the fun and exciting things you used to do."

"Ah, yes, our fun and exciting things. All basically pointless and a waste of time. Sounds like you're ready for me to leave."

He sat beside me and took a large bite of a pancake. "Not at all, but it's time you made some decisions. Back when you arrived you and I talked about having some goals and some plans and you didn't have either. Pretty sure you still don't, but I'm also thinkin' that some of your thinkin' has changed. Just want you to know you're not obligated to stay here if you have something better in mind for your future."

"But we're just a couple days from starting to combine the beans. Wouldn't it help you if I was here for that and the corn picking?"

"Sure it would," he stated, "but if you're here I want you to be here because it's your choice. Your decision. It's about to get really busy around here."

Legacy

"Nothing wrong with busy," I responded. "It's more fun when we have things to do."

"So you wanna stay?"

I paused for a few seconds then answered confidently. "Yeah, I want to stay. Seems kind of silly to be this close to a harvest and then not see it through."

"I agree but a lot of people do that, stop just before they finish something. You've had some ownership this year in our fields, and I'm glad to hear you say you want to see the finish. We may turn you into a farmer yet. What would you think of that?"

"Maybe," I responded with a smile. I couldn't tell for sure where he was headed with all this, but it was not our typical breakfast talk.

"Maybe, huh?" he asked with a shrug. "Let's get breakfast done and cleaned up. We need to get the combine all ready to go."

Fifteen minutes later the food was put away, the dishes were all washed, and we were outside standing beside the combine. Grandpa had the grease gun in his right hand and a bag with several quarts of oil and a new filter in his left. I carried some wrenches and a bucket to catch the old oil when we changed it and put in the new oil. I immediately crawled under the motor with the bucket and a wrench, and Grandpa walked around and checked everything else. No faulty hose or spark plug could survive Grandpa's scrutiny once he began his pre-use inspection. He was fanatical on maintenance as he had shown me at planting time, so nothing we did now surprised me. I knew he wanted the combine to be as ready as possible even though there was still no guarantee that everything about the harvest would go perfectly.

I had the oil drained and the plug replaced and was moving toward the front to put in the new filter when I heard a series of sounds that made me shiver. First there was the clank of a wrench hitting something, followed by the tearing of cloth. Immediately after that I heard a cry of surprise, followed by a loud thud on the ground. I dropped the filter and ran around the combine to see Grandpa lying on his back on the gravel, moaning steadily.

When I got to him I could see a small cut on the back of his head and his eyes were somewhat glazed, displaying a mix of shock and

Legacy

disbelief. I grabbed a rag and applied pressure to his head and tried to talk to him, but all he could do was moan. It appeared to me that his only visible injury was the head wound, which I thought was at least a small bit of good news, but I couldn't be sure. The right pant leg of his overalls had a long tear, but when I checked his leg I didn't see any cuts there.

My mind raced a thousand places in an instant. I knew I had to get him some help but I didn't know how I could do that without leaving him alone. I continued to try and talk to him and after a minute or two the glaze left his eyes, and he was able to communicate with me. I kept the pressure on the back of his head and thought more about the best way to get him the medical attention he needed.

"Can you hear me?" I began.

He squinted his eyes and grunted a weak, "Yeah, I hear ya."

"You've got a cut on your head and I need to get you some help. Can you understand that?"

He moaned loudly as he strained to raise his head, but he could not do it. "I can't move."

I held him still. "I know. It's okay. I need to get some help. Tell me your name."

"Carl."

"What town are we in?"

"Gowrie."

"Who's your favorite grandson?"

"I don't have one," he said and tried his best to laugh, but the attempt at humor hurt his head even more.

"Funny man," I stated. "But if you're cracking jokes you must be at least mostly all right. I really need to get some help. You think you'll be okay if I leave you here for a minute and go call the ambulance."

"I don't need any damn ambulance," he answered. "Just get me into the house."

"No," I responded sternly. "You're hurt, and we need to get you looked at. Holler if you want to, but this is one time you're going to take the orders instead of giving them. Understand? Do you think you'll be okay here for a minute or two?"

Legacy

He reached around and continued to press the rag against his head, and I could see he was in some pain. "I'll be okay."

I climbed up into the cab of the combine and retrieved a jacket he had stored there. I raised his head gently and placed the jacket under his head like a pillow. When I was convinced he was as comfortable as I could make him I sprinted toward the house and dialed the local ambulance service. The dispatcher assured me the ambulance would be there in less than ten minutes, which comforted me to some degree. After the phone call I raced through the house looking for anything that could serve as a bandage, and I also grabbed a blanket that I could place over him to keep him warm as he lay on the ground.

I ran back to him as quickly as I could and had probably been gone for less than four minutes. When I returned he was trying to sit up. "Stop it!" I ordered when I reached him. "Just lay back down and wait. Help is on the way."

He struggled again, trying to sit up but I pressed his shoulders down and made him lie still. "How bad does your head hurt?"

"Just a little bit," he answered. "It's really not that bad. I don't think that's the big problem though."

I gave him a confused look. "What do you mean?"

"I can't move my leg. That's how I fell. I was climbing up to the cab and my leg just stopped. Kind of locked up on me. I tried to move it when you went to the house, but I can't do it."

"Oh, God, I knew it," I stated. "Every time I saw you limping and you always giving me some weak excuse. Can you sit up at all?"

"I can try. Help me."

I placed my hands behind his head and shoulders and began to slowly raise him to a sitting position. Once that was accomplished, he immediately reached out and rubbed his right leg, and it was obvious that it was hurting him far more than the cut on his head. The cut was less severe than I had originally thought, which was good, and the initial pressure I had placed on it had seemed to help stop the bleeding, so now my attention turned fully toward his leg.

In the distance I could faintly hear the ambulance's siren and I knew they would arrive very soon. Grandpa heard it too. "Sounds like the cavalry is on the way. Guess I get to make a trip to Dodge.

Damn leg. I've got things to do here. Things that have to get done. I thought I could make it until we got the crops in."

I shook my head at him. "So you knew your leg was bad all along. I could tell too but you would never admit it to me, and apparently you were just as good at lying to yourself. What happened to facing a problem head on? That was you telling me that back when I dealt with Maxie, right?"

He leaned forward, wincing visibly, and he grabbed his leg tightly. "I thought I'd be all right until we got the crops in. Then I was gonna get it looked at."

The siren was much louder now and I knew the ambulance was really close to the farm. I left Grandpa again and ran to where the driver could see me, and I could direct them to where he was sitting on the ground. Once they parked and got to Grandpa I stood out of the way. The medics went through all their standard procedures, checked his vital signs, and cleaned and bandaged his head wound. I watched for a moment and then spoke up. "It's his leg, his right one. That's what caused his fall. It just stopped and locked up on him."

One of the medics, a stout middle aged woman, began to check out his leg. She moved it and pressed on several different areas up and down the leg, waiting to see Grandpa's reactions to her touches, but she didn't get one. "Does any of this hurt?" she asked him.

"No," he replied with a hint of fear in his eyes. "I can't feel any of it."

"Let's get him loaded up," she said to her ambulance partner.

It took all three of us to lift Grandpa onto the gurney, and I was surprised how heavy he was. I suspected that a third of his total weight was his pride, but I kept that to myself. I watched the ambulance drive away and I hurried back into the house to make some more phone calls before I drove to Dodge to be with Grandpa as he was treated. I called Rock and told him what had happened and I knew he would get the word out to some others who would want to know. I also called Mom who was naturally shaken and concerned by the news. We only talked for a couple minutes, but when I explained to her how I had noticed a problem with

Legacy

Grandpa's leg for quite a while she understood that it was probably something serious and she could not settle for just getting updates on the phone. She decided that she needed to be in Gowrie too to help however she could, so after we hung up the phone she bought a plane ticket to Des Moines. She was coming home.

When I arrived at the hospital I was more than a bit surprised to find that Grandpa was already in surgery. An x-ray had revealed a reasonably large blood clot in his lower right leg, and the doctor did not want to wait to remove it. I sat impatiently in the waiting room with half a dozen other equally impatient and equally uninformed people, each of us waiting for any updates on our particular patient and each of us hoping to only hear good news.

The minutes ticked away more slowly for me than any other minutes I could remember having to endure. Four of the others in the waiting room had gotten their news and had left with varying degrees of happiness, but I waited. And waited. I read through magazines I had never before been tempted to open, though I could not tell anybody anything that I had read. I paced around the room and the hallway, and I stared blankly out a huge window in the hallway and watched person after person go about his business, each one totally unaware that Grandpa had fallen and had a blood clot in his leg. I realized that just one day earlier I would have been one of those people, blissfully ignorant of those people who sat in this room waiting for news like I did now.

It took two hours before I heard anything of any substance. A tired doctor appeared from a room I was not allowed to enter, and as he sat next to me on the sofa he tried his best to paint on a weary smile, apparently his attempt to lessen my tension and stress levels. I wondered how many times he had walked through that door and delivered news to family members.

"Hello, I'm Doctor Swanson," he began as he extended his hand toward me. "You're here with Carl, correct?"

I responded politely and we shook hands. "Yes, I am. I'm Eli, his grandson. So what's the story with his leg? How come you had to do surgery on it so fast?"

He stared directly into my eyes and wore a really serious look. "It's fairly complicated medically and without getting too

Legacy

technical, the easiest answer is that he had a serious blood clot in his right leg. We felt there was a real danger of the clot moving into other parts of his body and we didn't want to take that chance. This was not a sudden thing, and I'm guessing his leg had been giving him trouble prior to his fall today."

"Correct," I explained with a nod of my head. "For well over a month but he would never admit it."

Doctor Swanson smiled at me. "Very typical. Denial is one of my biggest foes, especially if my patient is a farmer from around here who has something like this come up at harvest time."

"Yeah, well, I guess our harvest is going to be pushed back a while now. We were going to get started either tomorrow or the next day, but I can't do it myself. Don't even have a clue how to do it."

"You might want to learn fast," continued the doctor, "because Carl won't be doing any of that this year. We're going to keep him here for several days until we're sure we have his blood flow regulated properly and there is no danger of further clotting. And even after he is released he will need to take it really easy for a few weeks. Definitely no climbing up and down on combines and pickers and tractors."

I sat with a blank but serious look on my face. "What am I supposed to do about getting the crops in?" I wasn't sure why I had proposed that dilemma to a doctor who had no solution and probably not a great amount of interest, but the thought was inside my head and it came out verbally.

The doctor patted my knee reassuringly. "I'm not sure son, but this year Carl won't be part of whatever you do. There's another injury I need to tell you about too. His leg was just part of it. He also bruised his back when he fell and I'm equally worried about that. When he's ready to be discharged he will be in a brace that will prevent twisting and turning and help to absorb the shocks on his back when he walks. He will be moving much more slowly than he did before, and I wanted to prepare you for that."

"For how long?" I asked. "He will recover from all this, right?"

"He should, but it will be a process. It won't be fast and he's going to need your help and your patience. Sometimes the hardest

Legacy

battle for people in Carl's position is the struggle with their pride. Men who have spent their entire lives being independent often have a lot of trouble asking for help and even admitting they need help. Just warning you that there could be some frustration and even anger showing up in the days ahead. He's going to need help, and if he can accept that he can get well again. If not, the process will be difficult."

"Okay, thanks doctor," I replied. "When can I see him?"

"Not until tomorrow. He's still out from the surgery and will need to rest quietly the rest of the night. You should probably just go home and take care of whatever you need to do. No need to sit here all day for nothing."

We rose together and shook hands. "Thanks again," I continued. "I'll see you tomorrow."

My drive back to Gowrie was filled with uncertain thoughts, and the self-confidence that I normally possessed was nowhere to be found. I had no idea what to do next, especially with the harvest. I was a city guy who now found himself neck deep in unfamiliar waters, and I knew I needed help, so when I reached Gowrie I went and found Rock. He was in his yard waxing his car, and he gave me a wave when I pulled into the driveway. He finished wiping the wax off the trunk of his car and then put the towel down. Evidently he could see or at least sense the concern on my face as I approached him because our normal, friendly greeting was replaced with seriousness. "How is he?"

"Not sure, but I guess he's going to be okay. He already had surgery for a blood clot in his leg and he also hurt his back when he fell. He's going to be laid up for a while."

"Sorry to hear that, but I'm glad he'll be okay eventually."

"I don't know what to do," I conceded. "We were getting the combine ready, and I know it's time to bring the beans in, but I've never done that before. I don't even know where to start."

"Try not to worry about that," Rock stated. "After you told me what happened I told some people and I think your beans will be fine."

"What the hell does that mean? The beans will be fine."

"You'll see. Just try and relax if you can."

Legacy

"Right," I responded sarcastically. "I was thinking of going on a picnic or something."

Rock laughed. "I'm serious. Try not to worry. Surely you've been here long enough to know how this town works. Trust me."

"Oh, and I have to drive to Des Moines tomorrow morning to pick up Mom from the airport, and I'm sure she'll want to go straight to the hospital, so I won't even be around to get anything done." I threw a rock into the street in frustration. "I just don't know what to do."

Rock spoke calmly and confidently. "It'll work out. You hungry?"

"Starved," I replied.

"Let's go grab something at Hazel's. My treat."

My level of worry seemed to lessen with Rock's simple gesture and I found a smile. "You're treat, huh? Sounds good."

He set the towel on the ground, put the lid back on his container of wax, and we got into my car and went uptown to eat. My mind was still full of uncertainties but Rock had helped to somewhat calm me down. I was extremely hungry and devoured my chicken strips and fries quickly. We sat at our table for nearly an hour and in that short period of time I had to give four updates on Grandpa's condition. The power of communication in a small town surprised me again, and I wondered if the whole town already knew that Grandpa had gotten hurt.

I took Rock home and decided to return to the farm to get done whatever I could before sundown. I wasn't sure what all I would do, but I felt that I needed to do something. I also needed to clean the house and get things ready for Mom's arrival. For the first time in months I felt totally unsure of myself and out of place, and as I stood beside the combine and gathered up the tools we had been using, I felt extremely alone.

CHAPTER 38

I spent a really lonely night in the house. Television held my attention for a while and I wiped and cleaned the kitchen and the bathroom so it wouldn't completely look to Mom like two guys had lived there without much care or concern for dirt and things piling up in spots. I dug through some drawers and found a map that I could use on my way to Des Moines and the airport, because I really didn't know how to get there on my own. The only time I had ever seen Des Moines was the first day I had arrived in Iowa.

I was hungry again, so I threw a few hot dogs into a pan of water and boiled them, a simple meal that would require very little clean up. When I finished the hot dogs I sat on the couch. It was a little after ten and the news was on. I looked at the empty recliner and the house seemed even lonelier. A weird silence hung over everything and for some reason I could not make myself go upstairs to sleep. I went up and grabbed my alarm clock and a couple blankets and set up a makeshift bed for myself on the couch. Everything I had grown accustomed to regarding the farm had been suddenly turned upside down, and it took me a long time to turn my brain off and get some sleep.

I woke early and took a quick bath. I wanted to give myself all the extra time I could in case I got lost in Des Moines, because I had to be at the gate waiting for Mom when she walked off the plane. Half my drive was directly into the morning sun, but it was a crisp, clear morning and the traffic was light so I didn't mind. An hour or so into my drive I decided to stop at a Casey's store in Granger where I grabbed a couple donuts and a can of pop. From there it was only twenty minutes or so to the airport, assuming I didn't make any wrong turns.

I was happy to see that Des Moines had so many road signs along the interstate, especially ones indicating directions to the airport, because those signs actually made it relatively easy for me to find my way. I was ahead of schedule when I arrived at the airport, which was good, and I had forty-five minutes before Mom's plane was scheduled to land. I pulled into the parking garage and walked the short distance across the street and into the terminal, where it only took a few more minutes to find the correct gate.

The potential disasters that had filled my thoughts the day before were replaced with a genuine excitement for seeing Mom again. I had long since accepted that I did not miss my old friends and buddies back home, but there had been many times in the past several months that I had missed Mom, and I looked forward to the big hug that I knew was coming soon. It was announced over the loud speaker that her flight had just landed and I rose from my seat in anticipation. I looked around the reception area and realized I was standing in nearly the exact same spot where Grandpa had stood waiting for me. A couple minutes after the announcement people began to emerge from the same tunnel I had walked through nearly five months earlier.

She was about the thirtieth person to appear and when she saw me she couldn't contain her grin. She had her purse over one arm and a small bag in her hand, and it warmed my heart to see her again. We hurried toward each other and held each other tightly for several seconds. "Oh, it's so good to see you Eli," she began. "Let me look at you."

I grinned at her. "It's really good to see you too. I've missed you."

She pulled me close and hugged me again. "Oh, honey, I missed you too. So much. How's Dad?"

"The doctor told me his recovery is gonna take a while. They wouldn't let me see him yesterday, but we can see him today. Come on, let's go get your bags."

We pulled her suitcases off the luggage carousel and walked to my car, which she was about to see for the first time, even though she had paid for it. When I put the key into the trunk she looked the car over. "This one? I like it. Is it still running well for you?"

"It runs great," I replied with a smile. "Thanks again for getting it for me. Can't imagine being here and not having it."

"You're very welcome, sweetheart."

We took a different route to Dodge, one that was more direct and bypassed Gowrie, and the two hour trip allowed Mom and me the opportunity to have a real and substantive conversation, something she had attempted many times before with me. On all her previous attempts she had achieved only minimal results, but not this time. This time was different, as I was anxious to get here caught up on many of the things I had seen and done since I had been here. She seemed equally anxious to hear everything and I'm certain that I talked to her more in those two hours than I had in any month before I left for Iowa.

I told her about Rock and Kathy and the Jaycees. I spoke with pride about our garden and all the food we had grown there. I talked about the 4th of July, and I could see the memories of her youth coming alive in her eyes as she listened. I even told her about Maxie and the haunted house. She thought that was funny, clever, and dangerous all at once, and I had to agree.

When we reached the city limits of Dodge I had run out of stories and it was time to get back to the realities of the moment and Grandpa Carl's injuries. Mom turned to me with soft eyes and spoke gently. "Look at you. I'm so happy. I knew this version of you was in there somewhere just waiting to come out." She caressed my shoulder as I drove through town toward the hospital. "I'm proud of you."

I beamed. "Thanks Mom. You were right, and I guess I was too stubborn to admit it. This place is good. I actually don't miss the city at all."

"Yes, this place is good, but I couldn't tell you that. You had to find out for yourself and find your own way here. I knew you'd get a lot of the right kind of help here though, and I had to get you off that stupid street corner and away from your friends back home."

"They aren't my friends," I stated firmly. "I just thought they were. Took me a while to figure that out, and I know you tried to tell me that many times, but I never wanted to hear it or believe it."

"There are lots of things we all have to find out for ourselves, often the hard way, but we go through things and learn in our own ways and at our own pace. I just prayed you'd see it before it got too late, and I'm so happy you did."

"I know," I replied humbly. "Since I've been here I've thought about all the times you tried to talk to me and warn me about things but I didn't want to hear any of that either. It's funny but

Legacy

Grandpa subtly got in my face about three minutes after I met him, telling me all the lessons he thought I needed to learn."

Mom laughed when I said that. "That doesn't surprise me at all. He was probably testing the waters a bit with you to see what kind of hand I had dealt him for the summer."

"Could be. I was already mad about having to come here and he pretty much instantly made me madder."

"But look at you now," she exclaimed. "Seems to me that he has once again worked his magic and taught you some things about what is really important. I watched him do the same thing with others for twenty years, and he has never stopped teaching me, even today."

"I can believe that," I stated. "It's like he says stuff and you hear him, and then a while later you realize you learned something. Took me a while to catch on to what he was doing."

We reached the hospital parking lot and worked our way through the antiseptic corridors until we reached Grandpa's room. Two nurses hovered over him as we entered and we say him lying motionless on his bed. It was the first time I had ever seen him look weak and that surprisingly troubled me. He appeared to be somewhat awake, but not totally, and the taller of the nurses confirmed that for us. "He's still heavily medicated, so he may fade in and out on you for a while," she told us. "His back is hurting him and the doctor wants him to remain extremely still. You're welcome to stay with him though." The nurses finished whatever it was they were doing and then left the room. Mom and I stood beside Grandpa's bed, one of us on each side of him.

Mom leaned over and put her face close to his. "Hi Dad," she whispered. "I'm here and now it's my turn to take care of you for a while."

He seemed to recognize her voice immediately because he moved his hand and began to weakly wiggle his fingers. Mom understood and she took his hand in hers. He squeezed her hand as tightly as he could and I stood by quietly and let them have their moment. It was easy to see that the bond between them was strong and unbreakable regardless of time or miles apart. As the two held hands I saw him struggle to speak, and he spoke only one word which we could barely hear. "Molly."

She smiled and stood as close to his bed as she could, and while I watched them I thought again of the crops that needed to be brought in and my total uncertainty about how to do that. As I watched Grandpa lie there, the reality hit me that he could do nothing about the harvest, and it scared me to think that the responsibility fell onto my shoulders. I backed away from the bed and sat in a nearby chair, racking my brain for any possible solution that might present itself. None did. After a couple minutes I shared my dilemma with Mom.

"We've got a real problem here," I began. "It's time to bring in the beans and Grandpa can't do it. It's got to be done and I don't know what to do. Don't even know how to start. I stayed here so I could help and learn, but I can't do this by myself."

Mom walked over to me and hugged my shoulders. "We'll figure something out."

"That's what Rock told me too, but it's the only thing I've been thinking about since he got hurt and I haven't come up with anything yet. I need to get back to the farm to see what I can do, if anything. Do you want to stay here with him?"

"Yes, I'm going to stay here. You go on and you can come back and get me later tonight."

I rose slowly from my chair. "Okay. If there was ever a time for an inspired thought or two to come my way, it would be now."

Mom forced a smile. "I have confidence in you and so does your Grandpa. Go see what you can do, and I'll take care of him here."

I left the hospital, walked to my car, and began my drive back to the farm. All the way home I asked myself what the best thing was to do. Different ideas ran through my mind over and over, but each of the ideas finished in a dead end. I did not know how to run a combine. I didn't even know how a combine worked. Each mile I drove got me closer to a destiny I had not chosen, and I knew I had a strong desire to succeed, both for Grandpa and for myself. I just didn't know yet exactly how I would do that. It was time to come up with something, however, because it was already early afternoon and I was only two miles from the farm.

Legacy

CHAPTER 39

I turned off the highway and onto our gravel road, still somewhat caught up in my thoughts, and as soon as I did, what I saw in the field to my right nearly stopped me in my tracks. I turned away and then looked again to make sure what I saw was not a mirage. I slowed my car to a crawl and continued toward our driveway, unsure of what to feel as I stared at our bean field. I saw three combines moving across the field devouring the beans. Tractors with wagons hooked behind them waited in the end rows and the men on the tractors waved at me as I crept by in disbelief. It was Kenny and Herman, and they wore big smiles. When I pulled into the driveway my level of wonder and surprise grew even more.

There were half a dozen pickups and cars, as well as several tractors and wagons there. A group of men stood together talking near the garage and they looked at me as I parked my car and got out. Rock stepped out of the group and walked quickly toward me. I only half understood what I saw and had a difficult time comprehending even that much. "What is this Rock? What's going on here?" I asked.

Rock could not contain his smile or his pride. "Just helping out a little. Once everybody found out about Carl's fall we kind of thought you might need a hand with the beans, so we decided to take care of that for you today."

"Unbelievable," was all I could say. "Three combines?"

Rock shook his head. "Yeah, that surprised me too, but they all insisted on helping and I figured it would just help us get done even faster. Two of them are owned by guys your Grandpa had helped a lot over the years and they jumped at the chance to repay him. The other combine belongs to Josh. He was the most eager to help, and he told me he owed both you and Carl. He's still really happy you got his money and all his stuff back last July, and he said that Carl had been there for him many times when he was younger."

"These guys all have crops of their own to bring in don't they?"

"Sure they do, but that can all wait a day or two. You and Carl needed help, so we're here. You first."

Legacy

For a moment I wasn't sure how to respond. I looked at Rock, then I looked toward the combines in the field, and then I looked at the guys standing by the garage. "Wow," was all I could say. "Sounds great."

Rock slapped my shoulder and said, "Come on. We've got work to do." We walked over and joined the others by the garage, and they all greeted me cheerfully.

"Surprised Eli?" asked Lennie.

"Completely," I answered. "How can I ever thank all of you? Who got this all together?"

Crusher spoke up. "Several of us actually. Rock made some calls. So did I. Pretty sure Teaser did too. That's right isn't it?"

"Yeah, I told some people," confirmed Teaser. I had not seen him since he had ducked Grandpa at Sherm's, and I figured he would be mad forever from when Grandpa had made him walk back to town when we were walking beans. I realized again that I still didn't fully understand these people, but at the moment that didn't matter to me in the least.

Just then Kenny and Herman drove into the yard on their tractors, each one pulling a wagon full of beans. When they stopped, Teaser and Lennie quickly unhooked their wagons and guided them to the empty wagons that sat nearby and hooked them up again. Without hesitation or any real pause for conversation, they drove back to the field to await the next loads.

Arch and Captain then sprang into action and started their tractors. They carefully backed up to the full wagons and Lennie and Teaser hooked them up. They drove off, one behind the other, and took the beans to the elevator in town. With three combines running at the same time, the wagons filled quickly and there was no time to waste. Rock, Crusher, Lennie, and I stood together in the yard during the short lull between loads, and I tried hard to take in everything I saw. "What time did you guys get here and get started? " I asked.

"About 7:30," answered Rock. "Been going non-stop ever since and we'll be here til we're done."

"I still can't believe all this. You guys are incredible."

"What can't you believe?" asked Rock. "You've seen it before. You were part of it. Remember the tornado at Kenny's house? Same thing now."

"I guess so," I stated. "It just looks and feels different when you're on the receiving end of a gesture like this."

"It's all good," added Crusher. "You've done more than your share to help us and you've only been here a short time. Look at it this way. We're all here for two reasons. The first one is that it's the right thing to do, and the second one is because we want to be here."

I smiled the most appreciative smile I could generate and simply said, "Thank you all. What can I do? This is my first harvest you know?"

Lennie replied, "Yeah, we know. "Just do whatever needs done. Crusher and I will take the next loads to town and Arch and Captain will be back before long. You can hook and unhook the wagons to the tractors."

Rock added, "You and I can also help with the food. The women are inside cooking now and we can get that to the guys in the field when it's time."

"Sounds good," I stated. "Just tell me what needs done."

For the next several hours the process continued without a break. Everybody worked tirelessly, stopping only briefly for some food or bathroom breaks here and there. Twice we had to run fuel out to the combines and also had to put gas into the tractors that were driving back and forth to town. Eventually I remembered that Mom was still at the hospital and I needed to go pick her up.

"Rock, I forgot that my Mom is here. She's up at the hospital with Grandpa and I need to go get her," I explained.

"Go ahead," he answered. "We've only got a couple hours left and we should be done. I think we can handle it. You could grab a couple cases of beer though and bring that back with you. All of us will be ready for that when we finish."

"Deal!" I said with a smile. "Pretty cheap labor if all you guys charge is some beer."

Rock laughed. "Get out of here. Go get your Mom."

Legacy

The drive to Dodge went quickly. The weight I had felt hanging over me had been lifted off me completely by those amazing people who had taken it upon themselves to do what needed to be done without my ever having to ask them. In a couple hours all the beans we had would be in. I was full of energy and enthusiasm when I reached the hospital, and I couldn't wait to share the news with both Mom and Grandpa.

When I walked into his room it was noticeably different than what I had seen in there earlier in the day. There were dozens of balloons and flowers and there was a mountain of cards that were stacked up on the table near his bed. All of that had been delivered since I had been there earlier that morning. Grandpa was awake and Mom stood near his bed talking with him. He was still not allowed to sit up but he was coherent and alert. "Hi there," I began. Nice to see you awake. How are you feeling?"

"I've been better," he answered. "All the medication helps though, so it's not too bad. Makes me feel better though having your Mom here."

"Makes me feel better having her here too," I agreed. I gave Mom a hug and continued. "I think I can make you feel even better too."

"How's that?" he asked skeptically.

I hesitated for a second. "Well, I'll tell ya. The beans are almost done being combined."

Grandpa's eyes got wide and he wasn't sure he believed me. "What? Done? How?"

"When I left earlier I went back to the farm and there was a whole crew already at work combining the fields. They've been at it all day running three combines at the same time. In fact, they should be completely finished in an hour or two."

Grandpa smiled but did not speak. Mom squeezed his hand and said, "These people never change do they? If someone needs help they are always there."

"I turned our corner and saw the combines moving in the field, and I couldn't believe it. You've got some really good friends Grandpa."

He replied softly, "So do you it seems. Something tells me it's not just my bunch there helping out is it?"

Legacy

"No, it's not. Several of my Jaycee buddies are there too. Even Teaser. I guess he got over you yelling at him."

"I'm sure he was over that a log time ago, probably that same day. As soon as he calmed down and thought about it, I suspect he knew he earned what he got. Maybe helping today is his way of apologizing. He's a good guy."

Mom, who still held Grandpa's hand, took my hand as well. "My two favorite guys. Both very good men. A person's friends say everything about that person, and your friends are speaking very loudly for both of you today. I'm so proud of you two."

"So Eli, you still think you want to go back to the city or do you think you could handle this kind of life for good?" Grandpa asked.

I stared at him curiously. "What do you mean for good?"

"Do you remember our talk about Roy Dale?"

"Sure I do," I replied. "The legacy talk. His kids didn't want to stay and keep the farm going, everything he had worked so hard for. Is that what you mean?"

"That's it," he confirmed. "I could never interest your Mom in doing that either, but after five months with you, I guess I've sort of gotten used to having you around. Just wondered if maybe you'd consider staying on permanently and taking over the farm. I don't know how long it will take me to heal from all this, so I may be ready to hand over the reins even sooner than I had planned."

"Wow," I said. "That's an incredible offer. I don't know what to say."

"Just say what you really feel. If you do this, it has to be because it's what you want or it won't work. It can't be because it's what I want. I've seen the person you are and your friends are reinforcing that right now in our bean fields. It's a good life. A hard one at times but a good one, and I highly recommend it. You remember that first ride home from Des Moines when I told you that you had three big lessons to learn?"

I looked him directly in the eyes. "I remember. Humility, patience, and gratitude. I remember."

"Pretty obvious to me that you've learned all three, and that's very good. Now it's up to you. You once asked me how anybody could choose to live here, and I told you that in time you'd know the answer and would never have to ask again. You know that answer now don't you?"

"Yeah, I do," I stated with a wide grin.

"The offer is real. The farm is yours if you want it, with my help of course for as long as I can be here to do that. What do you say?"

I stood silently beside the hospital bed and allowed the realities of the offer to fully sink in. I thought about the city and my former buddies and our street corner stupidity. Then I thought about the tornado at Kenny's house and the 4th of July and the Firemen's Ball. I thought of Rock and Crusher and Lennie and all the Jaycees, but mostly I thought about our garden and the results I had seen from all the care we had given to it. I looked at Grandpa and then I looked at Mom. Grandpa was right. The only way his offer would work was if it was my choice and something I wanted for my future. I had known how I felt for a while but had never let the thoughts move to the front of my mind until that moment. I moved closer to Grandpa's bed and looked him directly in his eyes. "I'll take it. Thank you. And not just thank you for the farm. Thank you for everything."

Grandpa closed his eyes and wore a look of peace and contentment I had not seen him show before. Mom gave me a huge hug. "This is what I prayed for the day I put you on that plane to come here. It's perfect."

I looked at her and laughed. "Who would have ever thought? Your son, the farmer! Thank you too."

Made in the USA
San Bernardino, CA
12 April 2016